ECHOES OF US

Arden Coutts

Published by Wandering Creative LLC
United States of America

First edition

ISBN: 979-8-234-02631-6

When the world goes quiet, what echoes through the ruins is love, grief, and everything we couldn't outrun.

Content & Trigger Warnings

Echoes of Us contains themes and scenes that may be difficult for some readers. Content warnings include, but are not limited to:

- Apocalyptic and post-collapse settings

- Depictions of violence and injury

- Death and grief, including loss of loved ones and children

- Panic attacks and anxiety

- Trauma responses and emotional distress

- Survival situations and scarcity of resources

- References to illness and medical emergencies, and grotesque imagery

Reader discretion is advised. If you are unsure whether this content is right for you at this time, please prioritize your well-being.

Also by Arden Coutts

The Fall Series: A Queer Romantic Suspense Series
Prequel: Before We Fall
Book 1: Fall Into Midnight
Book 2: Fall Into Me
Book 3: We All Fall
Holiday Novella: A Nightclub for the Holidays

Poetry
Where We Once Existed: Poems about Love, Loss, and Grief

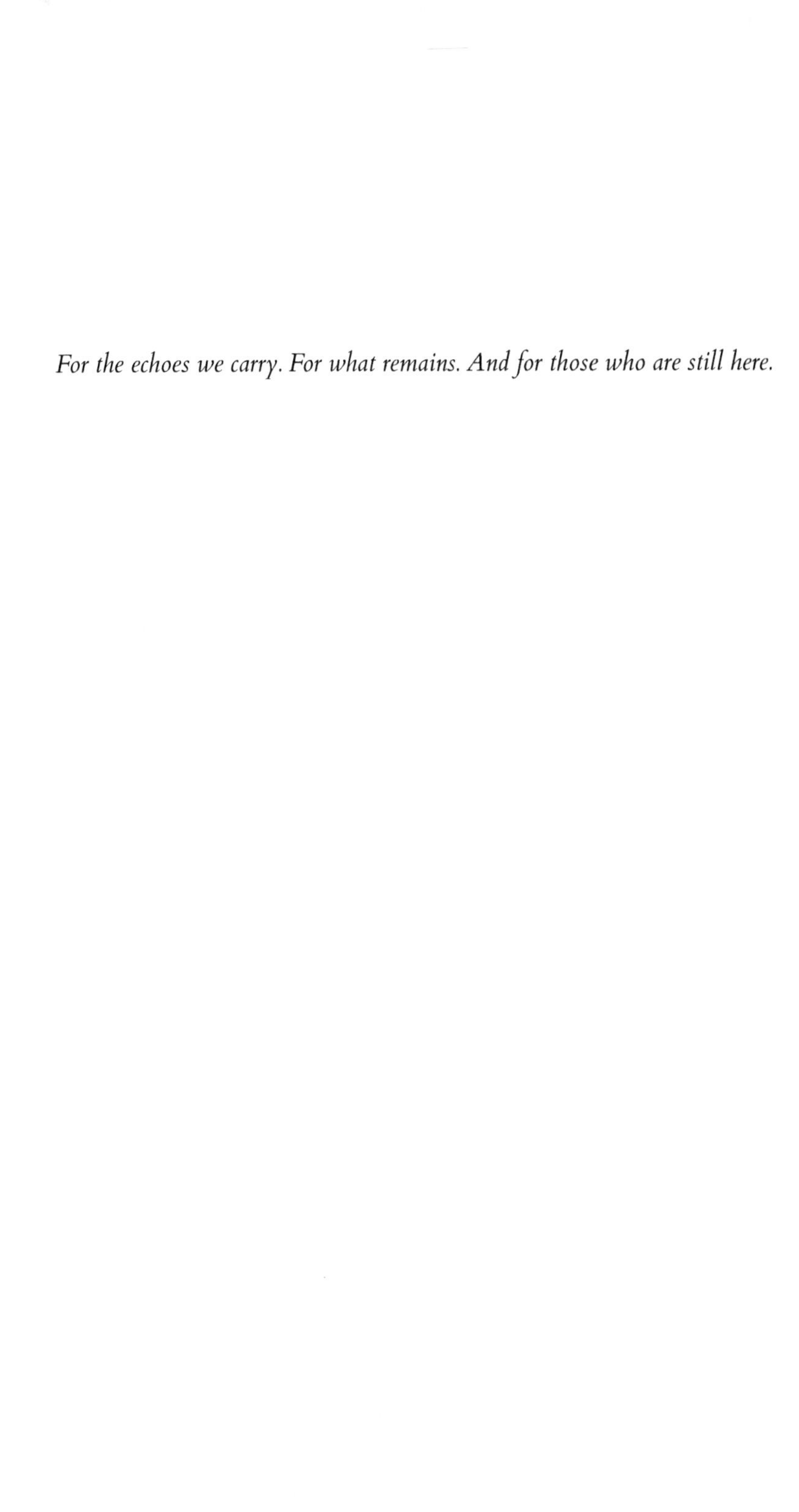

For the echoes we carry. For what remains. And for those who are still here.

Chapter One
When the World Ends

"*This is an Emergency Broadcast Transmission. We are interrupting your regular schedule for this emergency announcement.*"

I shut the water off and wipe the droplets off my face as I walk from the bathroom to the bed in my hotel room.

"*Ladies and gentlemen, the President of the United States.*"

A man's face fills the screen of my TV. He's too pale, too still. The kind of still that means someone has already told him that the world was ending and he hadn't had a chance to practice saying it out loud yet.

"*My fellow Americans, I never thought this would be an announcement I would make in my lifetime—*"

I'm waiting for the announcement as I stare at the TV, waiting for the punchline, something that tells me this is a joke. But the banner scrolling across the bottom of the screen isn't a joke.

EMERGENCY ALERT: ASTEROID HEADED TOWARD EARTH.

My stomach drops.

"*A large asteroid has been identified and is on a collision course with Earth. There's a high probability that pieces of the asteroid will impact us in approximately one year. Please stay calm and wait for further instructions.*"

One. Year.

The screen cuts back to the reality TV show I was watching before the announcement started, as if nothing had happened. There are bright lights, fake laughter, and a woman throwing a drink across the dinner table.

I look around the room in stunned silence before getting up to find my co-workers. I need other people. I need proof I hadn't imagined it. Walking out to the hotel lobby, I'm met by three of my fellow archaeologists and friends.

"Adrian, did you just see that news announcement?" Kay asks, breathless, eyes wide.

"It can't be real. There's no way it's real," Brian mutters, shaking his head as if he could shake the words loose.

"What the fuck is happening? This isn't real!" Greg grunts as he storms toward us, jaw tight.

Soon, all eight of us gathered in the lobby, looking at each other in confused silence.

Larry and Bryce, our crew chiefs, come out of their rooms and meet us.

"Listen, everyone, we don't know what's going on either, but we're making calls and seeing what the client wants to do about the dig."

"What? Like, they might end the project early?" Paul questions.

"Yeah, I think folks are scared and confused, which means things will likely start getting shut down. Remember what happened with COVID-19? This will probably be similar, and we should plan for that," Bryce responds.

The murmur is quiet at first before it fills the lobby. It's not only our team in the lobby now; more and more hotel patrons are joining us there. Everyone is asking, "Is this real?" and "What do we do now?" The confusion and fear are palpable in the small room, cloying. The smell of it clinging to everyone.

I've thought a lot about how I would react in bad situations. As an archaeologist, I've dealt with dicey situations before, when crew members had been hurt. Still, this was on another level. I wanted to believe that I'd stay calm and handle whatever the problem was.

I know I'm in shock. We all are. My mind goes blank, momentarily freezes, and then everything jumps into motion. Now's the time to decide if I'll be swept away by fear or frozen. The world is imploding, and reality is beginning to unwind. How am I going to react as everything starts to crack and shatter? When does the ordinary give way to chaos?

"Let's all go back to our rooms, and we'll meet in the conference room tomorrow morning instead of going out to the field. Maybe there will be more information by then." Larry speaks loudly enough for all of us to hear him over the other voices in the lobby.

"Right, maybe this is all just an elaborate hoax or something, and it'll be fixed in the morning." I look at Jessie, Brian, Kay, and the others in the group. We're all so hopeful that this isn't real. But something tells me that it is very real, and we need to prepare ourselves for what will happen next.

Nodding, I pat Brian and Kay on their shoulders and head back toward my room on the hotel's second floor. Brian and Kay are both on that floor, so we walk together, and none of us says a word.

"I guess I'll see y'all in the morning," I say, reaching for the door handle to my room. "Try to get some rest. I think we're going to be needing it."

I look them both in the eyes and see my fear mirrored back at me.

Nodding to them, I step into my room, hoping the terror I feel from the outside world will disappear once the door shuts behind me.

But it doesn't.

Leaning against the door, I let my legs give way, and I slide down, sitting on the gross, worn carpet of the hotel. Closing my eyes, I flashback to the television announcement that feels like it happened a lifetime ago.

At first, it all seemed like it should, but looking through the glamour of the President of the United States, I could start to see the truth. The illusion was of a well-put-together, calm, collected, and in-control individual. The reality was a slight tremor of the hand, resulting in a shaking paper; a sheen of sweat on the upper lip, revealed by a camera flash; a wrinkled shirt, slightly unkempt hair, and darting, bloodshot eyes, desperately trying to avoid eye contact.

Looking closely, nothing was what it seemed. There was a look on the President's face that I can only describe as a mix of fear and panic. It seemed like the fear was oozing out of his pores like a drop of sweat. There was a trembling in his voice that matched the shaking of his hands. He licked his lips as if he were parched and dying for water. It's burned into my mind, the look in his eyes. It reminds me of a cornered animal with fierce eyes—darting around, bared teeth, and pure panic. There was no escaping telling us all that we were doomed.

"I can't believe this is happening." My whisper bounces back to my shellshocked ears.

There is an asteroid that's going to demolish the world. What does one do with only a year to live and the world's end looming?

Chapter Two
Sinking

I've decided to keep a journal from now until the end. I'm not sure if it's the anthropologist in me or the need to write this down to try to make sense of it. It's 3:00 a.m., the day after the announcement. I'm having trouble sleeping, and I'm sure I'm not the only one. I can't help but wonder what will happen next. How will people react to the news? Will it be like in the movies? We saw people go crazy over COVID-19, and now this is happening again. If this project ends, I should go home and be with my family. It's the only thing I can think of doing. I haven't turned the TV on since the first announcement. I'm scared to see what else is going on in the world. I don't want this to be real. It can't be real, can it?

I set my journal down on the bed next to me. I haven't been able to sleep yet and can feel the fatigue setting in. I'm scared to close my eyes. What if I fall asleep and then wake up and it's all the same? That means that this wasn't a dream. I don't want it to be real.

Picking up my phone, I see a text from my mom. It's the first time she's texted me in months since my last visit.

"Will you be coming home?"

It is a simple, yet loaded, question. Will I be going home? Where, even, is home? I've been moving around since I left for college and rarely stay in a single place for longer than two years. Home was wherever I was, and I am okay with that. Yet seeing that text from my mom made me feel a longing I hadn't experienced since the first time I drove away from her worn, tattered house over 20 years ago.

Rolling to my side, I turn off the bedside lamp and sink into the covers, wishing the sun would come up and the wait was over. I seem to have trouble shutting my brain off. It's swirling with questions, and my anxiety is running rampant. This is just the beginning. What will happen as people start to lose their minds with fear? Does the government have a plan? What should I be doing?

As I lie in bed, I'm at a loss, letting my anxious thoughts wash over me like waves. My chest feels tight, and it's becoming increasingly difficult to breathe. Sitting up, I hang my legs over the end of the hotel bed and stare at the stark contrast of my pale feet against the ugly greenish color of the hotel carpet.

Just take deep breaths, in and out, in and out.

I inhale through my nose and exhale through my mouth, focusing on my feet and trying to think of nothing else.

In and out.

In and out.

The tightness slowly passes, and I take a full, deep breath, close my eyes, and flop back across the width of the bed. The old mattress does little to soften the fall. Looking over at the clock, it's only been 30 minutes. Getting up, I walk around to the small fridge and grab a beer from it. I might as well. Maybe it will help me sleep. Sitting down at the table by the window, looking out over the desert, I'm reminded of where I grew up: Sandridge, Nebraska. It's like Moses Lake, Washington, in that it's desolate in its own way—a sad place in many ways.

Sandridge is a small farming town located in north-central Nebraska, just south of the South Dakota border. It's surrounded by cornfields and cows, like here, except it has orchards and cows. Growing up there was uncomplicated, yet we all understood the importance of hard work at a young age. Sandridge is like many small farming communities in the rural parts of any midwestern state.

Everyone knows everyone else's business and is likely to share it with you. The kids are all looking to get out, and the adults are all wondering how they ended up there. People seem happy enough, but there's an almost tangible feeling of wanting something more.

Growing up there, I wanted nothing more than to get out and away. I hated knowing that anytime I did anything, everyone around town would know about it. It wasn't just that they knew, either. It was that they would talk about it, bring it up constantly, and bully you for it if they could. It was the way they'd talk: over coffee, in church parking lots, in the aisles of the grocery store, as if the town itself was one long-running group chat that you weren't invited to. They'd smile to your face and whisper behind your back while slowly twisting the knife they'd embedded there.

This was a place where being different wasn't okay. You needed to fit in and be like everyone else to make it out in one piece. My family was ostracized and considered too "poor" for many goings-on in town. We lived on the wrong side of the tracks, used food stamps, and my parents had health problems. These things made us easy targets for others to pick on. According to my mom, we were never good enough for others. I often wonder how much of that was true and how much of that was my mom's insecurities and anxieties.

People say that children can be cruel, but living in a small town, I found out that adults are often the ones who are cruel. Where do the kids learn it from? If there were differences, you were ostracized, bullied, and broken, but that's all part of being a kid, right? It helps build character. At least, that's what we tell ourselves to feel better.

I never fully fit in with any one group of kids growing up. I was a floater who could get along with everyone yet didn't fit in with anyone. I was always trying to fit in, trying to be one of the "cool" kids, but never quite getting there—always a supporting character, never the main character, not even in my own life. I was socially accepted enough to be invited to parties. I could hang out with the jocks and intelligent kids, yet I was awkward enough that I never fully felt like I belonged with them. I was never sure if I was being laughed at or if they were laughing with me.

The light from my phone makes me look down, pulling me away from my thoughts of home. A small pool of condensation has formed on the table under my beer. I've only taken a few sips, and it's already warm. The air conditioning in the hotel room is working overtime and is doing very little to ease the heat. I wipe the condensation off the table and grab my phone.

"Some of us are in the breakfast room if you want to join. We couldn't sleep."

It's from Kay. I look at the time at the top of the screen. It's 4:15 in the morning. I might as well join them, seeing as how it's not likely that I'll be sleeping. The breakfast room also has better air conditioning. What a weird thing to be worried about. Shaking my head at myself and my wandering thoughts, I dress in a pair of worn workpants and a t-shirt. Pausing, I look in the mirror next to the TV. I'm paler than usual, and my short, dark hair stands on end from running my hands through it. I catch a glimpse of my own eyes and pause. In my eyes, there's something I don't recognize. A look that I've not seen before on myself. Is this what fear genuinely looks like?

Chapter Three
Unraveling

"Hey, come join us." Kay pats the table next to her. There are more people here than just our archaeology crew. It seems that the hotel has started serving breakfast early, which is nice. It's giving us all a place to go to be with others and find some semblance of safety and community in a time of uncertainty.

Sitting down next to Kay, we lean toward each other, seeking comfort in closeness. I look at the others from the crew: Bryce, Brian, and Paul. They're my family. These people, who were strangers just nine months ago, are now my family. We live together, eat together, work together, and play together. All our time is spent bonding and weaving into each other's lives. A new dig means a new crew, which means a new family, and right now, this crew in Moses Lake, Washington, is my family. What's going to happen to all of us when we leave here? Will we be able to keep in touch? Will it matter as the world comes to an end?

"Everything okay?" Kay asks, leaning into me so that the sides of our bodies are pressed together.

"I don't know how to feel about all of this. I'm not sure what to do. How to act?" I look at her, seeking answers, and see the same haunted look in her eyes that I saw in my own a few minutes earlier.

Looking around at the table, I see it; we all wear the same expression. That's what it is: a shadow clinging to us. Now I understand when people say someone looks marked by something they can't shake. I see clearly the feverish glint in the eyes, paired with a hollow distance, confusion clouding them, and a strange slackness in the face. This is what it means to be carrying ghosts.

Someone turns on the TV, and everyone in the room turns to look.

"…again, we have no new information to report on the asteroid that is on a collision course with Earth, and we haven't heard anything from the officials at NASA. We know that the same information is being shared worldwide, and other countries are encouraging their citizens to stay calm until more information becomes available."

The TV is turned off, and conversation resumes. It's a mix of people making plans to leave the hotel and others discussing how it's all a lie and that the government is manipulating us. Something in my gut tells me this is the real deal, and the government is just as lost as we are. I know NASA has procedures in place for situations like this, but I wonder how effective they are and whether they'll work in this case. I guess we'll find out.

An odd calm has settled over me since I arrived in the breakfast room with the crew. The panic I felt earlier in my room is just a slight twinge in the pit of my stomach.

Kay grabs my hand as a fight breaks out across the room between two dads with different opinions on how the world will or won't end. Their wives and children gather around the two scuffling middle-aged men, trying to separate them. The fight is over before it even begins, with both men grabbing their wives and heading to separate sides of the room.

What was even the point, I wonder, watching both families. There are tears and real fear on the children's faces as their mothers cuddle them close to comfort them. This is just the beginning, and it will only get worse from here as more people begin to realize this is real. The man who started the fight by calling the other one stupid for believing in such "mainstream media bullshit" grabs his kids and wife. They leave the room, but not before he tosses a comment about all of us being sheep led to the slaughter, or something along those lines.

"What a bunch of idiots," Bryce says, leaning back in his chair, sipping his coffee. I try not to notice the trembling in his hand; maybe it's from too much caffeine. "What are you going to do?" I turn to look at Kay. She's slightly disheveled, as we all are, as the clock ticks over to 5:00 a.m.

"I'm probably going home to be with my family in California. My sisters and brother are already going to my grandmother's house. I'll meet them there in the next couple of days." Kay's smile is sad as she looks around the room. I wonder what she's thinking. "What about you? Will you go home?" she asks, looking back at me.

I wonder what I look like to her right now. Do I have the same dazed look on my face as everyone else?

"I guess so. I don't know where else I would go. My mom texted me asking me the same thing. I suppose it's what I should do."

"What do you want to do?" she asks, swaying into me and out again.

"I don't know," I say, leaning into the swaying, "I suppose I'll go home. It's the right thing to do, to be with family."

"We're family." The swaying stops.

"Yes." I don't know what else to say. I'm not sure what she wants from me. To say that I'd go to California with her? I don't think I could do that. Shouldn't I do what everyone else is doing? Go home and be with my family, even if it's not what I necessarily want to do.

Kay's eyes search for mine briefly before sliding away, focusing on nothing in particular as she avoids my gaze.

"I'm sorry."

"It was silly anyway. It makes sense that you would go home. It's what you should do, and you always do what you should, right?" Kay's words sting. She isn't wrong, though. I always do what I should, whether I want to or not. It's how I was raised, a people pleaser. I am never one to speak out, and I am always willing to do whatever I can to please others. I am always seeking affirmation from others and struggle to speak kindly to myself.

"Sorry," I say again, as Kay shakes her head, leaning into me.

"It doesn't matter." A whisper filled with so much more than words can say.

We sit in silence as time slowly ticks by, eventually watching the sun come up through the dirty windows of the hotel.

Larry and the other crew members join us in the breakfast room, taking up most of the space. Many people who had been with us throughout the early morning hours had already packed and left.

"What's the word, Larry? Are we shutting down the dig?" Brian asks. We all look at Larry as he settles back into the flimsy hotel chair. It creaks under his weight and, for a moment, I envision him tumbling comedically to the floor as it gives way. I almost smile.

"Yes, the company has decided to terminate our contract and end the dig until they know more about what's happening. For all non-local people, you can start heading out today or tomorrow. We'll cover the hotel for you for one more day. After that, it's out of your pocket." I nod my head along with everyone else as we digest the information.

"I'd suggest that you all try to get some sleep and leave either later tonight or early tomorrow. I'm guessing the roads will get crazier the longer you wait to leave." Larry looks at each of us. He doesn't have the same harrowed look as the rest of us. He seems…fine, resigned almost.

"When will you leave?" I ask, looking at Kay.

"Today, probably this afternoon. I want to get home as soon as possible, and you know the traffic in Southern California will be wild."

"Makes sense." I look at her again, wanting to hug her, show affection, and comfort her more than leaning in.

"I'd better get to packing." She moves away from the table, and I find myself reaching for her as she gets up and starts walking away.

"Wait up! I'll come with you." I get up from the table, saying rushed goodbyes to the rest of the team and jogging to catch up with Kay.

"Kay! Wait! I…"

"You…what? You, what?" She turns on me, the vacant, scared look in her eyes now one of sadness and anger.

"You've had nine months to decide what you want, and you've been too scared of being yourself to accept it, and now it's too late. We're out of time, and you're still too scared to let yourself go!" It's a hushed whisper but carries so much force that I step back.

"Kay, I…thought we would have more time. I wasn't ready for a relationship or anything; I couldn't have known that the world would end."

"Let's not do this. Let's leave each other on a happy note, with all our great memories. Let's not make this a thing and make it any sadder than it already is." Kay leans in, gently kissing me before turning away and unlocking the door to her hotel room.

Once again, I'm left not knowing what to say. Before closing the door, Kay turns, leans into the open space between us, and looks me in the eyes.

"It could have been great. Us. We could have been great. But now, we'll never know, will we? If you get lonely in Nebraska, come see me before the world ends." Kay shuts the door before I can tell her how I feel, that I want to go with her. That I would love for there to be an "us"; that would be great. I want to tell her all of that, but I don't. I can't.

Chapter Four
A Place Called Home

May 16, 2030

It's 6:00 a.m. the following day, and it's real. I managed to get some sleep even though my anxiety ramped up again once I returned to my room. I woke up about an hour ago, knowing I needed to get on the road. I know I need to return to Nebraska and be back home. It's a long drive, almost twenty-four hours on the road, so I'll have to make a pit stop somewhere along the way, probably in Montana. I don't know what to expect on the roads, and I'm scared, or maybe I'm more nervous. I'm not sure.

Closing my journal and capping my pen, I drop both into my backpack. I've already said my goodbyes and am anxious to get on the road and get out of town. I've driven this route twice and know it well, but I still get nervous when traveling long distances. Not to mention how people will be driving given the world's end.

As I carry my suitcases to my car, I pass Bryce and Brian. They're headed to Spokane, where they live, and have short drives ahead of them.

"Adrian! You heading out?" Bryce asks, coming over to help me load up my shit.

"Yup, figured I might as well get an early start. When are y'all heading out, again?"

"Here in a bit, we'll caravan our way home, just in case we run into any issues."

"That's smart. I hope y'all get home safely," I say, giving Bryce a warm hug that lasts longer than any other hug we've shared. Brian also comes in for a hug, and we spend a moment in silence together. These two are my favorite team members. We spent so much time together as dig partners and outside work, drinking and getting into trouble. I will miss them both.

My chest and throat grow tight with tears as I drop my backpack into the passenger seat of my car.

"Be safe, and good luck," Bryce says, as he and Brian wave to me.

I wave back and brush a tear from my suntanned, freckled cheek. I want to believe I'll see them again, even though I know I won't. This is the last time I'll see the family I've built here. I cry silently as I merge onto I-90 East and start the drive back to Nebraska, back to the place I once called home.

As I drive, I can't help but think back to my childhood in Nebraska and what it was like growing up there. The early years of my life were spent in a tiny town of about 45 people called Prairie Bend. Its name comes from the rolling fields of prairieland that make up the landscape. It was beautiful there. We just had corn fields, so it was nice to drive 45 minutes away and it was like you were in a different world—all green, with rolling sandhills and creeks.

I remember spending summers outdoors, taking in the scents, feeling the sun's warmth on my skin, getting chickenpox and being confined to the house, and playing with our rabbits in the grass around the house.

I can't remember a single winter in that place, even though I spent a few there. It's nothing but summer days, the smell of sun-kissed skin, and colorful houses.

The community consisted of large Queen Anne-style homes of all shapes and colors. We moved houses regularly, and because the town was so small, we kids would pack our toys in trash bags, throw them into our red wagons, and pull them down the street to our new home. I can remember going through this process at least three times.

We lived in blue, pink, and white houses before I was in the first grade. I only remember the places we lived in by the color of the house. I have clear memories of all the houses, but the one that stands out the most is the pink house. I loved that house. I had a large bedroom with a bay window that I was obsessed with.

The pink house was full of happy times and great memories. We got our first karaoke machine in the pink place. Our evenings were spent singing to artists like Amy Grant, Cher, and Bon Jovi, as well as many other classic '80s bands. I remember getting my first cat, Princess, meeting my best friend, Hannah, and falling asleep to everyone yelling "I love you" through the house. The pink house was our family at its best, and the white house was the beginning of the end.

My memories of the white house consist of a massive staircase that we used to throw our toys down and a bullet hole in one of the upstairs windows. I used to stare at that bullet hole and make up stories about how it got there, surmising that whatever had happened in that house hadn't been good. There was a feeling in that house that was off; we could all sense it, but we didn't understand what it meant. Arguments became more frequent, yelling overtaking the love, and the music faded.

We weren't in the white house for long before moving into a farmhouse in the country about 10 miles outside of Sandridge. When we moved in, the former residents shared a story with us. They said the house's original owner had died on the property after getting his arm caught in a combine and bleeding to death in the fields behind the house. Leaving all of us to believe that his ghost haunted the house.

It was also rumored that he had buried a large amount of money on the property. We never found proof of either statement, but there were times in that house when my skin would crawl as I lay in bed, feeling eyes on me from the open closet door. My older brother, Garrett, also had an experience where he woke up to a man with glowing red eyes looking at him from his bedroom doorway. This was when all of us kids stopped sleeping upstairs. For us, it was real—and it was terrifying.

Things started to change in this farmhouse for my family: I gained a new sibling, Adam, in the house where we grew up, where my mom fell ill, and where my parents' love for each other began to fade.

I also recall spending our nights at the town's only bowling alley during this time. That bowling alley was a constant presence throughout my childhood and early adulthood. My parents loved bowling and went every week, sometimes on weekends. They would give us kids handfuls of coins and send us back into the arcade so we didn't interfere with their bowling game. It was an ideal picture of a family night out in the '90s.

Journey, Eddie Money, and Def Leppard sang us through the night. The bowling alley smelled of mold, cheap fried foods, and spilled beer; the air was full of cigarette smoke.

The sounds, songs, and smells comprised most of my childhood. I often returned to the bowling alley for birthday parties and Saturday night hangouts throughout high school. When I was in my early 20s, I would return yet again to work at the bowling alley bar as an unemployed recent college graduate. It was precisely the same as when I was younger, maybe a little smellier, but the people were the same, the songs were the same, and there was still the smell of mold and bad fried foods. That bowling alley was a keystone in our family. It was there at the beginning and end of my parents' relationship, and their attendance at bowling events ebbed and flowed like their love for one another.

Chapter Five
Billings, Montana

Billings, Montana, is the perfect spot to stop between Moses Lake, Washington, and Sandridge, Nebraska. It's almost halfway between the two. It's also the largest city in Montana, so I'll have better luck finding a hotel and can stay close to the interstate just in case I need to make a quick exit.

Pulling off I-90 East, I take the last exit in town and find a hotel right off the interstate. It's nothing fancy, and it doesn't need to be. I've been on the road for around ten hours, and I need to crash for a bit before I get going again.

"Made it to Billings."

I hit send on the text to my mom as I head into the hotel to see if they have any availability. There isn't anyone at the front desk, and the place smells like old food and smoke.

"Hello!" I look around the empty lobby, holding my breath as I wait for the clerk to materialize.

A younger man comes out from somewhere behind the counter.

"What do you want?"

Rude. "A room, please."

"Three hundred dollars."

"For one night?" I can't keep the surprise out of my voice as I look at him.

"Haven't you heard? The world is ending. I can charge whatever I want now." I'm pretty sure that's not how it works, but I don't have the energy to argue with him, and even if I did, he has a point.

"Two-fifty," I say back, looking him dead in the eye.

"Two-seventy-five," he counters. Nodding, I hand over the exact amount in cash. Something I learned a while ago was that when shit goes down, having cash is one of the best things you can do. I went to the bank yesterday and withdrew all my money. I know carrying so much cash is unsafe, but I also know that many places would now be cash-only.

The man behind the counter passes me a room key for a room on the second floor. It's not ideal for a quick exit, but I'm losing steam at this point, and I need to sleep.

Taking the key, I head up to the room. It smells and doesn't look like it's been cleaned in a while. It probably has bed bugs, I think to myself as I pull the sheets and comforter back to inspect the bed and see what's going on.

I won't be sleeping in the bed. I can't see any bed bugs, but the stains on the sheets don't do anything for me, either. I take out the food I've packed from Moses Lake and sit at the small table by the window. I can see only the parking lot and a small part of the Billings skyline. Turning on the TV, I settle back in the smelly chair for a quick bite. I'm unsure if I will stay the whole night, but I need to eat and get at least a few hours of rest before I hit the road again. If anything, I can pull over and sleep in the car somewhere along the way.

"In today's news, riots have begun breaking out in larger cities in the U.S. According to our international correspondents, other countries appear to be handling the situation more effectively, with minimal riots and many citizens adhering to government restrictions.

Billings has not seen any unrest, although there have been a few minor encounters with law enforcement as the day continues. It's mainly smaller stores dealing with individuals stockpiling of goods and complaints about stores' price gouging."

Turning the TV down, I look out the window and focus on my plan for the next day. I need to finish my drive, so it's another twelve hours until I get home to Sandridge, if everything goes right. I'll get through Montana and South Dakota and then work my way down to Sandridge along the Nebraska-South Dakota border. It's a drive I've made before, and I typically enjoy it. Still, I have massive anxiety about driving through the Badlands right now, knowing that gas will be expensive, and in short supply, in that area.

Putting the rest of my food back in the cooler, I turn the TV volume up just enough to hear it and bring the other chair around so I can put my feet up on it. This is how I'll be sleeping tonight. No way in hell will I be sleeping on that bed.

I don't know how long I've been asleep, but my neck has me groaning in pain when I wake up. I must have been slouching weirdly in the chair. What woke me up? Looking around, everything looks normal, but something definitely woke me up.

The TV is static, casting the room in an eerie glow, and nothing seems right. Looking out of the hotel window, everything looks normal, until I look a little closer at Billings's skyline.

I can see the faint glow of something on fire…no, wait. There appear to be fires burning throughout the skyline. Just as I start to stand, a massive explosion rocks the horizon, illuminating the night sky and sending shockwaves rippling through the air. The glass in front of me rattles but doesn't break. Chills sweep through my body as I watch the horizon ignite.

Holy shit, Billings is burning.

I need to get the fuck out of here. Springing up, my heart is in my throat, and panic fills me. I need to run and get out before the roads fill up. I grab my bag and cooler and bolt for the door, wrench it open, and tear down the outdoor walkway. Doors bang open around me. Someone shouts. Someone else screams. The air buzzes with panic as people spill from their rooms, colliding, swearing, dropping keys and bags. Everyone surges toward the parking lot, toward their cars, desperate to get out before whatever happened downtown crawls its way to the edges of the city.

The parking lot is chaos. Engines roaring, horns blaring, tires screeching against asphalt. I hurl my gear into the backseat and fumble for the keys, my hands slick with sweat. The engine turns over once, twice, then catches. Relief barely has time to register. I have enough gas to get away from Billings, but not enough to disappear. Not enough to feel safe.

I slam the car into reverse and nearly plow into a family of four as they sprint for their minivan two rows down, the parents shouting, kids crying, the sound sharp and panicked in my ears. I jam the brakes, heart pounding, lungs burning, the lot pressing in on me from every side as if the city itself were trying to keep us trapped.

Fuck, that was close!

Taking a deep breath, I try to calm myself. I need to focus so I don't get in a car accident. Focus. It's hard to think clearly with my heart beating in my ears and my adrenaline making me shake.

It's okay, everything is fine.

I'm stuck behind three other vehicles as we try to get out of the hotel parking lot and back onto the interstate. Maybe I'm leaving too late. Perhaps the roads are already backed up. Fear causes my stomach to clench, and I check my mirrors to ensure my doors are locked. We finally start to creep forward slowly. So fucking slow. My fingers drum on the steering wheel as I chew on the inside of my cheeks. We need to move.

I look in the mirrors again at the cars lining up behind me and then glance out the driver's side window.

Fuck.

People are emerging from the tree line around the hotel. They're running from something. Running from whatever the fuck is happening downtown, and they're heading right toward us. Looking from the mob of people racing through the parking lot to the cars in front of me, I decide to go off-road and around the three vehicles blocking my exit. I'll drive on the shoulder or the grass, if I need to. I'm not waiting for people to try to get in my car.

I slowly pull out, start driving around the cars, and make it to the front of the line, where a continuous stream of traffic from Billings is clogging the road.

Fuck it.

I merge onto the shoulder and start slowly driving next to the traffic that's moving on the main highway. Looking in the rearview mirror, I can see flames and smoke as Billings continues to be engulfed in flames. Whatever blew up must have been highly flammable.

Several cars from the hotel follow me along the shoulder. We create our caravan, leaving the fleeing people of Billings behind us.

The interstate is running smoother than I thought, given the number of people trying to get on it. I easily merge into the main traffic stream and take off, not looking back. I don't want to see what's behind me. I'm great at running from my problems; this is just another one to avoid.

Chapter Six
Nebraska

Driving through Nebraska is like finding yourself on a different planet. Small, struggling towns occasionally break their remoteness with crumbling buildings and potholed roads. Yes, there are bigger places, like Omaha and Lincoln, but where I'm going, there is nothing but single-lane roads, gently rolling hills, crops, and cows.

My brothers and I used to work in fields like the ones that I drive past. We all started working on the farm when we were young. I was eight when I started. My older brother, Garrett, and my younger brother, Adam, began working around that age.

It was demanding work, and the hours were long. I've always enjoyed being outside, so perhaps that's why I liked it. I also got to spend time with my dad and work with my siblings and some of my closest childhood friends. There's something about being outside, in the sun, doing physical labor, that I find freeing.

Standing outside, breathing in the fresh air, and letting the sun kiss your skin—it's something I'll never forget. It's like the colorful houses. Fresh dirt, sunburned skin, drying sweat, cow feed, birds singing, tractors in the background, '80s music on the radio, and the smell of diesel make up my memories. They create a world in my mind. Even without specifics, I can still revisit those places and moments. All it takes is the slightest hit of a familiar smell or a note of music to bring me back there.

Individual songs, sounds, and smells transport me back to my child-hood, to our old country house in the middle of nowhere, surrounded by cows, cornfields, and abandoned buildings.

My childhood was not all terrible; there were some rough patches, but others were much worse off than my family. We had problems, as all families do, mainly dealing with my mother's health, money, and the fact that my parents had five children and no plan for how to care for all of them. They had no expectations for our futures, which, in a way, left us free to make our destinies. But no foresight was involved regarding our prospects, education, and financial needs.

Even with those difficulties, my brothers and I would run outside through pastures, dodging fresh cow manure and playing pirates, using cow bones as swords, which is how we spent our time as children. I can still smell the freshly cut grass, feel the sun on my skin, and hear the birds' songs whispering in the wind. It was mostly a carefree childhood spent outside, digging through old, abandoned barns for lost treasures left behind by former inhabitants, and running barefoot through the front yard as we played tag.

My mother and I would walk along the dirt roads and collect rocks that caught our eye. She even bought me a rock tumbler so that I could make them into jewelry. On those same walks, we would take casts of different animal prints that we saw along the way. I had a collection of animal casts that occupied an entire shelf in my bedroom. She also made a small pouch that I wore when I went bow hunting with my father. I collected rocks as we wove through the trees, stalking deer and turkey. I had quite a rock collection. Some turned out to be prehistoric artifacts, while others were merely aesthetically pleasing. These moments influenced me and led to my career as an archaeologist, as well as my desire to live outside and avoid being trapped in a cubicle.

Sometime later, I discovered that my mother wanted to be an archaeologist when she was younger. It all made sense, in a way, that her desires would color the way that she raised her kids. She gave me a love of the past and for things left behind by others.

We were surrounded by the artifacts of those who had lived there before us. We would dig through old burn piles and find the most exciting things. I had a keyring full of skeleton keys that I would try on all the doors throughout the house. My mother had shelves of historic glass bottles that we had liberated from collapsed buildings in our backyard. It was perfect, living in the present but surrounded by the past. We often find ways to carry things from our past with us, whether we realize it or not. We are forever living with ghosts.

When I cross the border, I'm almost overwhelmed with memories I usually keep tucked away within myself. I'm trying to keep Nebraska in its box in my mind. I'm overwhelmed with the need to leave again, even though I've just arrived. This place was never mine. No matter how hard I tried to fit in, it never worked. I always floated between friends and activities, never genuinely finding my place.

Not much has changed.

I pull into a small gas station that still has pumps from the 1990s. There's no pay-at-the-pump option, and I'm forced to go into the deteriorating building. It smells of hot dogs and gasoline. The floor is scuffed and covered in mud and dirt, which the farmers track in.

I give the heavy-set woman behind the counter a nod and a tight smile as I walk to the back to pick out a soda. I grab a few snacks and glance at the TV behind the counter. There's a football game on. The normalcy of it makes me uncomfortable. Do they not know about the asteroid that's barreling toward us?

"How ya doing, sweetie?"

"I'm well, ma'am. Can I get $30 on pump two, please?" I pull cash from my wallet and slide it across the counter to her.

"Have y'all heard about the asteroid?" I ask cautiously. She glances up from the cash in her hand and smiles.

"You don't believe that now, do ya? I think the government is playing with us, trying to make us panic, so we spend all our money to improve the economy. Don't believe everything you see on the news now." She chuckles, handing my change back.

"Right," I say, giving her another tight smile, and taking my change, I head toward my Kia Soul. Its dark blue paint is already covered in dust from driving along the backcountry roads.

Standing at the pump, it hits me that I'm back in Nebraska—back in a place I told myself I would never return to. Panic builds in my chest, and the urge to cry overwhelms me. I turn from the gas station and let the silent tears stream down my face. I feel like I did as a child: removed, and like I don't fit in. I don't understand how people can completely remove themselves from the rest of the world.

The farther I drive into Nebraska, the farther I get from reality. The radio stations, not 100 miles ago, covered the impending doom. Now, nothing but country tunes fill the stations, broken by bursts of static when the frequency cuts out. I turn the Bluetooth on and let my K-pop playlist fill the car as I drive toward Sandridge. Losing myself in the music and the gently rolling hills of the countryside.

It's late in the evening when I arrive at my mom's house. It's a tiny house on a dirt road next to the train tracks that have been turned into a walking trail. The white stucco siding is dotted with gray and black filth, and the roof sags in the dim light from the streetlights. I've tried to get her to move several times, but I think she'll go down with the house. The Earth is swallowing both. I can't bring myself to go in just yet, and I sit in my car in silence, mentally preparing myself for my family.

From my mom's texts, I know that my brothers have made it home and are staying with her. My older sister, Grace, is with her family in Grand Island, and my other brother, Mitch, is with his in Valentine.

Everyone is accounted for and is currently in Nebraska. My nerves are fried from driving, and I'm exhausted. I'm unsure if I'm ready to deal with my family and their shit. We haven't been close since I came out as trans and started my transition from female to male, and now I am about to be stuck in a house with them until the end of the world.

Chapter Seven
Sandridge, Nebraska

I t takes everything I have to go inside, but I manage, and it's not as bad as I thought it would be. The house is small but clean, and my mom has food ready for the whole family. My siblings seem happy to see me. I wonder if I've built up our reunion in my head so much that the actual thing isn't as big a deal as I thought it would be. I feel calm after walking into the house and greeting everyone. There's still a weird sense of not knowing the people here with me because so much time has passed, and we've all changed so much since the last time we were together. I'm unsure what to do or say, so I settle at the kitchen table and let the conversation flow around me.

"Do you think it's real, Mom?" Garrett asks, sitting across the table with a plate full of hamburgers and fries.

"I don't know what to believe anymore, but I'm leaning toward yes. It doesn't make sense to make something like this up." Mom moves around the kitchen while fixing and preparing food for us all.

"What about you, Adam?" she asks, placing another burger.

"I think it's real," he says, glancing around at each of us as we start to settle into being around each other again. "What about you?" He looks pointedly at me; his eyebrows raised in expectation.

"I think it's real," I mumble, my mouth full of burger. I'm famished from the drive and, right now, feeding myself is my top priority, along with not saying the wrong thing to set anyone off. As a chronic people-pleaser, my entire life has been around helping and ensuring that others are comfortable. Yet my entire existence makes my family the most uncomfortable. It's a mindfuck.

We were all once so close when we were younger. We were close in age and did everything together, from sports to playing after school. As we approached high school age, everything changed. I started playing sports, and my older siblings thought that our parents loved me more because of the support that I got. I also tried hard in school and earned good grades, which can be attributed to my tendency to be a people-pleaser. I had to be the best and did everything I could to accomplish that. In the meantime, my siblings grew to hate me more and more, and the animosity spread from the older ones to the younger kids, until those I had been closest to wholly abandoned me.

I was all alone by the time I got to high school. All my siblings have grown apart from me. I still feel like they hate me, maybe on a lesser level. That feeling of never belonging is still there, sitting in the pit of my stomach, making me feel like I'm on the verge of tears with every passing second.

When I came out, my older siblings made several comments about transgender people that still echo in my head. I don't know if I'll ever be able to forget or forgive them for the things they have said.

As I chew my burger, I look around the kitchen. I can tell that it's well-used, which doesn't surprise me. My mother has always been an avid cook and baker, often making large orders of pastries for events around town. I miss her cooking—it may be one of the things I miss the most.

The floor in front of the oven is worn and scuffed, the stovetop is dirty from use, and dishes are piled in the small sink. It's nothing like what we used to have when we lived in the country house.

Mom would stand in our large kitchen with the windows and front door open. Our kitchen had an entire wall of windows, and my mother would go down the line opening every window, creating a wind tunnel through the house as she cooked, the curtains billowing.

My father would be outside mowing the lawn, and the smell of fresh-cut green grass, wet soil, and dew would ride through the house on the back of the wind. There was warmth and a calming effect as the wind wove through our home. It created a sense of serenity, like how the house feels right after I wake up. It was warm, with light streaming in from the windows, and everything would be quiet. There was a softness around it.

The calm never lasted, though, as the house filled with the sounds of children as they rose for the day. At other times, it would be punctuated by yelling as my parents fought, often over money. I found myself escaping to the outdoors more and more throughout my childhood. It was my safe space.

I would climb onto the roofs of the old barns and look at the stars. I always looked at the stars, wondering what else was out there, where I belonged, and if everyone else's world was like mine. Never feeling like I fit in and never knowing how to explain it, the country house had dark moments of sad songs, stars, poetry, and suicide notes written and hidden amongst my toys.

Our old, historic country house was full of ghosts, some that existed before we arrived and some that we left behind. I sometimes wonder if the house was, indeed, haunted. Our family was deeply affected by that house; it was a trying time, and we didn't all emerge unscathed. I think the decision to move the family into town came at the perfect time; we needed to get away from the country house and start fresh somewhere else, and that's precisely what we tried to do.

We moved to the house in town in an attempt to keep our family together, and now, to find myself sitting in the house that had once saved our family during a time when we were all doomed, seemed slightly ironic and very fitting. This house had brought us together before, and it seemed we were doing it again, coming together for one last time.

"What are you going to do now that you're home?" Mom asks, finally sitting with the rest of us at the table.

"I suppose we need to watch the news and figure out what other people are doing. They must have a plan in place for situations like this. They have programs specifically for near-Earth objects and space debris. Maybe they will try something like that to destroy or move the asteroid off its path." Adam nods along with me as I talk, and Garrett grabs another burger, seemingly unfazed.

"I meant, what will you do now, as in tomorrow? How are you going to spend your time now that you're home? Do you have to keep working?" The questions seem odd, given the state of the world.

"I…I'm not sure. I guess I'll hang out here. I might drive around some in the next couple of days and visit places in town, but I'm not sure what to do. I mean…what do you do when the world is ending?" I look from my mom to my brothers. There are no answers here.

Mom nods, gathering our discarded plates and moving them to the sink. "You should probably get some rest. You've all had a long day today. I've got the pullout couch ready for someone and an air mattress in the spare room where the two of you can sleep."

We all look at each other briefly before Garrett and Adam get up and head toward the spare room, leaving me with the pullout couch in the living room.

Mom has already gathered her things and is moving toward her bedroom. There's a silence that fills the space, making it almost hard to breathe. I feel like I did when I was a child—trapped and alone.

I lay down on the couch and pulled out my phone.

"Did you make it home all right?"

"..."

"Kay? Are you still angry with me? Please just let me know that you're okay."

"This is Kay's sister, Janice."

"Hi Janice, where's Kay?"

"She never made it home."

"What?"

"They found her belongings on the side of the road about 50 miles from home. Her car was parked along one of the cliffside viewpoints."

"I don't understand. Where is she?"

"The authorities don't know and don't care. They're saying she was likely mugged and maybe killed for her gear in the car. She had all her camping stuff with her from work."

"What the fuck?! Did they even look for her?"

"We all did; we couldn't find anything. Our family is holding a funeral for her next week. Everyone says there's no way she's still alive, given how everything is falling apart. Everyone is going crazy out here."

"Janice, I…I don't know what to say. I'm in shock. I'm so sorry. Please let me know if there's anything that I can do to help. Kay and I were close."

"I know. She talked about you a lot. She mentioned that maybe you would be coming home with her this time. I wish you had. Maybe she would have made it home."

My heart is pounding so hard I can hear it in my ears and see it behind my eyes. How is this possible? Kay, gone? It doesn't make sense. Why did she stop? Would she still be here if I had gone with her?

"I'm sorry, Janice. Please let me know if anything comes up."

I don't know what else to say, and I stare at the bright light of my phone in the darkness as I wait for her response. It never comes. Sighing, I roll to my side and let the tightness in my chest break free, along with the tears I've been holding back. I hold my sobs in as much as possible so my family can't hear them. I cry quietly in the living room, letting despair take hold.

Chapter Eight
The Death of Childhood

May 20, 2030

"He wanted to care, and he could not care. For he had gone away, and he could never go back anymore. The gates were closed; the sun was down, and there was no beauty left but the gray beauty of steel that withstands all time. Even the grief he could have borne was left behind in the country of youth, illusion, and the richness of life, where his winter dreams had flourished." — F. Scott Fitzgerald, All the Sad Young Men

Morning seems to take forever, but eventually, the darkness fades, and dawn starts to break, filling the living room with dampened sunlight.

Was it all a dream?

Was Kay really gone?

Kay being gone is a reality that I can't get behind. She was the only person who accepted me for who I am, and now she's gone. That doesn't make sense, and it can't be real. I roll over and tuck myself back into the sheets, hoping to hide from this new, fresh hell I live in. There's a part of me, deep down, that knows that this is just the beginning, but I can't go there yet. I can't accept it.

Adam and Garrett come out of the room and sit at the table. Mom follows soon after, getting the coffee brewing and instructing the boys to make eggs and bacon for everyone.

Wiping the remaining tears from my eyes and the salt tracks left behind by last night's cry, I pull myself together enough to get up and meet my family at the table.

"I think I'm going to drive around today and check out town. It's been a while since I've been home." I announce this to the table, as if any of them care what I'll be getting up to.

"That will be nice. Maybe you'll see some folks that you know."

I hope not.

I force a smile to my face and dig into the eggs and bacon that the boys have put together. I add cream to my coffee, enough to make it more like creamer than coffee, and drink it as fast as possible. I'm dying to get out of the house, to escape the cloying atmosphere that thickens the air around me.

Having showered and put myself together, I leave the house, breathing deeply as I step out into the mid-morning light. It's overcast and feels like it could rain. The weather perfectly matches my mood as I trudge toward my dust-covered car.

Pulling out of the dirt driveway, I drive up to Main Street. This was where we would spend our nights skateboarding down the street, and to the right, we would lie on the grass under the wind turbines, listening to the wind whistling through the blades and the music playing on the radio.

A few blocks from here is the local pool, where we used to go skinny dipping. High school, while socially tricky, was also a time of freedom and self-discovery, especially in the summer.

I loved that specific time of summer night when the sun began to set and the temperature was perfect. It's the ideal temperature and time of night to get in trouble. The air smells of mischief, and the night creatures come alive.

My nights were filled with laughter and running from the police. I sat on couches, listening to my friends playing guitars and singing to their favorite bands. I smoked my first joint on an abandoned railroad bridge, feet dangling into the darkness below me, bats swinging wildly in and out of the sky above me, and a beautiful night sky full of stars going on forever, uninterrupted by light of any kind.

I miss the freedom and carefree nature, not having to think or worry about what tomorrow brings. I miss being able to run the streets at night and the complete freedom and vulnerability that comes from floating naked in an empty pool with nothing around you but the night sky. I miss the smell of mischief and the sound of laughter in the night air.

There was an overwhelming sense of freedom in those moments. We were all so carefree, and none of us realized that life would not be what we had expected when we left this place. We were completely unaware that everything we wanted for ourselves would come at a price. I struggle with always trying to find that feeling again, of wanting to return to how it was when we were young and wild, completely untethered by the adult world around us.

Making a left turn, I pull onto Main Street and drive slowly down the deserted road. There aren't any cars parked on the street yet, and light fog lies undisturbed over the town. It's as if no one lives here. I drive slower, taking in the state of the buildings. Some look brand new, while others are falling apart, abandoned and condemned.

Pulling onto Highway 20, I continue through town, driving toward the park where I worked as a lifeguard, played softball, practiced track, and skinny-dipped on those perfect summer nights. It's just as quiet here as it was on Main Street, and I wonder if the entire world has disappeared overnight. Where is everyone?

It's almost ten in the morning; people should be out. On my way to the park, I drive past the dollar store and see my first sign of life. There are three cars in the parking lot. I turn down the side road and drive to the park. Pulling into the gravel parking lot, I get out of my car. I don't know why or what's driving me, but I walk to the swings and sit in one, letting my legs take over and focusing only on the movement.

My mind settles as my legs pump. I don't know the last time I was on a swing, but my legs know what to do, and before I know it, I am swinging through the air, and the cool, damp air is rushing past me with every upswing of my body.

Kay.

I can't keep her at bay any longer, and the damp air becomes wetter with each tear that rolls down my face, which is swept away by the wind.

Kay was one of the first people to accept me for who I am. She didn't question anything. She just accepted everything. Kay was my escape from reality, much like Hawai'i had been when I was younger. It was a moment of escapism. There wasn't any stress. No one cared what you looked like or what you did.

It was a time full of freedom. A time full of warm breezes, saltwater, and sand. Rides in the back seat of a jeep with Bob Marley's "Three Little Birds" strumming through the air, our hair blowing in the wind, her head on my shoulder while her fingers danced to the rhythm of the music over my bare, sun-kissed leg. I stood on the beach, watching the sun go down, holding her hand, and not worrying about who might see it. I don't think there was ever a time when I felt so free and more like myself than in those moments.

Kay made me feel the same way—like myself, even though I didn't know what that meant. Now she's gone, and I'm here swinging at my childhood park, crying for all the things that have already been lost.

Chapter Nine
Grief

May 20, 2030

Can you explain what grief is and how we should respond to it?

I was in my early 20s when my father died. That day is still burned in my memory; it feels like it happened yesterday. The phone rang around six in the morning, and all I could hear at the other end of the line was my sister sobbing, followed by my mother's calm voice telling me that my dad had passed from a massive heart attack.

I didn't know what to do. I didn't know how to act. I was sad but felt I needed to be strong for my siblings. I broke down when I saw his ashes for the first time, but after that, I kept my grief to myself. I felt a lot of sadness for my younger siblings because they never got a chance to see our parents at their best. They never heard "I love you" ringing through the house, nor did they experience the love our parents had for one another. Their childhoods would not be made up of the good. They wouldn't have those moments of freedom in the arcade of a bowling alley or running through the fields, playing with cow bones. Instead, their childhoods would be punctuated by the death of a parent.

Grief, for me, isn't endless mourning or soft remembrance. It's an acknowledgment. It's naming the loss and accepting that the person is gone, fully and finally. Once I do that, I bury them somewhere deep inside myself where the pain can't reach the surface every time I breathe.

I don't linger. I can't afford to. If I let myself sit with the loss, turn it over, feel it fully, it would hollow me out from the inside. So, I move forward, carrying

the weight of what was, sealed away and heavy, because staying with the dead
has never saved the living.

Lying my journal on the grass next to me, I look up at the dreary sky and find the sun barely peeking through the cloud coverage. It must be nearing noon. I've been at the park for a few hours and should probably head home for lunch. Getting back in my car, I find myself continuing out of town, and before I realize it, I'm at the cemetery, at his grave. It's well-maintained, and his headstone is littered with figurines and flowers from family and friends. It's been over a decade since he passed, but people still come to my dad's grave to leave behind things that remind them of him.

Sitting down, I pull my journal out. I can't help but wonder if this is what life is all about. To live and to die, is that all that matters? What about the ability to believe?

I suppose I began to lose the belief that anything was possible as I grew older. Life seems to have worn me down and made me tired. I've forgotten about my imagination and about the ability to turn a cow's rib into a sword. I've become bogged down in reality and my grief. The truth is that reality is never what I wanted or thought it would be.

As I got older, things changed in my life. Finding those moments to take my shoes off and run through the dew-covered grass became more complicated and more challenging. I changed, and the people around me changed. The world has changed. Those simple times are lost in the day-to-day struggle. I had to adapt, or the world would have eaten me alive.

How do I survive when everything is changing around me? Why must everything get so confusing and complicated? Kay always told me to close my eyes and think of something happy, but what if I didn't have anything pleasant to think about? What if there is only sadness, bad memories, and nightmares that follow me through the night into my waking moments? How do I get back to that smell of freshly cut green grass and sun-filled kitchens? How do I wake up from the nightmare, and what happens if the dream is real?

I feel the panic tightening my body as I sit in the grass in front of my dad's grave. It grows with every stunted breath until I can barely draw another breath in. My chest is so tight. I curl over onto myself and try to force air into my lungs. Tears sting my eyes as I clench them tightly shut. I let the waves of panic roll through me as I tighten my arms around myself and focus on the feeling of my arms wrapped around my body.

Deep breaths.

I hear Kay's voice in my head as I breathe in through my nose and out through my mouth. The tightness lessens. The world sharpens around me as the panic subsides and the tears stream down my face. I need to get over this and pull myself together. I'm the one that my family is going to lean on when shit gets hard. I need to have my act together so I can help them. If there's a way to survive, I need to be able to take advantage of it; I can't be frozen in panic when the time comes. I can't let them down like I let Kay down, and how I did when Dad died. I need to be there for them. I can't run away back to college this time. I need to stick with this and see it through to the end.

I pick myself off the damp grass, grab my journal, and return to my car. I'm determined not to let anyone else down. I have to be able to keep my family safe. It doesn't matter if they all hate or don't trust me. My only goal in life is to keep them safe.

Chapter Ten
Deidamia

June 20, 2030

I've been home for a month, and every day has been a waiting game, today included. I get up, help around the house, and we do business like the world isn't ending. It seems like everyone else around us is doing the same. Everyone settled down after the initial shock and the riots that followed the announcement, it would seem. At least here in the Midwest, it seems to have calmed down some. There are still cities in the south that are rioting, and there have been attacks on D.C. in the last month. It's different around the globe, though. Some countries have established councils for humanity and are implementing lotteries and other systems to save their people. Russia and China are working together to devise a plan to destroy the asteroid, but here in the United States, we've heard very little in the last month regarding what our leaders are doing to save us.

The blaring of the emergency alert system pulls me from my journaling, and I direct my attention to the TV in the living room.

"This is an emergency announcement from the President of the United States. We've worked closely with NASA's Planetary Defense Coordination Office (PDCO) to manage and monitor the situation. The PDCO has been tracking and characterizing the asteroid and is working with experts worldwide to strategize how to mitigate the impact threats of this near-Earth object.

NASA and FEMA are collaborating to ensure that an effective emergency response plan is in place, should impacts occur. We are also working to coordinate efforts with the multinational International Asteroid Warning Network and the Space Missions Planning Advisory Group.

"If you recall, a few years ago, we conducted the Double Asteroid Redirection Test (DART), and this is the perfect scenario to apply those test findings to our advantage. The DART mission successfully demonstrated that it is possible to deflect and change an asteroid's motion in space through kinetic impact, achieved through a purposeful collision. We will recreate that initial DART mission on the Deidamia asteroid, hoping it will generate enough energy to move the asteroid out of direct impact with Earth."

I start to zone out as the droning voice on the television continues spewing words at me that I can barely comprehend. I suppose they will launch a rocket into the asteroid in the hope that it will be moved off its path. I'm not sure if I believe that will work.

Tracking space debris, asteroids, and meteors is complex. Once a near-Earth object is identified, there are many paths it can take based on gravity, orbits, and other factors. This is the case with the asteroid that is headed toward Earth. They have an idea of how it will travel, but with so many unknowns, there is no telling whether it will have an impact.

Interestingly, they named the asteroid Deidamia, which means to destroy and to tame. It also has a meaning associated with battle and war. Deidamia is the lover of Achilles in the Trojan War, only to be left behind as he departs for war with Patroclus. This is not how I imagined using my Classical Studies minor, but I can't help but wonder who decided to name the asteroid after two Greek words that mean "to destroy" and "to tame." I also can't help but wonder if this announcement will have the same impact as the first one they made, or if people have become too unhinged even to care.

When the announcement about the asteroid first aired, everything changed. It shifted my world, tilted its axis, and shattered everything I thought I knew about humanity. I don't know what I was expecting, but the way people slowly became unhinged is not what I pictured happening. I've been home for a month now, and I've been watching everyone. I am watching them unravel.

It starts slowly—a bad joke, a burst of anger—and then builds. Bad jokes can escalate into verbal attacks, followed by physical beatings. Guns are pulled before words can even be exchanged in some instances. Everyone is on high alert, yet some still don't believe that the asteroid is real. It doesn't make sense.

The details change continuously throughout the weeks. At first, they insisted that it would just be a passing phenomenon, but as the year progressed, the story evolved from a near miss to a direct hit and a possible mass extinction event. It would take us all out, just like the dinosaurs.

I've started to question what exactly makes us human. Is it our ability to know right from wrong? Our ability to distinguish what is moral and just? What happens when that all goes away and we revert to our primal instincts? Do we, as humans, fundamentally cease to exist? If we lose our humanity, how can we regain it?

I don't think I ever realized how dark and terrible people could be. When they lose touch with reality and stop giving a shit about societal norms, anything is possible. Everything we thought we knew is a lie, and humanity ceases to exist when people realize they have nothing to lose.

People become desensitized. Things that were once thought impossible become commonplace, and people start to care less and less when they occur. This is the world that we live in. Natural disasters occur worldwide so frequently that people often no longer consider them a concern. So many terrible things happen daily, and people don't care because they've seen so much of it that it has become routine. We are desensitized to the events we should care about most, or perhaps it's how our brains cope to keep us moving forward.

Even with scientists, subject matter experts, and governments worldwide confirming it, many people choose not to believe it. In the end, sometimes, it's just easier to ignore something than to address it: ignorance is bliss.

The Chelyabinsk meteor that struck Russia in 2013 was a fragment of a near-Earth asteroid, approximately 66 feet in diameter. There was a massive explosion, and over a thousand people were injured when the meteor exploded. The shock wave was the most impressive part, damaging thousands of buildings and could be felt across several cities.

They had no idea it was coming; they were aware of the asteroid but not the meteor. That meteor was the most significant natural object to enter Earth's atmosphere since the last monster meteor in 1908, which wiped out a forest in Siberia.

If something like this happens once, it can happen again. Only this time, it will be worse.

"What did they say on the TV?" Mom asks as she steps into my makeshift bedroom.

"They're going to try to blow it up and push it off course," I reply, not looking up from my journal, where I've started doodling.

"Your brothers and I are going out tomorrow for food. Do you want to come with us?"

"No, I'll stay here; I don't like going out in town."

"I don't understand why you're like this. It would do you good to get out."

"The world's ending, Mom. I don't think what will do me good at this point matters." I look up from my journal to see that she's already walking away, tired of my self-pity. It's weird how we've switched in the last month. My mother was always one to seek pity from others, always the victim, and now I'm looking for pity. I am looking for anything from anyone to make me feel seen and alive.

Chapter Eleven
Humanity Lost

"And now there is merely silence, silence, silence, saying all we did not know."
— William Rose Benet

The house is quiet when I drag myself off the rumpled pull-out couch. A slight spasm ripples through my lower back as I swing my legs over the edge. Sleeping on the thin mattress has caught up to me, and my body resists every movement until I stretch it out.

I wander into the kitchen, my bare feet cooling on the linoleum floor. The fridge is almost empty, but two eggs are left in the carton. Will this be the last time that we have eggs to eat? I go to the pantry and feel my stomach drop as I look at the bare shelves. We will never make it if we don't start preparing for the end. Anxiety creeps up, tapping me on the shoulder and curling around my insides. I lose my appetite and put the eggs back in the fridge. Hopefully, Mom and the boys will be able to find food today. The store shelves have become just as bare as those in the pantry as companies have halted production of goods for public consumption.

I quietly make my way into the bathroom and turn on the shower so it can warm up. I then relieve myself and brush my teeth. Pulling back the shower curtain, I reach out my hand to feel the warm spray from the shower, but it's not warm. It's frigid. I pull the curtain back farther and look at the handle; it's turned up to the "H," yet the water is still freezing.

Stepping back from the shower, I take a moment to look around the bathroom. There's natural light coming in through one window, and the light is off. I reach out and try the light switch.

Nothing.

I quickly grab my pajamas and put them back on before rushing out of the bathroom, the shower still running.

I try the TV—nothing. Then I try the light switch—still nothing. I pause and listen for the air conditioning over the beating of my heart. The stillness in the house becomes cloying. The only sound is that of my breathing.

We don't have power.

I pull out my cell phone and look at the top right corner, where there should be service bars and a signal strength indicator. There's nothing there.

We don't have power, and we don't have cell service. I've seen enough disaster movies to know what this means.

I grab a pair of jeans and a T-shirt out of my suitcase after pulling it out from under the bony mattress I've been sleeping on. My heart is racing so fast that I can see it in my vision. Are we the only ones without power, or is it a city-wide issue? What if it's worldwide? Will this be how the panic starts?

I step out of the house, letting the screen door slam behind me, and waiting to hear the screams echoing throughout the town as chaos erupts. But I don't hear anything. It is eerily quiet. I don't see or hear any vehicles, people, or machinery noises.

I grab a bike from our porch and start pedaling my way down Main Street. There are several cars along the street, but there are still no people. Where have they all gone? Am I the only one left? Where would they go?

I'm breathless from pedaling and from the panic that's taking over. I decide to head toward the only grocery store in town. That's where people tend to gather, and if the world is ending, everyone is going to need food. Plus, I need to find Mom and my brothers. Rounding the corner, I slam on the brakes and almost go headfirst over the handlebars of my bike.

It's almost as if every person in town is at the store. But it's not the bloody, chaotic scene I'm expecting. They're all listening to something. I can barely make out the voice of someone on a radio from where I've stopped.

Swinging my leg over the seat of the bicycle, I dismount and let the bike fall to the warming asphalt. As I walk closer to the crowd, I start to make out the words coming from a handheld crank radio—the kind that I didn't know were still in existence, let alone still working.

"…there will be a lottery. This lottery will be held in two days, and it will determine the individuals who will be evacuated to underground shelters. A secondary lottery will be held in a week to decide which individuals will be evacuated to space stations. We are doing everything we can to ensure the survival of the human race. We ask that you remain calm and refrain from panicking. Radio channels broadcasting this information include FM 97.3, FM 100.4, and FM 92.5. Stay tuned for more details, and again, please remain calm."

There's the briefest moment of silence as what I assume is confusion ripples through the crowd, my panic adding to the tide. I catch a glimpse of familiar faces as people shift with the motion of the panic.

"Adam! Garrett!" I call out to my brothers and move toward them as the crowd shifts. People aren't leaving, but they aren't standing still, either. It's like everyone is shifting around, looking at each other, wondering what to do. Will anyone from Sandridge, Nebraska, be chosen? I grab Garrett's arm as I manage to wriggle my way through the now-crushing energy of the crowd.

"What's going on!" I shout, as a hundred people start to question their lives.

"We need to get out of here, now!" Garrett shouts back, grabbing Adam's arm.

"Where's Mom?" I look around and don't see her anywhere. I turn a full circle while elbowing the people around me to get some space.

"I don't know, she was just here."

"Garrett, we can't leave without her. Who knows what's going to happen?" I grip his arm tightly as the three of us turn slowly, looking for any sign of our mother's strawberry-blonde hair in the crowd.

Someone pushes me from behind, and I lean against them, trying to get space and keep on my feet. I get pushed again and turn. I can see that the crowd has become so clustered that it's almost impossible to move without pushing people out of the way.

"We're going to be crushed if we stay here!" Adam shouts.

"Back up!" A loud shout comes from the front of the crowd, and like one, we all turn.

The store owner stands on a bench in front of the shop's doors, a shotgun in hand.

"Everyone needs to leave and go home. There won't be any shoppin' today!" He cocks the shotgun.

Those close to the front start to panic as those in the back continue to push them forward toward the shop owner and his gun. We're somewhere in the middle with no idea where Mom is.

"Garrett, lead the way, get us out of here!" I cry out as someone pushes me into my brothers. Garrett is the largest of us all and will be able to use his bulk to help us escape. I hold on to the back of his shirt, and

Adam follows behind me as we make our way to the right side of the crowd. It's quicker to go this way than back to the left, from where I came from. I've given up hope of finding Mom or getting back to my bike. Right now, I'm just worried about getting out of here alive.

Garrett forces his way through the crowd, as people push and pull and dissolve into panic. Screams tear through the crowd as people topple over, get trampled, and are moved around.

I've heard people scream in terror before, at haunted houses and other fun, yet scary, events. Yet I've never heard people scream like they are now. It's as if all of the air in their lungs is being forced out of a constricted windpipe—some of the cries dying as soon as they start, as the person is crushed in the crowd. I've never heard anything like it before, and the sound makes the hair on my arms stand up and goosebumps spread across my skin.

Garrett breaks through the crowd, followed by me and Adam, all of us breathing heavily from the effort of navigating through the crushing crowd. Once we're free of the crowd, we look back, hoping to catch a glimpse of Mom. What we see instead is the crush of humanity taking its toll on the unfortunate souls that came out today.

"Jesus." Adam's whispered voice can barely be heard over the screaming and overwhelming surge of noise coming from the crowd. I've never seen anything like this before, and my heart clenches in my chest for those still stuck in the crowd. Everything in me longs to help them, but I know there's nothing I can do until the crowd settles and we can easily access those injured.

"Garrett! Adam! Adrian!" Our mother's voice rings out, clear as a bell, above the clamoring voices of the crowd, and the three of us turn as one toward it.

Mom is a little disheveled, but nothing compared to others who are stumbling from the mass of moving limbs. She has a small cut on her cheek that is leaking bright red blood down her pale, drawn face. I've never seen my mother look like this before. So scared and vulnerable and small. My brothers and I run toward her, Adam scooping her up in a hug as Garrett and I watch, pushing aside the stray pedestrians as needed, as they break free from the cloying cloud of body parts next to us.

"Are you all right?" I shout over the growing noise around us. She nods, and I reach out for her hand as we start to move away from the grocery store and the ever-increasing chaos around us.

The walk home is quiet. None of us says a word as we slowly make our way to the house, each of us lost in our thoughts, pondering what we just witnessed.

Finally, I can't hold my thoughts in any longer. "That was fucking insane," I whisper, looking around at the shellshocked faces of my siblings and mother.

"What just happened?" Adam replies. "Should we have stayed and helped?" he continues.

"I don't think there's much we could have done. I don't even know if it will have calmed down yet. People were losing their shit," I say, and silence falls over us again, the only sound that of the gravel beneath our soles.

"What about the lottery?" Garrett says, as we near the house. "Do you think anyone from here will get picked?"

"I doubt it, and if they are, it'll be the rich folks," Mom says as she huffs out a breath, winded from the walk back to the house. She always believed that people were out to get us and that only the rich mattered. I couldn't help but wonder if she was right in this case. If people had enough money, could they buy their way to space or an underground bunker?

As we walked in the mid-morning heat, all I could think of was the lottery. What about us? What are we going to do? The likelihood of us being picked in the lottery is slim to none, and we need a plan for when the asteroid hits. I have a feeling that things are going to get crazy now that they've announced the lottery; there's no telling what people will do.

I pause in front of our house, looking at it as if I'll find the answers written in the grime coating the white stucco exterior.

"You coming?" Garrett asks, turning around at the front door to look back at me.

"I'll be in in a minute or two." I'm not sure if I can stand the suffocating interior of the house just yet. I need to be outside, to feel the sun and the fresh air on my skin for a bit longer. Pulling up one of the abandoned plastic chairs on the front lawn, I sit down and let my skin bake in the sun while my mind wanders.

If today is a glimpse at what's to come, the world will be torn asunder in no time. People will get angrier: they'll blame the government at first, then they'll blame each other, and before we know it, we'll have set the world alight with our hate before the asteroid even enters our atmosphere.

My stomach turns as the anxiety rolls through me, making my body tingle. I need to do something to keep my mind off the impending doom of our planet, so I pick up the shovel lying in the grass next to the house and start digging. The smell of fresh dirt prickles the inside of my nostrils as the pile next to me grows ever larger, the more I dig.

I dig until the sun goes down and exhaustion tugs at my every limb. Stopping only when I can't see the difference between the blade of the shovel and the dirt it cuts into with each pass.

July 2030

It took far less time than I thought for people to start to lose their shit. The day after the grocery store stampede, people started running the streets in gangs of five to ten. Every person is armed to the teeth with various weapons. I don't know what to do or who to trust in this town anymore. I'm afraid that it's every person for themselves. The fact that people are already going crazy makes me worried about what will happen tomorrow, when they draw the lottery. When people know for certain that they aren't picked, I'm sure things will get quickly out of hand. What do we do now? How do we prepare for the end of the world? It's possible to prepare for a hurricane or ride out a tornado in the basement, but when it comes to an asteroid barreling through space, there's not much that can be done. One minute, the world will be fine, and the next, we will all cease to exist.

Chapter Twelve
Lottery Day

I can feel the tension in the room as we gather around the battery-powered radio, waiting for the lottery to start. They're doing it by social security number and are selecting several thousand people to go to the underground bunkers. It's seven in the morning. The lottery will last all day, as it is being conducted using a random number selector set up in conjunction with the Social Security agency. I'm not sure how this will work, but I can imagine it won't work very well. Will they let families go together, or is it just the selected person?

They haven't shared any further information since the original announcement, and I know we're not the only ones who have questions. This is what the United States has decided to do, but what about the rest of the world? Is Europe conducting a lottery as well, or do they have a different approach?

Now that communication has been cut off with the rest of the world, we can only get our information in bits and pieces from the disembodied voices coming through our radios. How do we know if they're telling us the truth?

They said the towers are down because of grid failures and overload, but I can't shake the feeling it is also about control. It's a lot easier to manage panic when people can't connect with anyone outside their own town.

"It's starting! It's starting!" Adam whispers excitedly, and I turn my attention back to the radio that we're all huddled in front of. The announcer's voice sounds like it's a million miles away, fighting through the airwaves to reach our eager ears, as he starts reading off the first number.

We've been here all day, waiting for our number to be called. Hoping for it to be called, yet here we are at the end of the lottery, still huddled around the radio, but feeling less alive than we did when it started. It's evident as the man on the radio wraps up that none of us have made it. Now we need to start thinking about what we're going to do. I glance around at my brothers and my mom. I imagine we, all of us, have the same look on our faces: one of defeat and confusion.

"What now?" I ask.

"What the fuck do you mean, 'What now'?" Garrett says, standing angrily. "We're screwed! There's nothing for us to do, nothing can save us from an ASTEROID!"

It's panic, and I know it is because I can feel it clawing at the edges of my brain as well, feel it tightening my chest.

"We can't just sit here and do nothing." I look around at them, only to get incredulous looks back from my family.

"I think that's all there is to do," Mom says, sitting back in her chair and taking a drag of her half-smoked Misty Menthol 120, the long white body of the cigarette bouncing in her mouth as she sucks on the end of it.

"I can't do that. I won't do that. I'm going to find a way for us to get underground. Perhaps we can find a nearby bunker or build our own. We have time to do that, right?" I'm trying desperately to keep the panic from my voice, but it creeps in at the end, causing my voice to rise before my throat closes around my vocal cords, cutting off the question.

"We might be able to do that," Adam says. He's been quiet this whole time, leaning back in his chair and not making eye contact with anyone.

"How, though?" I ask, turning to face him fully.

"What about the bunker at the old house in the country? Could we keep digging that out and turn it into something else? Something bigger and more secure?"

"That's a brilliant idea! I hadn't even thought of the old bunker!" I can't contain my excitement and jump out of my chair, smiling hugely at everyone.

"If we all chip in, we should be able to construct something pretty nice before they say the initial impact will happen." I glance around again, hoping to see some hope and acknowledgement from Garrett and Mom. But they don't seem to get it; both look dejected and hopeless while Adam and I give each other nods. If Garrett and Mom don't want to help, the two of us will do this alone.

I'm not quite ready to give up just yet.

It's been a few days since the lottery announcement, and here we are, huddled around the radio again as they announce who will be going to the space station. I have no hope this time; I fully expect them to take the rich and the brightest among humankind to the space stations. It would make sense for them to take some action to ensure that our species will survive and be able to rebuild if there's anything left. This is precisely what they did. They didn't share the names of individuals chosen, but had a moment of calling out social security numbers, and then the voice on the radio shared what I had been waiting for:

"In coordination with our colleagues around the world, we have decided that we will be bringing several scientists, doctors, and experts to the space station to help preserve our existence. Some of these individuals have already been informed of this decision, and others will be informed in the next day or two."

"That's bullshit!" Garrett yells, pushing back his chair so quickly that it topples behind him as he walks out of the living room and out the front door. I understand how he feels, but I also know that they're trying to save the world, literally, and they have to do something. They can't accommodate every person who wants to go into space or give everyone a spot in the bunkers. There's only so much room and so many supplies. What else can they do?

"He'll calm down," Adam says, getting up and following Garrett out of the house.

I look over at Mom and watch as she gets up to follow the boys out of the house, leaving me alone with the droning voice on the radio repeating the message about space and who they'll be taking.

I swallow around the lump forming in my throat and look around the empty house. Its walls are covered in photographs documenting our childhood but also stained with a film of cigarette smoke. I know that if I took a photo, the outline would still be visible on the wall, a brighter shade of off-white than the browning walls around it. I look down at my clenched hands, taking a deep breath of the stagnant air.

I need to get out of here, but I can't leave my family. I need them to come with me, to get on board with a bunker at the old house. How do I convince them to do this?

It takes Garrett thirty minutes to calm down and for the family to return home. I'm still sitting where they left me in the living room, except the radio is now off.

"Adam says that the bunker at the old house is our only option if we want a chance," Garrett says, looking from Adam to me. I nod; Garrett has never been one to listen to me.

"When are we going to get started?" he asks.

"Tomorrow," Adam and I say in unison.

"Mom, I need you to gather canned goods if you can without running into trouble," I say, looking at her as she nods in agreement. "We'll make the move out to the old house in a day or two. I think it'll be safer out there, with fewer people around. I think things are going to get crazy around here once people start to realize that no one is going to save them."

Again, I'm met with nods and a regretful sense of compliance.

"We need to make sure we have everything that we need to survive. We don't know how long we'll be underground, but we should plan for at least six months, if not longer."

I stand up, feeling the need to move and get out some of my anxiety, "I'm going for a walk, but we should start packing tonight so we can get moved as soon as possible."

"Be safe," Mom says around her dangling cigarette.

"Right," I say back and walk between Adam and Garrett, almost running to get out of the door. What if I'm doing the wrong thing? What if we should be doing something else? How do I know if this will work?

The panic subsides a bit as I step out into the cooling evening air. I tilt my head back and close my eyes, taking deep, settling breaths. I open my eyes, letting them slowly focus on the stars overhead. I used to be obsessed with stars, begging my mom to get me a planetarium for my room so I could lie on my floor and feel like I was outside. I have many memories of lying on the ground, looking up at the stars, and wishing I were up there with them. And now they were coming to me, crashing into my world, destroying everything.

I walk out to the dirt road in front of the house and turn a slow circle, looking for the asteroid. They said on the radio earlier that it could be seen now because it was closer. They also stated that debris from the tail would likely begin to fall to Earth within the next week. They didn't know how large the pieces would be or where they would fall, just that they were coming. I didn't share this with the family. I don't see how it would make a difference; plus, they'll hear it later when they turn the radio on again, as they've been broadcasting the same information repeatedly. Right now, we need to focus on building our bunker and finding food.

I continue my slow turn and stop once I catch a glimpse of something that seems "off" in the sky. It looks like a shooting star, but it's huge, and behind it is a smoky tail, like the kind of trail left behind by a plane. That must be it. Standing in the middle of the street, looking up at an asteroid that's going to destroy the world. How is any of this real? How is this happening?

The tightness in my chest returns, and a small sob escapes before I can catch it. My chest is so tight I can barely get a breath in or out as the squeezing continues. I drop my hands to my knees and bend over, trying to catch my breath. My tears fall to the dirt-covered ground in front of my scuffed shoes and are immediately soaked up by the dry earth.

ARDEN COUTTS

Is this how we all die?

Chapter Thirteen
Into the Dark

"Sometimes the sound of silence is the most deafening sound of all." — K.L. Toth

August 2030

It's been two days since they announced the space station lottery winners, and everything has gone to shit. People have lost their damn minds, and our small country town has been thrown into chaos. People in town are angry, scared, and in a state of denial. I was driving through town today and saw a man get shot. He was trying to take food from the store, and Gary, the store owner, shot him, right there in the street. He didn't pause or warn the man before he opened up, firing on him. Am I any better, though? I didn't stop, didn't even pause, when I saw it happen. I just kept on driving. Does that make me just as responsible for that man's death?

I'm still thinking about the dead man in the middle of the street, surrounded by the canned food he had with him, as I pull into the dirt driveway of our old farmhouse. It's a good ten miles outside of town, and there's nothing around it. The house itself has been abandoned since we moved out all those years ago and is slowly collapsing. We've been driving back and forth from town to the country house every day for the last couple of days. Eventually, I know we will have to move out of here, as it will become too dangerous in town. The faster we can get our bunker fixed up, the better.

Climbing out of my car, I take a deep breath, and for the briefest moment, I'm transported back in time to my childhood. I'm suddenly ten years old again, running through the fields, now overgrown and unkempt, chasing after my siblings as we play tag. Opening my eyes, I look up at the sky, looking for the weak shadow of our incoming doom. Not finding it, I give up and head to the backyard, where both brothers are digging. We need to clean out all the debris that has built up at the bottom of the bunker, and then we must continue digging. Not only down, but we needed to dig over, through the walls toward possible cave systems. We don't have a way to reinforce the entrance of the bunker, so our best bet is to dig down and over, away from the opening as far as we can, as deep as we can.

I conducted some research on the geology in the area with the hope of finding cave systems nearby, only to find that what lurks beneath the Sandhills is almost as scary as what the surface had transformed into. The Sandhills were an old ocean of sand, layered and shifting, a landscape that swallowed water and kept it hidden, feeding it down into the aquifer like a secret it refused to give back. Digging here didn't feel like carving into earth so much as disturbing something that had been settling for thousands of years. The deeper we went, the colder it got. The air changed. The soil darkened. Every shovel of sand felt too easy, like the land was letting us in on purpose. They said Nebraska didn't have caves the way other places did. There were no grand limestone cathedrals, no tourist trails, but the plains still had hollows, old channels, buried pockets where water had moved and moved and moved, carving unseen spaces through softer layers. Not caves, exactly. Something worse. Something unfinished. And the farther down we dug, the more it felt like we weren't building a bunker at all; we were reaching for a hidden underworld that ran beneath the state, beneath the borders, beneath everything we thought we understood…stretching north through the bones of the plains toward South Dakota, where the land turned rough and ancient and the dark had been waiting a lot longer than we had.

I'm terrified that we won't find the hollows, that we won't find any caves and that we'll be digging until we die. I don't have the heart to tell my family that even if we do this, the likelihood of us living is damn slim.

It's okay to lie to them if it's for their good, right?

My heart races with my secrets and lies as I walk up to the bunker. Which, right now, is just a slab of cement with an opening in the ground at one end. We used to play in it as kids, using it as a hiding place. I never liked going down there; it was full of spiders and creeped me out. It felt like someone, or something, was going to reach out of the depths of the debris and snatch me up if I wasn't careful. Now the danger is coming from above rather than below.

I don't immediately jump in to help with the digging. I'm too lost in my thoughts to realize I'm even at the edge of the bunker, my body seemingly stopping on its own. My mind flashed back to the dead man on the street and the rumors that had started popping up in town about the military killings.

"Yo, are you gonna just stand there or are you going to help us?" Adam's voice cuts through my mental fog, and I drop the supplies I'm holding next to the bunker. I managed to scrounge up some canned goods from an abandoned house in town before being run off by other looters.

"What's on your mind?" Garrett asks, both brothers now pulling themselves out from under the cement roof of our bunker.

"They're talking about military killings in town. The National Guard has been deployed to bigger cities to deal with riots."

"What's the point in rioting?" Garrett says, looking from Adam, then back to me.

I shrug, even though I know it's purely of desperation and hate.

"Who cares. If we don't have to deal with them, we've got enough to focus on." Adam throws a shovel in my direction, "It's your turn to dig for a bit."

I put the rest of the supplies down and pick up the gritty, dirt- and sweat-covered shovel. The hole to get into the bunker is small, and I have to suck in my stomach as far as I can and shimmy back and forth until my lower body passes the smallest part of the entrance. Once my waist is past, I drop the rest of my body through. We'll need to fix that.

I pause in the darkness and wait for my eyes to adjust. My nostrils are assaulted by the smell of fresh, moist dirt and decay, two smells I'm already familiar with, but know I'll be getting much more of in the upcoming weeks.

Most of the bunker has been cleared out, and we've started digging into the far side, in the direction of where a cave system should exist, that is, if we can find it. Picking up the shovel, I move toward the opposite wall and start digging. It's not the precise strokes of a flat shovel that I'm used to using in archaeology, but rather fast, hard chops into the side of the dirt wall. All I'm hoping for is to knock larger chunks out so that I can move more mass with less shoveling.

"One of you should work on making the entrance bigger and making it easier to get in here," I say between breaths. When I don't get a response, I pause my digging, listening for my brothers. Hearing nothing, I turn and keep digging. It's best to keep digging.

The rhythmic sound of the shovel piercing the dirt wall soon takes over every part of my body. All I can hear is the soft crunch of the shovel slicing and the sound of my breathing. I don't know how long I dig, but when I stop, my shirt clings to me, and the dirt below my feet is spotted with my sweat.

The shovel slips from my numb, blistered hands and falls to the floor as I gasp for breath. It isn't panic, not yet, but it's close. The tightness is there, and I'm having trouble breathing. I can't tell if it's from digging so much or from the ever-growing anxiety swirling through my body.

I glance toward the entrance of the bunker and can't see any light. I've dug through the daylight into the night, and no one came to check on me. I close my eyes, and what little light is left from the setting sun is blacked out by the back of my lids. I slow my breathing, taking deep breaths of the earthen, moldy air. It's rich in its scent, almost making me gag in its heaviness. I fight through it, one hand on my chest, grounding myself in the feel of my steadying heartbeat.

I open my eyes and let the darkness of the bunker consume me. This is what it's going to be like from here on out. We'll be underground soon, and sunlight will be something that we dream about as we cast shadows on cave walls with our flashlights and candles. I don't move for several minutes, allowing my body to acclimate to my new surroundings.

How will we survive like this, and how long will we be able to?

I find the shovel in the dark. Placing my hand on the dirt wall in front of me, I start digging again. The slicing of the shovel is the only sound echoing through the darkness.

Chapter Fourteen
World's End

September 2030

The news came in whispered waves. Parts of the world have been destroyed.
Smaller pieces of debris from the asteroid had entered our atmosphere, burned
in the night sky, and crashed to the surface. We had watched the meteorites
burning through the atmosphere at night, but it was impossible to tell where
they had landed and how bad the devastation from the impact would be.
It was beautiful to watch as the smaller pieces exploded in the atmosphere,
shooting off brilliant sparks and lighting up the night sky with a flash of light.
The sky was ablaze with hundreds of bright streamers that ended in light
bursts, resembling fireworks. I spent time outside every night, watching the
bursts of light fill the sky. Closing my eyes, I would see them streaming across
the backs of my lids.
Then the whispers came. I don't know where they started, but information finds
a way, and this was no different. The world was burning from the impacts, and
if the asteroid didn't kill us all, the fires just might.

I pause writing in my journal to look at the flickering candle next to me. We've started sleeping in the bunker recently, the four of us clustered together in our tents, each of us with our candles and flashlights. I try not to burn mine too often, but the darkness gets to me, and I find myself using more candles than the rest of the family. We've made significant progress on the bunker and found the cave after three weeks of digging. It's massive and gives me some hope.

We haven't ventured too far away from the house yet, though. I think we're afraid to leave behind the last semblance of humanity that we know—still yearning for the feel of the sun on our skin in the daytime. I know I'm not willing to give that up just yet.

"Anything on the radio?" Adam's hushed voice whispers through the darkness.

"No, there still hasn't been an announcement. They were supposed to launch tomorrow, right?" Garrett's hoarse voice seems to fill the entire space even though he's whispering.

"Yeah, the DART mission is supposed to happen tomorrow, and then the launching of the ships to the space station after that. I think they are launching at the same time, but I'm not sure," I whisper back.

We all fall silent, the heaviness of the cool, moist bunker air cloying in its thickness. It is almost as bad as the air outside. In the last week, the air above ground had taken a turn. Filling with ash and smoke from all the fires, it is hard to breathe when we go outside, but we still do, trying to soak up as much sunlight as we can through the smoky atmosphere before we move underground permanently.

"Do you think we'll be able to see it from here?" Garrett asks. I hear the tent fabric rustling as he turns over, his silhouette splashed across the tent wall.

"No. I think they are launching from Florida and North Carolina, and with all the ash and smoke in the air, I doubt we'd see it even if we lived in those states," I respond, shifting in my tent, trying to find a more comfortable position on the dirt-covered floor of the bunker.

"I heard in town today that a meteor hit in Iowa just over the state line. There's nothing left of Iowa now. It wiped the entire state out." Adam's whispered news brings nothing but tense silence.

I can't help but be thankful that we weren't impacted by it, but I'm also devastated by the loss of life, so many people.

I had wondered if the rumbling I'd felt in the ground the other day was a meteorite making impact somewhere, and it seems like I was right. We've been lucky so far, only seeing the small meteorites burning up in the atmosphere, but there are so many now that it was only a matter of time.

"Try to get some sleep," I manage around the lump in my throat.

Turning over, I try to take my advice, but the whispers in my mind are too loud for me to ignore. They're telling me to get up, to dig, to run. They're telling me that I must survive and that death is coming for me.

I almost sob as the time ticks by, the only sounds the muffled breathing of my family around me and the slight electric buzz of the battery-powered clock next to my head. I swear I can hear the numbers switching over as every minute passes.

At two in the morning, I leave my tent, moving silently through the bunker and out into the night. It's cold, and a chill runs through my body. I didn't bother putting my shoes on; it's easier and quieter to move without them.

I pad over to where my bike is leaning against the porch of the farmhouse. Pausing for a moment, I close my eyes and let the feeling of the grass under my feet ground me in the world of the night.

Getting on my bike, I start the ten-mile ride into town. I've gotten fast at it and know it won't take me too long. I've been biking into town once or twice a week to look for supplies in the cover of the night. Many people have fled, and that means they've left behind things that might be useful. It's dangerous, but we need supplies to survive.

I concentrate on my breathing and the sound of the tires on the dirt road as I ride, noticing the subtle changes in the sounds as I transition from gravel roads to paved ones. Soon, the dark outlines of the houses of Sandridge loom on the horizon, backlit by the faint light of the moon.

I head toward the library and the block of houses to the east of it that I haven't checked yet. Many of them were abandoned before the world went wild, but it doesn't hurt to check them out.

The first house I check is directly across from the library and empty for as long as I can remember. I drop the bike behind some bushes and walk through the doorway. There isn't a door, so getting in is easy. Pulling out my flashlight, I shine it around the room before moving. I hold my breath, scanning the darkness for any signs of life. Seeing none, I breathe out slowly and start to move through the house, going first to the kitchen. It's been picked clean; the drawers and cabinet doors have been thrown open, with some items missing. I move through the house like a ghost, picking through the rooms and finding nothing that will be of any use.

I turn the flashlight off before I leave so as not to draw attention to myself. I crouch down at the door and listen. There's the distant sound of a truck, but it doesn't sound close enough for me to worry about.

Grabbing my bike, I move to the next block. The houses are clones of each other, their silhouettes blurring together in the darkness. There aren't any cars on the streets or in the driveways, which leads me to believe that most people have left. I bike down the road, looking at each house as I pass it, pausing to look for cameras and any signs that they might still be inhabited. Seeing none, I park my bike at the first house and go to the front door.

It's slightly ajar.

I push it open with my foot as I go into a crouch. I stay low as I move into the living room, using the couch next to the door as cover just in case someone is home. Pausing, I let my eyes adjust to the shadows of the house and start to move, slinking through them as if I were a shadow myself.

I check the whole house first and find it empty. Now I can hunt.

I find a duffel bag in the first room I enter. I pause to take it in. There are posters of a pop group on the light blue walls, Polaroids in the mirror, and drying flowers hanging by the window. I would have loved this room as a kid. I grab the duffel from the closet and search the rest of the room for anything that we might be able to use. I find a few batteries and a flashlight in the desk drawer.

I move to the next room, gathering any items that run on batteries that could be beneficial. I stop at the bathroom and empty their medicine cabinet, taking all the basic pain medication they have. I find a well-stocked medicine kit under the sink and grab that as well.

I slither down the stairs, barely feeling the carpet on my bare feet as I move quickly and quietly, not giving them long enough to even creak under my weight. My last stop is the kitchen. I find a few reusable grocery bags and fill one of them with canned foods from the pantry. The person who lived here left in a hurry and didn't take anything with them. I'll have to remember this address so I can come back for more food. I fill the bag and reluctantly start heading back to where I had left my bike. I would take more, but it's challenging to go back with too much weight, and I want to get back before the sun starts to rise.

I pause at my bike, listening. The sound of a truck ripples through the night air, disturbing the silence. It sounds closer than it was before; the hair on my arms and the back of my neck stands up, and something tells me to hunker down and not move. I take the bags off and set them down next to my bike, behind some bushes, and lie flat next to them.

They don't have their lights on, but their truck is loud enough to give them away. The truck is black and rolls around the corner on my right, the direction I need to go to get home. It moves slowly, and I can barely see three figures in the front seat illuminated by the dashboard lights.

This can't be good.

It doesn't look like they're looking for supplies, as they're not stopping at any of the houses, which means they're looking for someone or something to fuck with. I try my damnedest to sink into the ground and duck my head as they drive past. I can hear them talking, but not well enough to make out what they're saying.

The truck rolls down the road, slowly turns the corner, and continues down the road to the south of me. I jump up as soon as it's out of sight and get on my bike. I grab both bags, sling the heavy duffel across my back, and put the bag of food in the small basket on the front of the bike.

I start pedaling down the road, heading west toward home. I've just made it to the end of the block when I hear the truck. Looking over, I can see it at the end of the road and know that they can see me.

The headlights suddenly blaze on and blind me as the truck's engine roars to life, and they floor it toward me. I'm momentarily stunned by the light, but my instincts kick in and I start to pedal faster, flying down the road, hoping that they won't follow. The headlights turn in my direction as they make it to the street I'm on, and I'm illuminated from behind. I can hear their laughter over the roar of the engine.

I know I can't outrun them, but I can't seem to focus or think of any way to get away from them. My brain is full of chaos, and I'm panicking, which makes me much more winded than I should be. At this rate, I'll run out of energy before they catch me. I pedal faster; my legs and lungs burn with every spin of the tires.

Okay, I'm on a bike, I can go places a truck can't.

I make a quick turn down a narrow dirt alley and hope that it's too small for their large, jacked truck to follow, but they do. The sound of the engine vibrates off the building walls, seemingly shaking them as I pedal past.

Shit. Shit. Shit.

My lungs are so tight that I can barely pull air into them as I continue to race down the alley and make a fast right turn onto one of the side roads back by where the grocery store used to be.

I pedal down the road, almost losing control as the road gives way to gravel. There's a bike trail ahead that I can take. It's wide enough for bikes, but I don't think the truck will make it. I risk a glance behind me and almost crash my bike. They're close and getting closer with every second. I can see their faces clearly, and all I see is pure unadulterated joy. They have guns and are dressed as if they are going deer hunting, except they're not hunting deer; they're hunting people.

I focus on my breathing and pedaling, finding a rhythm that I can maintain. I'm almost to the trail when they pull up beside me.

They're just playing with me.

The realization hits me as I look over and hear their laughter tinkling through the whooshing of air around me. I'm not going to make it, and we all know it now. I was the last one to figure it out.

They nudge the truck over, and I swerve to miss getting hit, which effectively causes me to wipe out. The bike slides away from under me as I hit the ground hard, and what air I have in my lungs is pushed out abruptly as my body meets the ground. My teeth clatter together, and I taste blood as I bite down hard on my tongue. The duffel bag of stolen goods somewhat cushions my fall, but I find myself rolling down the road embankment, unable to stop.

The bike and bag of food are lost; there's no way I'm getting those back.

I sit up, dazed and confused. I'm at the bottom of the embankment, next to a small stream and a culvert. I have enough awareness to move toward the culvert. I can fit if I take the bag off. Shoving the duffle first, I follow it and inch forward into the cold water at the base of the culvert.

Above me on the road, the truck stops, and the men get out. Again, their voices are muffled, but the intention is clear. I know it's only a matter of time before they find me, so I keep crawling. Maybe I can make it to the other side and sneak away before they notice. The cold water and mud seep into my open wounds as I continue to crawl through the muck. I grit my teeth against the pain, but I can feel my body starting to shake, probably from shock and pain. It's only as I make it to the other side of the culvert that I realize how cold the water is. My teeth are chattering, and it feels like it's the loudest sound in the world.

I stay in the culvert, listening. I can still hear the men, but it sounds like they're on the other side still. I slide out of the culvert on my stomach and plaster myself to the side of the ditch, hoping that the tall grass will cover my escape. It hurts to move.

I can't seem to slow my breathing, and it's coming in short bursts, exploding around the chattering of my teeth. The gravel and rocks are cutting into my cold feet, and everything in me wants to stop and rest. But I know I have to keep going, I know if I'm caught, I'll be killed. This isn't a game of hide-and-seek; it's a matter of life or death. Hugging the duffle to my chest, I keep moving, slowly inching farther away from the men and their truck.

"Fuck, there's a culvert here!" The exclamation is loud, and I know it's only a matter of seconds before they find me.

I move faster, crouching low and moving with the flow of the grass in the hopes that they won't see me.

I make it to the bike trail as they continue to look around the culvert's ends. I stay in the ditch, but I move closer to the tree line, where the shadows are darker, and I keep going.

Faster, faster. I need to go faster.

I can't hear them anymore, and when I look behind me, I can't see the truck. I think I'm far enough away so that I can move to the trail where I can make time faster. I'm only a few miles from home at this point and can use the trail most of the way before cutting over. There are a few houses on the way, and I'll stop to see if I can find another bike or something I can use so I don't have to walk the whole way.

I climb up the embankment and stand on the trail for a moment. Finally, I can rest and catch my breath. Every inch of my body hurts, and I can feel a sob rising in my chest. I'm so tired.

The hardest thing to do is to start walking again. My feet are bloodied and bruised, as is the rest of my body. I limp along the trail until I come to the first farmhouse. It's dark and quiet, like everything around it. I try the garage first and can't believe what I see.

A bike!

I grab it and make a run for the trail, not caring how much noise I'm making. I hope no one is home. It only takes me a minute to get back to the trail with my newly procured bike. It's better than the one I had before. Sturdier.

Pedaling brings a new kind of pain as the scraped skin on my legs pulls with every movement of my legs. Silent tears track down my dirt- and sweat-covered face as I ride, the cool air of the night chilling everything as I go.

Before I know it, I'm pedaling up our driveway, and the sun is rising beside me. I can finally see where I stand.

I get off the bike slowly, take off the dirty and torn duffle, and look at my body.

The skin on both of my palms is scraped, with a huge chunk missing on my left hand. My pants are torn in numerous places, and under the denim are scrapes full of debris from the gravel road. I lift my shirt to find brushes and a few scrapes on my ribs. I won't be able to hide this from my family. I feel my face and find a scrape on the right side of it, just under my eye. I'm definitely not going to be able to hide this.

Making my way around the front of the house to the bunker, I slide down the opening and find everyone still asleep in their tents. The exhaustion hits me so hard that I can feel the heaviness in my eyes and limbs. I toss the duffle in the corner and crawl into my tent, ignoring the pain of crawling on my hands and knees. I feel sleep pulling me under before my head even hits the pillow.

As I start to wake up, the pain in my hands and knees begins to radiate through the rest of my body. Waves of fire lick their way down my nerves, causing me to suck in a breath before opening my eyes.

I lay in the cool tent, surrounded by the scent of freshly disturbed soil, for several minutes, letting my body and eyes adjust. Every inch of my body is sore. My muscles scream as I flex them, feeling out how badly I've hurt myself.

My wounds are dirty still, crusted over and weeping at the same time. I sit up slowly in my tent, looking at my shredded palms. It's going to be so painful pulling out all the gravel and cleaning the wounds. Luckily, I have the first aid kit that I took from the house last night, and it's fully stocked.

I can hear the muffled voices of my family above me, and I know they are outside, not in the bunker with me. Opening the tent flap, I extend my legs through the opening in the nylon material and pull out my lamp, turning it on so it illuminates the interior of the bunker.

My pants are soaked with blood and pus and stuck to my open wounds.

Where do I even start?

I use some water to wet the cloth of my pants, loosening them where they're fused to the wounds. Wincing, I unbutton my pants and slowly pull them off without standing up. Slipping them off, I'm left in a long-sleeved shirt and my boxers. I can now fully see the extent of my leg injuries. I'm covered in scrapes of various sizes and depths on both legs. My upper thigh, having taken the brunt of my fall, has a large patch of road rash that needs to be cleaned of rocks and gravel.

I'm going to have to ask for help.

"Mom! Can you come help me?" I call out from the bunker and listen to the voices above me as they pause.

"What do you need?" she asks from the top of the opening.

"I had an accident last night and need help cleaning out my scrapes." She doesn't know that I've been going out at night for supplies. None of them do.

I hear shuffling, and soon Mom is standing in front of me, looking down at my demolished legs and hands.

"What the hell did you do?"

"I had an accident on my bike. I went for a ride last night and hit some loose gravel. I crashed."

"No shit. It looks terrible."

"It feels terrible," I mutter, turning on my side so she can access my upper thigh better. I rest my head on my forearms as I lie there, letting her slowly pick the gravel out of my body. Every pebble sends zings of pain rippling through me.

I fall asleep at some point and only wake up when she pats me on my shoulder. Rolling over and sitting up, I've barely opened my eyes, but

I know that she's cleaned my legs, arms, and hands. I've been out for a while.

"Sorry, I fell asleep," I whisper.

"It's okay, you must have been tired. All your midnight supply runs are catching up with you."

"You know about those?" I ask, looking at my bandaged hands.

"Of course, we all do. Supplies don't just magically appear. We've noticed all the things that you've been bringing in lately."

"I don't think we have enough."

"Don't be silly. I think we have more than enough. You know that we probably won't even need to be in this bunker for that long. I hate that we're already living down here. I don't think it's necessary."

If she only knew what town was like, I think she'd have a different opinion.

"Right," is all I say. I've given up trying to reason with her and trying to explain that the world is coming to an end. She's in denial, and there's no speaking to her about the fact that we might be underground for a long time.

"One of your brothers heard from a trader that they're launching the rockets tonight."

"It seems like they're launching them earlier than they initially said they would. I wonder if that means something?"

"I doubt it." She pats my leg as she gets up, leaving me sitting in the darkness of the bunker, my shadow bouncing off the dirt walls around me.

I sleep through the entire day and am still so tired. I can barely keep my eyes open as I find some canned tuna to eat. Moving hurts, sitting hurts, and opening the can of tuna hurts. I've never experienced so much pain at one time before. My body is shaking as I stand in the bunker eating my meal. I want to go outside for a bit, but I don't think I can climb out of the bunker or get back in without hurting myself further.

I change my clothes and settle back in my tent, zipping it and dozing throughout the rest of the day. I wake up briefly when the rest of the family comes down for the night, and then the darkness takes me.

"Wake up, wake up!" Garrett's shouts ring through the space of the bunker's opening where we all are sleeping. I have no idea what time it is or what is going on, but I can smell smoke. I sit up, ignoring the screaming in my body, and scramble out of the tent. Garrett, Adam, and Mom are already out of their tents and standing below the entrance of the bunker, looking out into the darkness of the night.

Except it isn't dark. I can see an orange glow flickering through the night air.

"What the fuck is going on?" Adam whispers as we all stand transfixed.

"We should pack up our stuff and move deeper into the caves," I say, looking around at their upturned faces. This might be it. This might be the end. What if a meteor hit near us?

"Don't be silly, it's just a bit of fire," Mom says.

"I think it's more than that," Adam replies, and then he moves to go outside.

"Be careful!" I shout as he scrambles his way up and out of the bunker.

"Holy shit!" His shout comes almost immediately as he stands up and looks around. We look from underground as he turns in a circle before climbing back down into the bunker.

"Adrian is right. We need to grab our stuff and move deeper into the tunnels."

"What's going on?" Garrett asks.

"The world is burning."

Chapter Fifteen
A World on Fire

October 2030

I imagine this is what hell looks like. Flames raging uncontrolled through the world, leaving nothing but her charred skin behind. Embers blowing on the wind as it gusts through the flat plains of Nebraska, nothing there to stop it. The world is on fire, and there is no stopping it. It is burning. People without shelters underground burned with the rest of the surface. I've been told that the smell of burning flesh flowed over the blazing landscapes of the Earth; her body blackened and littered with death. But this is only the beginning.

We fled from the surface, choosing to survive in the ground, when the air turned toxic, and the sky stopped looking like the sky. We sealed ourselves in and listened to the world above us die. We kept digging until the bunker shifted, a little at first, as if the Earth were settling into a new shape, and then the wall gave way into a hollow space that shouldn't have been there. Cold air spilled through the opening, damp and old, carrying the scent of stone and water. Crawling into the darkness, the small hollow opened wider the farther we went, a hidden underworld fed by the aquifer and carved out by time and pressure, and moving water appeared before us.

Others had been digging as well, bunkers being punched into the earth, tunnels reinforced with scavenged lumber and sheet metal. Everyone looking for the same thing: water, shelter, and a place where the fire and destruction couldn't touch. It became apparent that the hollows weren't isolated; they were connected, like veins. Linking us with strangers and pockets of survivors below the burning plains.

I sit up as Garrett and Adam come into the new cavern that we had moved into after the fires started. We'd moved about two days ago, going deeper into the cave system, hoping to escape the smoke and heat from the flames above us. So far, it seems to have worked. We used small, collapsible wagons to move all our goods, along with hiking packs filled to the brim. We managed to move everything easily, and the natural cave floors were relatively smooth and flat.

We ran into a few other people and heard that the launch of the rockets hadn't gone well, which is what started the fires. They said that only a few of the rockets launched made it past the debris field of the asteroid; the others exploded in the atmosphere, with flaming pieces falling back to Earth. That's when the fires started. There were parts of the United States that were still burning after several days had passed.

Whispers through the caves said that the sky itself was on fire—the results of the failed DART mission. Apparently, the ship contacted the asteroid but didn't move it enough to impact its trajectory toward Earth, so Russia sent up several nuclear payloads in the hopes of blowing the asteroid up. It worked to some extent, breaking the asteroid into millions of pieces. There was so much debris that the sky was on fire as it entered the atmosphere. It was a single massive rolling cloud of fire raining down fireballs and chaos as everyone fled the surface.

Every bit of news came to us as people passed through the cave system. Garrett took it upon himself to go out on scouting missions to see what was waiting for us further in the caves. He gathered a great deal of information as he spoke with others and shared it with us. It was the only way for us to get news.

"You know how we felt that tremor the other day?" Garrett whispers into the dank, dark air.

"Yeah, it felt like a pretty big earthquake," I whisper back. The darkness has a way of making you want to whisper, as if speaking too loudly will wake the things hiding in it.

"Apparently, there have been several large meteorites that have hit us. Not big enough to wipe us all out, but large enough to devastate the areas they hit, causing earthquakes and tsunamis. Someone said the sun was blocked out now by all the dust and debris, and I heard that, like, 75% of the population was wiped out with the last one that hit." Garrett's hushed voice grows louder as he talks, almost like he's excited to share the news.

"I wonder how much of that is true." Adam's voice comes from the darkness to my left; neither of us know that he's there and listening to us the whole time.

"It's hard to say. But I do think it's safe to say that every time we feel the earth shake, it means there's been another impact." I nod at Garrett's last statement, forgetting that they can't see me.

"I think that's a safe assumption," I finally respond. I think it's safe to say that our planet will be left pockmarked, barren, pillaged, burned, and uninhabitable. The once beautiful blues and greens are likely now nothing but blackness and ash. The world has gone dark, blanketed by darkness, and there is no way to save her. This is how the world comes to an end.

October 2030

We've been underground for several weeks now. Many things about living underground are unpleasant. The worst is the silence. It is crushing, a heaviness that hangs in the air and settles in your bones. Silence can be so loud that it leaves your ears ringing. The atmosphere is thick with it, and your lungs feel like they are coated in oil, always heaving to pull in a full breath. It snatches your breath before you can pull it into your lungs, stealing it and setting it free to whistle through the darkness. Everything is crushing you, and you are already buried.

Even with my family around me, the silence seems to be all-consuming. We've found several people in the darkest parts of the caves who have lost their minds, whispering to themselves. I imagine they're so desperate to fill the silence that they do so with their own mad ramblings. I watched a man claw at his ears the other day, screaming about how loud it was—the silence. Darkness is a mindfuck. You see things that aren't there; you hear things that aren't there. It slowly drives you mad.

I place my journal on the mat next to me and turn off my lantern. I know I need to conserve the battery, but I need to journal to keep my mind right. I feel like I'm one whisper away from turning into one of the people that we'd seen in the caves that had lost their grip on reality. I don't want to end up like that, but I can feel myself slipping deeper and deeper into a depression. I've been thinking about death a lot lately and how, in a world of chaos, nothing is certain except for death. It happens, always, and is unpreventable. Life in the tunnels is becoming a dangerous game of hide-and-seek with Death. We never know where we will find Death and who will go into Death's beckoning hand.

The thing that scares me the most is that I'm starting to get used to it, the dying. No matter how hard we try to survive, death is always nipping at our heels, waiting for us around the next corner; it's unavoidable.

Death and silence are my greatest enemies as I sit huddled in my tent, surrounded by the darkness. Pain and sadness linger and whisper through the silence, and my moments of quiet are filled with the memories of those I've lost on the surface and the life I used to have. The ghosts of my past life are always there, whispering through the dark, reminding me that I'm alone and haunted by my memories. I feel an emptiness where they once were, filled with silence and screaming memories. It's a constant struggle, a want to forget, and again, in the same breath, I never want to let those memories go. I'm never truly alone, as I'm constantly walking with the ghosts of what once was.

"Adrian?" Garrett's voice breaks me out of my ponderings as his shadow dances on the tent wall.

I turn my lantern back on, breathing a sigh of relief as the light floods my small space.

"Yeah, what's up, Garrett?" I open the tent flap.

"Do you want to come with me on my next scouting run? I was thinking of leaving soon. I need to take something to trade for more medication for Mom. Her cough is getting worse."

I pause, listening to her breathing whistling through the dark, and the slight catch that comes at every inhale as her lungs work overtime to fill.

"Yeah, I'll come with. Did you want to leave now?"

"As soon as you're ready," he replies, getting up and moving back to his tent.

I close the flap, grab a jacket, and put on some thicker socks along with my hiking boots. The caves are cold, and you never know when you'll run into water, so wearing layers and waterproof boots is vital when going deeper into the caverns.

I climb out of my tent, my lower back protesting every movement. I take a few moments to stretch it out, along with my legs and shoulders. Everything resisting the sudden change in position.

"I'm ready," I call out to where I can see his flashlight sitting.

Garrett emerges from the darkness, carrying a backpack filled to the brim with gear and goods that we can trade. It's a mix of electronics, batteries, and food.

Mom started coughing when we moved deeper into the caves and hasn't stopped. Her immune system was already compromised, and I think we all knew that it would be challenging for her, but I don't think any of us thought she would get sick so soon.

We ran out of cough medicine and antibiotics two days ago, and her cough had already worsened.

Garrett walks up, nodding to me, and we both move off into the dark of the tunnels. I have a small hiking day pack with me that contains basic supplies, just in case we're gone longer than expected.

Neither of us says a word as we walk through the tunnels, and as we walk, I'm reminded of a vivid recurring nightmare I had as a small child.

I'm standing at the end of a long hallway lined with doors. It looks like an old, abandoned hotel; the carpet is ancient, stained, and smells of mold. The walls are covered in lousy wallpaper and are out of focus, as if I'm looking through a foggy window. I'm not looking at any of this, though, because Death is at the end of the door-lined hallway. Death doesn't move. It stands at the end of the hall, eerily waiting for me. I don't want to run because I'm afraid that Death will give chase if I do. I can hear my heartbeat pounding in my chest. It starts slow and steady, filling my chest before it picks up speed, traveling from my chest up to my throat, and soon, I can hear and feel it pounding in my ears; I can see the pounding on the backs of my eyelids. I can't breathe. I'm frozen in fear. I can't stand there forever and need to move, but I can't. I also know I need to pick a door to go through, but I don't want to because Death will be waiting for me on the other side, no matter what door I choose. I also know I'm dreaming, stuck in my recurring nightmare, and can't wake myself up.

I pick a door, jiggle the handle, trying to open it. Death moves closer, and the door won't open. I panic, turning to another entrance. Death is a step closer. This door opens. I throw myself through it only to find myself back in the same hall of doors, Death inching toward me. Death is always there, steps away. Waiting. I snap awake, my heart pounding in my ears, and my hands shaking with adrenaline. It's just a dream, but the fear and panic are real. I lay in bed, attempting to fall asleep, to think of something happy. Eventually, I fall back to sleep.

The nightmare would always end, and I would think of something happy and bright to help me fall back asleep.

Walking through the tunnels is like walking down one long hallway after another, and thinking of happier times to help stave off the fear is becoming harder and harder. Most of the time, I'm unsure if I'm awake or still dreaming. The panic, the fear, it's realer than ever. Darkness has a way of changing everything around you. Sometimes I'm so overwhelmed by it that I can't breathe. It consumes me. I tell myself to think of something happy, but all I can think about is the deafening sound of my heartbeat and that Death is one step closer.

"What are you thinking about?" Garrett asks as we walk in silence.

"Honestly? Death," I mutter back, looking at the shadow of his back as he walks in front of me.

"Nice, and so like you."

"I know, how very typical, right?" I say, with some light in my voice.

We both scoff at the statement.

"How far do you think we will have to go before we find someone to trade with?"

"It's usually an hour or two before I run into folks. I think they have a camp in the area and venture out, just like us, to trade. We always seem to meet in the same location," Garrett replies, holding his flashlight out in front of him. My lantern lights the area in front of me, barely reaching the darkness around Garrett.

"Okay." That's all I can think to say as we continue our walk in silence. The next hour and a half pass without either of us saying anything, and suddenly, voices can be heard echoing off the walls of the tunnel.

"We're close," Garrett says.

"Are they nice?" I ask, trying to ready myself for a quick escape if we need one.

"Usually."

The tunnel opens up into a large cavern that's full of people. So many people! I haven't seen this many folks in one location since the riot at the grocery store before we moved underground. It steals my breath.

There's a sound that seems so foreign to this new world that it makes me pause. They have a generator and have lights strung throughout the cavern, ensuring the area is properly lit.

"Holy shit."

"It's impressive, right?" Garrett says, smiling at me as he walks into the trading post.

"I thought it would be like two or three people milling about with things to trade, not an actual city!" I can't keep the shock out of my voice as we move through the crowd. I pull my backpack close to me, trying to keep my belongings to myself. I'm sure there are pickpockets around.

"They have chickens," I whisper in awe as we walk by a small pen of birds.

"They have almost everything," Garrett says, making his way to a small table in the back of the cavern.

As we weave through the crowd, I can't help but notice that some of them look ill. Their skin is pale, with dark circles under their eyes and red noses—the coughs of the sick echo through the chamber.

I pull a handkerchief out of my bag and tie it around my face, over my mouth, as we continue on our path to the trading post medical vendor. Garrett does the same. As we approach the medical point, a line starts to form, and the sounds of coughing grow more consistent.

"Are the people here usually this sick?" I ask Garrett, looking around at all the pale faces.

"No, it's never been like this before. Something must be going around."

"These people look like shit." I can't keep the worry out of my voice. If they have something contagious, we could catch it and bring it back to Mom and Adam, and Mom already has a weakened immune system.

"Do you think they'll still have meds in this?" I ask as we line up.

"I hope so," Garrett says, looking around as he ties a handkerchief around his face as well.

It feels like hours pass as we wait in line, but finally we reach the front. The man behind the table looks just as sick as those waiting for medicine.

"If you're here for antibiotics, we don't have any."

"Do you have anything that could help with a cough or with lupus relief, steroids maybe?" I feel stupid for even asking, as I know the man likely has neither, given the amount of sick people in the cavern.

"No, I'm sorry, we're out of everything."

"We brought batteries and electronics to trade as well as canned goods. Are you sure you're out?" Garrett insists, pushing forward and putting a pack of batteries on the table.

"Hey Garrett, listen, I know you've been here before for your mom but I really don't have anything left. Whatever illness is spreading through the caves is causing people to fall ill. A lot of folks have already died from whatever it is." The doctor covers his mouth as a fit of coughing racks his body.

We watch as he curls in on himself, clutching his chest with his free hand.

As he pulls his hand away, I note the blood on it.

"He's coughing up blood," I whisper to Garrett.

"We should go," he whispers back.

Nodding in agreement, I grab the pack of batteries from the table, give the doctor a sad smile, and leave with Garrett. We move through the crowd quickly, trying to avoid contact with others as we go.

"Help us, help us!" The cry goes up from somewhere in the cavern behind us as a crowd forms around a woman and a man. The man is lying on his back on the floor, coughing up dark red blood as the woman holds him.

"Please!" Sobs break off the woman's cry as the man continues to choke on his blood.

I look at Garrett and we speed up, jogging now to escape the chaos of the sickness. Breaking through the crowd, we keep jogging, desperate to put as much space as possible between us and the illness before we stop and remove our face coverings.

"What the fuck was that?" I ask Garrett, taking a breath after removing the handkerchief from my face.

"I have no idea. It's never been like that before. Whatever illness that is, it happened fast. I was just there two weeks ago, and everything was fine." Garrett is panting beside me, and he takes his handkerchief off his face as well.

I imagine we both have the same look of fear in our eyes as we look at each other.

"That was some scary shit," I whisper.

"We should get back to Adam and Mom," he says back, and I nod my agreement. We move off in silence, and neither of us says a thing until we're almost back to camp.

"Do we tell them about the illness?" I ask, breaking the silence.

"I think we have to, right? Just in case we've brought it back with us." His response sends chills down my spine.

Right, we could have brought it back with us.

"Okay." I follow behind him as we enter the cavern where we've set up camp and find Mom and Adam sitting around one of the lanterns playing a game of gin rummy.

"You guys are back fast," Mom says, looking up from the game and smiling at us as we walk in. Her smile fades immediately as she looks at us. Our faces give away the news before we can say anything.

"What happened?" Adam asks, looking from Garrett to me.

"We didn't get any meds; they didn't have anything." Garrett's voice is solemn, and Mom's face falls even more before she gives us a small, sad smile.

"That's okay, I'll be fine. Was there any news from the surface? Has anyone been able to go above for news?"

Garrett and I look at each other before either of us speaks, as if saying it will bring it to life.

"Well, it seems like there's some virus going around in the caves. There were a lot of sick people. It's why they were out of medicine," I say, settling on one of our camping chairs, away from Adam and Mom. Garrett follows me over and sits next to me, effectively distancing ourselves from them just in case we brought the virus back with us.

"Like what kind of virus?" Adam asks, looking back and forth between us.

"There was a lot of coughing, and it looked like they were coughing and throwing up blood. There was a lot of blood." Everyone looks at me as I speak, and my stomach drops with the attention.

"That sounds pretty serious," Adam says, and a heavy silence falls over the camp.

"Do you think you brought it back with you?" he says after a few moments.

"We can't be sure, but I think it would be smart for Garrett and me to maybe stay away from you two for a little bit just in case."

"I think that's a good idea," Mom says, agreeing with me.

I nod in agreement and get up to put my bag in my tent. Garrett follows suit.

"I think I'm going to lie down for a bit," I say, and crawl into my tent, leaving the rest of the family to chat about the cavern.

I fall asleep to the sound of their muffled voices.

Chapter Sixteen
The Plague

"It is a curious thing, the death of a loved one. We all know that our time in this world is limited, and that eventually all of us will end up underneath some sheet, never to wake up. And yet it is always a surprise when it happens to someone we know. It is like walking up the stairs to your bedroom in the dark, and thinking there is one more stair than there is. Your foot falls down, through the air, and there is a sickly moment of dark surprise as you try and read just the way you thought of things."
— Lemony Snicket, Horseradish: Bitter Truths You Can't Avoid

I wake to the sound of wet coughing coming from Garrett's tent. It's not the same kind of cough that Mom has; it's thicker, wetter, and deeper. It sounds the same as the coughs that permeated the cavern we visited yesterday.

Whatever virus is in the caves travels quickly.

Getting up, I crawl out of my tent and find both Adam and Mom up and sitting across the cave against the far wall. Well away from Garrett and my tents.

"I'm worried about him," Mom says, looking at Garrett's dark tent.

"How long has he been coughing for?"

"It started about an hour ago," Adam says, getting up and pacing the small area that we've been calling home.

"What do we do?"

"I don't know if there's anything we can do. I guess give him water to keep him hydrated, and if we have any pain medication left, we can give him some of that to keep the fever down if he has one."

Mom and Adam nod in agreement, then both of them turn to me. "You'll have to care for him, since you've already been exposed," Mom whispers.

"Right, right," I whisper back, my mind already racing. I don't want to be responsible for the well-being of another, let alone keeping someone alive. I'm also terrified of getting sick myself.

"Sure, I can do this. I got this," I say to myself as I move toward Garrett's dark tent. Picking up my lantern, I turn it on and move toward the tent. I unzip it slowly and am hit with the smell of sickness. It's sweet and sickly, clinging to the air and making it almost unbreathable. I step back and go back to my bag, rummaging through it until I find my handkerchief from yesterday. I put it on, looking up at Mom and Adam as I do so.

"Maybe you two should wear some kind of mask," I suggest, turning back to the tent and Garrett.

I unzip the tent flap the rest of the way, letting the stagnant air wash over me and flow into the open space of the cave. It feels as if I'm letting some living creature out of its bag to destroy the safe space that we've created.

Garrett looks like death. His skin is waxy and oh, so pale. The only color is from the red around his nostrils and the corners of his mouth, and the dark, dark circles that have formed under his eyes. His pale skin is pulled tight across his cheeks, as if he's lost a tremendous amount of weight in a short period.

He opens his eyes slowly, hissing as the light hits the pale blue of his irises. He struggles to sit up before flopping back on his sleeping mat, exhausted from the effort it took to raise his head from the pillow.

"Drew the short straw, did ya?" His voice is soft and wobbles with the effort it takes for Garrett to speak.

"I volunteered," I say back with a smile. Reaching out, I put the back of my hand on his forehead and pause. It's hot and clammy at the same time.

"Well, you definitely have a fever," I say, smiling again.

"I could've told you that."

Trying to keep the smile on my face, I help him sip from a water bottle and hope that he can keep some of the water down. I need to keep him hydrated. I take what medicine we have and help him take that as well.

"I'll come check on you again in a bit. Try to get some rest."

As he nods, his eyes are already closing, and he's drifting away into unconsciousness.

"How's he doing?" Mom asks, still sitting on the other side of the cave.

"He's got a fever and looks like shit. I got him to drink some water and take some meds. But that's about all I can do."

She nods, looking from Garrett's tent to me to Adam, "Should the two of us move camp so we don't catch it?"

"You want to leave us here? I don't know what I'm doing! I can't care for him by myself." The panic is instant, hitting me in the chest and overwhelming me.

"I mean, Mom has a point. It doesn't make sense for us to stay here and get sick along with Garrett and you. Plus, Mom shouldn't risk it; she's already weak."

"I can't believe this. You seriously are just going to leave us here?"

"Adrian. Calm down. It's only until he gets better, and if you don't get sick, the two of you can come find us when he's better." Mom looks from Adam to me; Adam nods his head in agreement.

They don't wait for me to say anything else. Both rise and gather their belongings that they'd already packed. I hadn't noticed that they were packed; they must have done it when I was helping Garrett.

"What if he doesn't get better?" I whisper, stepping closer to them.

"Stop. Don't come any closer; we can't risk getting sick," Adam says, holding up a hand that freezes me in my tracks.

I can't wrap my brain around this. I don't understand how they can leave us here, how they won't help us.

"We're only going to the cavern that's down the tunnel on the left. It's not too far away, and you'll be able to come and get us when he's better," Mom says, as she's already walking toward the branch in the tunnels.

"Please, don't leave us here." I hate that I can hear the whine and weakness in my voice, but I need them. I need their help to do this.

"We won't be far," she says, as if that makes all this okay, as if she wasn't abandoning us when we need her the most.

They leave; without so much as a backward glance, they leave. Garrett is coughing in the tent as they walk away, and I have nothing to help him except for some water and anti-inflammatory medicine.

I turn away from the darkening tunnel as Mom and Adam disappear into the hazy darkness and turn back to Garrett's tent, where his coughing continues to grow louder and louder. For the briefest moment, I think about leaving, running after them, begging them to take me with them. But I can't leave Garrett. I can't leave him here to suffer alone.

I go to his tent, unzipping it and holding my breath as the smell wafts from inside it. I help Garrett drink more water and assist him in rolling to his side so he can cough up the phlegm in his throat more easily.

I leave the tent flap open, letting his illness permeate the air of our cavern. If he's already sick, there's a good chance that I'll get sick soon, too, so why fight it? There's no reason to keep him confined in such a small space, where the sickness can fester.

I stay up with Garrett for hours, helping him sit up eventually so he can clear the gunk from his lungs. Except it's not phlegm, it's mucus and blood. It hasn't been that long since he first got sick, and he's already starting to cough up blood. Whatever this illness is, it progresses rapidly and is relentless.

I'm trying to stay awake so I can help Garrett when he needs me, but I'm so tired that I keep drifting off. The feeling of my head falling into space as I fall asleep keeps waking me. But eventually, I fall asleep to the sound of Garrett's coughing.

Consciousness comes slowly to me as I start to wake up. My eyes are dry and feel like they are full of gravel as I rub them.

As I stretch, it hits me. It's quiet. Garrett isn't coughing anymore. My breath hitches.

Is he feeling better?

I get up slowly, stretching my back and legs that are stiff from falling asleep while sitting up. I approach Garrett's tent slowly, scared of what I will find but hopeful that it will be him, sleeping soundly.

I crouch down and immediately know that Garrett is dead. His eyes are open, and pink foam coats his mouth, running down his throat. His skin is gray and cold to the touch.

I fell asleep, and he died. I should have been awake; if I hadn't fallen asleep, maybe he would still be alive.

My mind starts to run and spin in circles. I can't breathe. I stumble backward, away from the tent, and slam into the cave wall behind me, knocking myself to my knees. One hand on the cave floor, the other across my mouth, I let out a silent scream and watch as my tears are absorbed by the dirt floor as if they never existed.

Garrett is dead.

It's all I can think about, the only thing bouncing around the inside of my skull to the fast beat of my racing heart.

Garrett is dead.

I don't want to be alone with his body; I can't be alone here.

Grabbing my pack, I shove my lantern and a few supplies into it and take off down the tunnel, following the path that Mom and Adam took just a day ago.

The only sounds I hear are my harsh breathing and the thud of my feet on the cave floor. I run for what feels like an eternity and eventually find myself in the next cavern, where Adam and Mom have set up camp.

It's quiet; maybe they're sleeping.

I walk into the camp, fear making the hair on my arms and the back of my neck stand up; a tingling courses through my body from the top of my head down my spine.

I reach for the first tent's zipper and slowly unzip the flap.

Adam lies on his side, eyes closed, seemingly asleep. As I look over his face, I realize that he's too still. His chest isn't moving, and there's a pink tinge to his lips. I look closer, holding my lantern higher, and that's when I see it. The pillow under his head is covered in red and soaked with blood that he coughed up.

Jesus.

I scuttle backward away from his tent, bumping into Mom's tent behind me.

"Adrian?" It's a weak whisper, brittle, like dry tree branches blowing in the wind.

"Mom!" I spin around and move to the front of the tent, hurriedly unzipping it, desperate to get to her.

"Mom!" I practically shout as I struggle in my desperation to open it.

I finally manage to open the tent, and the first thing I see is the large amount of blood coating her face from her nose down. She's been coughing up blood for a while. Too weak to roll to her side.

I reach in, pulling her toward me and propping her up against my chest as I sit behind her.

"Are Adam and Garrett okay?" Every word is forced out on a weak breath, leaving her exhausted after she speaks.

"They... they didn't make it, Mom. I'm sorry."

"You... you did this... to us." It's barely a whisper, but I hear what she said.

"I didn't do this, I didn't know there was an illness in the caves, how could I have known?" I whisper back.

"I'm sorry, I'm so sorry, I didn't know," I continue to whisper, holding her closer to me as each breath rakes through her body. I can feel them crackling through her lungs and know that she's not long for the world.

"Please, Mom, I love you, I didn't know." I'm crying, my tears soaking into the matted hair on the back of her head as I bury my face in her hair.

"You . . . did this." A last rattling breath leaves her body, and she slumps into my embrace. She doesn't take another breath, and I lose track of how long I sit there with her body.

She's cold by the time I move, and my tears have dried. I feel numb as I bury my emotions; it's better not to feel anything than to be hurt by what she said.

I move to a dark corner of the cave and curl in on myself, waiting for the coughing to start. The darkness has taken everything from me, including the love I had for my mother.

I loved my mother dearly and had always wondered what life would be like without her. When I was younger, the thought of her not being there was terrifying. Her many health issues meant she continually had surgeries, and I was scared she would not return every time. I didn't know it then, but the feeling of being out of control, the tightness in my chest, and the fear were anxiety. Severe anxiety related to the fear of my mother dying while in surgery, and what that meant not to have her around. I spent my childhood terrified of her death, and now she was dead, and I didn't feel anything.

Chapter Seventeen
The Other Side

"No one can tell what goes on in between the person you were and the person you become. No one can chart that blue and lonely section of hell. There are no maps of the change. You just come out the other side. Or you don't." —
Stephen King, The Stand

I 've been with their bodies for what feels like days, but I know it's only been a few hours. I already feel like that's too long, like I should be doing something, like I need to do something for them.

Standing slowly, I wait for the blood to flow back into my cramped limbs before I move. Adam and Mom look peaceful, not like how Garrett had looked. It's as if they simply fell asleep and didn't wake back up.

I don't know what to do with the bodies. Do I leave them here? Do I bury them? Burn them?

Looking at the walls and floors of the cavern around me, I don't think it would be possible to bury them here; everything is too hard. I can't move them, either; it's just me, and it would take a lot of time and energy that I don't have to do that.

I decide to leave them where they lie. It feels wrong, but I don't have that many options. I'd seen similar camps when out exploring, abandoned with a body left behind. Maybe the person died from old age or took their own life, but it was a common thing to see when walking through the caves. So, I would do what others had done, and I would leave the bodies behind.

It feels weird touching their bodies now that they've passed. Skin isn't meant to feel like this, cold, waxy, and thin. I move Mom farther into her tent, folding her arms across her chest and pulling her blanket up to cover her face. The blanket is actually a quilt, one that my grandmother made.

It makes me pause. I feel as if my hands belong to someone else as they linger on the coolness of the quilt before zipping the tent, sealing the corpse inside.

I move to Adam's tent next and do the same for him. It's all I can do, and I hope that it's enough to give them peace in the afterlife.

I gather their packs and go through them, picking out the batteries and any food that I want to take. I can only carry so much, so I need to be smart about what I take. Food that's high in vitamins and protein, which will last a long time and provide multiple meals, and fresh batteries fill my pack.

I go back through the tunnel to our original camp and put Garrett's body to rest, gathering a few more supplies before setting out down the tunnel to the right.

I don't know where I'm going, but I know I can't stay here, and there's only death in the other tunnel.

November 2030 (I think)
Darkness has a way of warping your world until you don't know what is up or down. Everything you thought you knew no longer exists, everything takes

on a new personality, and nothing is what it should be. Your mind is always playing tricks on you, making you think you're seeing or hearing things that aren't there. Darkness confuses and transforms everything around you until you don't exist.

Surviving underground for an extended period is almost impossible. When you come out on the other side, if you come out on the other side, you won't be the person you were when you went in. Fear does weird things to the mind and body. It slowly breaks you down until your perception of reality no longer exists. Who you may have been going into the underground is not the person you will become. The complete and utterly overwhelming sense of fear consumes, erases, and rewrites your soul.

My lantern flickers, and I put the journal down, looking to where it sits a few feet away. I don't know how long it's been since I left their bodies or how long we've all been underground. I've lost track of the time of everyone and everything I came into this place with, including myself.

I let what was left of my family slip through my fingers. I couldn't save any of them. After all we had been through to survive the initial impacts, to dig the tunnels, after all of that, I couldn't do anything to save them. . . I couldn't go back to the surface, not after the impacts. The air up there was poison, thick with ash and burning metal, and the heat still rolled over the plains like the world was refusing to cool down.

I cough as my throat begins to close, and black dots dance in front of my eyes. Anxiety comes forward full force, making me feel as if I'm suffocating in the little cavern I've found. Thinking about them always brings anxiety, shame, and guilt with it.

I put my head between my knees and take deep breaths, in through my nose, out through my mouth, until the panic subsides.

I've been roaming the tunnels aimlessly since the deaths of my brothers and mom. I like being by myself, it means the only person I have to take care of is myself. I'm responsible only for myself, and there's a weird sense of freedom in that.

I don't have to depend on anyone, and no one depends on me. It's just me, and that's all I need. This is how it should have been, how it's supposed to be. Being alone allows me to move quickly when I need to, and I go where I want, when I want. I don't have to consider anyone else.

I've come across a few groups in my travels, and the more I see them, the more I think I've made the right move. They have to move slowly; there's never enough food, and if trouble finds them, they won't be able to escape fast enough. At least, not all of them.

The tunnels have become dangerous. Some people run them like packs of rabid animals. Their feet create a dull thrumming sound that is similar to the sound a herd of stampeding horses makes at a distance.

The first time I heard the thrumming, it was almost magical; the vibrations in the walls, the ground, and the air were all around me. Everything was charged, and I could feel the beating of their feet in my chest. It started with a dull building until the sound was so overwhelming that it was as if you could hear every individual footfall.

That first encounter was terrifying. I managed to hide in a small side tunnel as the massive group of mostly men went whooping through the tunnel. But once they were past, I felt... invigorated. Alive.

That scared me more.

I come back to reality and out of the past as I catch my breath. The anxiety is gone, and the dullness is returning. I look at my pack next to me and dig through it, finding my last granola bar.

I need food.

I've been avoiding going to the trading cavern, unsure if the illness is still spreading through the tunnels or if people are still trading. The thought of being around a group of people makes my skin break out in goosebumps.

But I need food, so I'll have to go.

I tuck my journal into the deflated pack and grab my flickering lantern, turning it off quickly so I can change the batteries.

For a moment, the darkness closes in, and I swear I can hear Death whispering to me, begging me to come join it.

I half expect to see Death waiting for me when I flick the lantern back on, but no one is there. It's all in my mind.

I take a breath and get up, my body feeling weakened by the lack of food and water. I know I've waited too long this time to try to find supplies, but I couldn't bring myself to move, to care.

I know it's anxiety and depression, but there isn't much I can do about it. I don't have medication, and "pushing through" isn't a thing that's always possible.

Today is more manageable than others, and I know I need to move now before the depression grabs hold of me again.

I walk through the tunnels with my lantern held high and in front of me, my eyes straining against the darkness, expecting people to emerge from it with every bend in the tunnel.

I don't see anyone, though, and as I get nearer to the trading cavern, I don't hear the typical chatter. It's much quieter; it's still there, just not as prominent.

I walk into the lit area, and I'm surprised by how much it has changed. There aren't groups of people huddled around tables like a farmer's market. There are a few people wearily walking around the almost empty space.

I head to the closest table that has food.

"How much for those cans of pears?" I ask, my mouth watering at the thought of eating them.

"What do you have to trade?" the greasy-haired man asks; I notice that he's missing most of his teeth.

"I have batteries."

"How many?"

"You tell me how many you want, and I'll tell you if I can make it happen."

Scoffing, he pushes two cans of pears toward me. "Five packs of unopened batteries, double-As."

"Four packs of double-As and one pack of triples," I counter.

He raises a bushy eyebrow, "Fine."

I can tell he's not happy, but I don't care; he took the deal. I pull the batteries out and hand them over as I grab the cans with my other hand. Putting the cans in my bag, I nod to him and back away from the table.

I move to the next table and spot a can of Spam.

"I can give you some batteries for that can," I say, nodding to the Spam.

"You can have it," the old woman says, waving her bony hand in the direction of the can.

"What?" I hesitate to take it, waiting for her to change her mind.

"Just take it, you look like you need it more than some of these folks."

I look from her brown, depthless eyes to the Spam before quickly grabbing it and stuffing it into my bag.

"Why don't you sit down and have a meal with me?" she asks, pointing to the empty stool beside her.

"A meal? What... kind of meal?" I'd heard rumors that people had started eating rats and also each other when a body became available.

"I have some ravioli warming up on the camp stove." Her finger moves from the stool to the stove that's set up slightly behind her.

I pause and sniff the air. The smell of red sauce and oregano hits me slowly, and my stomach clenches with hunger.

I nod.

"Sit," she demands.

I do.

"What happened here? The last time I came, there were way more people and supplies." I settle on the stool and take my pack off, keeping it between my legs.

"The Roamers came." She stirs the ravioli, and my mouth waters.

"Roamers?" I ask, eyeing the food and trying to concentrate on the conversation.

The old lady chuckles as she turns to me, "Where have you been hiding? Everyone knows about the Roamers."

I raise my eyebrows and shake my head, "I don't know what you're talking about."

"The packs of wild men that roam the tunnels? You've not seen or heard them?"

"Oh, yes. I guess I didn't know they had a name."

"Yes, someone started calling them Roamers, because they roam the tunnels looking for people to kill."

"Why are they killing people?"

"To eat." She says it so nonchalantly that I almost don't realize what she's said.

"What? To eat? Are you serious? This sounds like a myth."

"I've seen it. When they attacked this place, they came in packs of five; their teeth and nails were filed down to points to make it easier to rip into the flesh of those unfortunate enough to be caught by them." She scoops up a serving of the ravioli and passes the bowl to me.

I can barely contain myself as I shovel a piece of the scalding pasta into my mouth.

"Easy! It's hot!" the old lady says, shaking her head.

"What's your name?"

"Adrian. You?"

"Lori."

"Nice to meet you, Lori, and thank you for the food."

"We need to help each other out now more than ever."

"Can you tell me more about the Roamers. I've only seen them once, and I was hiding, so I didn't get a good look at them." I can't keep the curiosity from my voice.

Lori looks at me strangely but continues, "I don't know what you want me to tell you. They kill and cannibalize anyone they come across in the tunnels. I've seen it. That day they came here, they killed so many, and I watched one man rip the throat out of another with his bare teeth."

I stop with a ravioli halfway to my mouth when she says that. It sounds like something out of a movie, and it's hard for me to wrap my brain around it.

"I also saw them take some of the men to join them. They said they could come with them if they filed their teeth and let the Roamers cut off one of their ears as a show of loyalty. Several of the men here did it."

"You saw all of this?"

"Yup, happened right over there." Lori points toward the far tunnel opening in the cavern, opposite us.

"That's . . . wild," is all that comes out as I shove more food into my mouth. The truth is that I'm more than intrigued. I want to know more about the Roamers. Are they surviving this way? How many groups of Roamers are there? I have so many questions.

"Why don't you stay here and rest for a while. The lights will go down soon." Lori's voice breaks me out of my thoughts about the Roamers.

"Oh, I don't know if that's necessary. I've already taken up enough of your time and supplies."

I don't trust her, or anyone around here, and staying makes my skin crawl.

"Are you sure? I have an extra tent that you can use if you don't have one."

"I'm good, thank you, though." I don't like the way she's pressing me, like she needs me to stay the night.

"I'm actually going to get going. I've got to make up some time still before I rest, so I'll just get going." I make an awkward motion with my thumb and start to get up.

Lori grabs my arms before I can distance myself from her.

"You should really stay the night."

My skin crawls, and I look around the cavern. The man I traded with earlier is watching us with a toothless grin, and two other traders are watching as well.

I'm not safe here.

"I'm leaving." I deepen my voice and push her hand away. Grabbing my pack, I make a move to the far tunnel, the one she said the Roamers came from. I don't make it there, though.

I'm so focused on getting to the tunnel that I overlook one of the men coming up behind me. He grabs my pack, dragging me to the ground.

"What else you got in that pack, boy!" He throws me to the ground, his stagnant breath and the impact knocking the air from my lungs.

He tries to rip the pack off my back, but I roll with the impact and knock into his legs, dragging him down with me as I continue to roll.

"God dammit!" he shouts as he hits the ground, and I keep moving. I can't stop or I'm dead, I know this inherently as I struggle to force air into my lungs.

I'm so stupid. I should have figured it out sooner, but my hunger distracted me. They knew it would.

I'm almost to my feet when the other man reaches us, pushing me back down and holding a knife out in front of him.

"Just give us the pack," he hisses.

I kick out, hitting the hand that holds the knife, and something snaps. I bare my teeth as I dive for the knife, picking it up and swiping out.

I feel the tug of the knife as it connects with the second man's arm as he reaches for me. I don't stop there, though. As he pulls his arm back, I follow, dodging inside his reach, and I plunge the knife into his stomach.

Screaming, he falls back.

I turn, ready for the first man to come at me, but he doesn't. He stands by Lori, if that's even her name, and they both look stunned at what I've done.

"Give me my fucking pack," I grind out, wielding the knife in front of me.

The toothless man takes a step forward and tosses it to me.

"If you take another step toward me, I'll gut you," I hiss, my body is full of adrenaline and something else.

They both nod as I move forward, grabbing my pack. I walk backward until I'm in the tunnel, and then I run. I run and I don't look back.

I don't know how long I run for, but I stop eventually, completely exhausted, adrenaline long gone.

"What the fuck?" I mutter to myself in the darkness.

As I pace the small cavern I stopped in, I start to giggle, then laugh. I have no idea why, but I can't seem to stop; it's bubbling out of me as if I'm not in control of my own body.

Fuck, I think I liked that.

That thought kills the laughter in my throat, and I cough.

What's wrong with me?

I was never one for violence, although I think I've always had a darkness inside of me. A bit of a temper would come out when I was frustrated and didn't know how to articulate my feelings. I always thought of myself as more of a healer and not one to harm another.

The darkness has changed me, though. I've done things I never thought I would have to do. I've had to throw everything I've ever believed in away and have prepared myself to do anything to survive.

That's how I justify what I've just done to myself. I had to do it. It was me or them. Maybe that's what everyone is doing, even the Roamers.

If I killed because I had to in order to survive, does it really count as doing something wrong?

How do I know if what I'm doing is right or wrong when the norms of society no longer apply?

How can I justify this to myself?

Chapter Eighteen
Roamers

November 2030

None of us is good or evil. We are just trying to survive, so who gets to make that distinction? Is it me, is it you, is it the group of hungry cannibals running through the tunnels? Who has control in a situation like this? The answer is no one and everyone. We all get to make those decisions and hope to come out the victor on the other side.

I know I need to keep moving in case the people from the trading post come after me, but I'm exhausted. My legs feel like jelly from running, and my lungs are just now starting to catch up with the rest of me.

I look around the small cavern that I've stopped in, my laughter long gone now that my sanity seems to have returned.

I pick my pack up and start back down the dark tunnel to my left. I'm not quite sure what I'm doing or why I have a desire to find the Roamers. What will I do if I find them? What if they see me first?

I use a headlamp instead of my lantern and cautiously move down the tunnel toward the unknown. I've only been walking for what feels like a few minutes when I feel the vibrations through the tunnel floor. It's like feeling the bass of a good song vibrating through your whole body, rattling your teeth a bit.

It's intoxicating, in a way, knowing that death is racing toward me through the darkness. I can't seem to move, and I'm unsure if I even want to. If I stay here, will they kill me, or will they let me join them? The idea of joining them makes me nervous, but perhaps it would make everything easier. Am I willing to give up parts of myself to survive?

The vibrations grow stronger, as if I'm getting closer to the epicenter of an earthquake; the sounds of their feet and breathing bounce off the walls. I swear I can hear their breathing; it's like a midnight freight train racing toward me. I can feel the anger, hunger, and energy pulsing in the air, rushing out in front of them, seeking out anything in their path that it can consume.

I like it. I like it a lot, which terrifies me. The fear, the rush, it makes me feel something. It makes me feel alive again. It makes me want, and what I want is to kill them or join them.

I 'm deserving of living like my hands are clean, like I'm innocent. I've likely just killed a man, and the Roamers are my punishment for what I've done.

It's easy to think in terms of "good" and "evil." When all of this started, I thought of myself as being good, but now, I'm like them—tainted, bad, evil. I deserve whatever the Roamers decide to do with me.

As I stand frozen in the center of the tunnel, I'm living for a moment with one foot in and one foot out. I'm minutes away from life or death. All I need to do is make a decision.

My heartbeat seems to sync with the sounds of the pounding feet approaching me. My breathing stutters and almost stops, and a tingling starts at the small of my back before spreading up my spine and curling around my shoulders, before it cramps into my chest.

I don't have a choice now; my body has taken it away from me. I'm frozen in fear as terror takes hold. This is why I can't be responsible for another. I'm incapable of making decisions when they are needed the most. The panic consumes me entirely, leaving me utterly useless. I can't breathe; I can't see or move, and the darkness around me seems to swirl, tilting everything in a way that doesn't make sense.

I am incapable.

Chapter Nineteen
Hope

"Hope in reality is the worst of all evils because it prolongs the torments of man."
— *Friedrich Nietzsche*

My feet are glued to the tunnel floor as I struggle to breathe around my fear and panic as the Roamers roar toward me. I manage to take a deep breath, and my mind clears for the briefest of moments.

Maybe this is the peace that I want, something only death can offer. Life seems too damn long sometimes, filled with so much struggle. Perhaps this is my way out, my escape?

My brain resets as I catch a bit of movement in the dark. It's as if a shadow is slowly detaching itself from the rest of the darkness around me, racing toward the thin beam of light my headlamp is putting out.

I assume it's a Roamer, and I brace myself for the impact and the pain. I've never felt anything like this before. Like everything in my body wants me to run, but I'm completely frozen in place. My mind is telling me to give in, while my body is desperately trying to get me to move.

Every muscle in my body tightens as I prepare for the impact, my heart is in my throat, and the creature in my chest is wrapping its hands tighter around my lungs, making it harder to breathe.

Breathing becomes an afterthought as the Roamer gets closer to the beam of light.

Darkness swirls on the edges of my vision as I start to pass out from holding my breath.

The Roamer bursts into the thin ray of light and doesn't stop. They run past me, right past me, as if I don't exist.

Am I already dead? Am I a ghost?

I'm shocked and frightened even more now and can't make myself move. I almost jump out of my skin as a pale hand reaches out of the darkness behind me and grabs my forearm.

The hand is cold, small, and stark white against my dirty arm. For a moment, my mind stops racing, and all I can see is the hand clutching my arm. I snap out of my panic. The slight woman shakes my arm, and I suck in a deep breath and push the creature in my chest back into its box. I take another breath and focus on her moving lips.

"We have to run!" she says, pulling at me as she moves backward, away from the thunder.

Nodding, I turn and run with her, my mind and body finally working in tandem. I lock hands with the stranger and run through the tunnel, my lungs bursting with the effort as we're chased through the darkness by the thundering devils behind us.

We run until the thunder becomes a dull thumping and every breath feels like fire racing through my chest. My legs shake with exhaustion, and dots dance in my vision. It's at this point that we finally stop, and the stranger turns to me.

She's stunning even as she bends over to put her hands on her knees, trying to catch her breath. I can't take my eyes off of her.

"I'm Lily," she exhales.

"What?" I can't seem to hear over my breathing and the pounding in my ears.

"Lily. My . . . name," she says again, still trying to catch her breath.

"Adrian," I say back, assuming a similar position as it becomes easier to breathe with each passing moment.

"Why weren't you running?" Lily asks, as she plops onto the tunnel floor, leaning against the wall.

The light from my headlamp highlights her face. It's narrow, and she has high cheekbones. Her skin isn't as pale as I thought, but it's a light brown; it's darker than mine when I'm not covered in dirt. Her eyes are a beautiful shade of blue, electric. Her hair seems to be red or maybe auburn, but I can't tell as it's in a knot at the nape of her neck.

"I... I just couldn't." I manage to squeeze the words out around each inhale.

"They would have killed you. You're not one of those trying to find a way out, are you?"

"What do you mean?"

"I don't know where you've been, but a ton of people down here have started going to the Roamers. *Asking* them to kill them. You're not one of those, are you?"

"No," I lie. That's exactly what I was thinking.

Lily narrows her eyes at me; it's clear she doesn't believe me.

"Does it work?"

"What?"

"Going to them and asking them to kill you?" I ask, not looking her in the eyes.

"I don't know. I don't have a death wish," she replies, leaning her head against the wall and closing her eyes.

"Where are you from?" I'm desperate to learn more about her.

"South Dakota. You?"

"Nebraska. Do you know whereabout we are now?"

"I think we're still in South Dakota, but I could be wrong."

"How long have you been down here? Do you know anything about the surface?"

"I've been underground since the fires, and I haven't heard anything about the surface in a while. The last thing I heard about was that the fires had wiped out anyone still living above ground."

"Same."

"Are you alone?" Lily asks, lifting her head from off the wall and looking into the light from my headlamp.

I angle it down, so it doesn't shine directly into her eyes.

"I am now. I wasn't before, but now I am." It's all I can bring myself to say. I don't want to tell her about my family, not yet. I don't want her to know that I couldn't save them, that I let them all down.

I want—no, I *need*—her to like me.

"What about you?" I say, driving the conversation back to her.

"I'm alone; have been since the beginning."

"That must have been tough."

"It has been. I've tried joining some of the groups but haven't had very good luck with any of them."

"Really?" That seems weird. Why wouldn't she get along with groups?

"Yeah," she says softly and looks away, and I can tell that she doesn't want to discuss it any further.

"We should keep moving."

"We?" I ask, my chest tightening for a different reason.

"Yeah, I mean, that is, if you want to come with me." Lily stands, holding out her hand. She doesn't have anything with her, not even food or supplies. It's just her. There's no benefit to going with her, yet I can't stop myself from reaching out and taking her hand.

I'll stay with her for a little while, that's it. Just long enough to feel whole again, and then I'll leave.

Lily doesn't let go of my hand as we walk; she holds it as if I were her lifeline and not the other way around. We walk like that for hours, neither of us talking, just navigating the tunnels in silence together.

"Tell me about yourself," I say after what feels like hours have passed.

"What do you want to know?" Her blue eyes flick to me in the low light of the headlamp, and I barely catch it before she looks ahead again.

"Anything... everything." I feel like the air in the tunnel is charged, and I squeeze her hand gently.

"I was going to school in South Dakota, to be a nurse, but had dropped out before the end of the world happened. I was living with my grandpa."

"Why did you drop out?"

"I didn't like it. It was too much blood, too much pain. I couldn't handle seeing people, especially children, in pain."

"I can imagine that was hard." I squeeze her hand again. I feel close to Lily already, like I've known her for a long time, as if we're two old friends catching up after a few years apart.

"I hated it. My grandpa was super disappointed, but there's a part of me that thinks he was proud of me for quitting and for exploring other careers."

There's a sadness every time she mentions her grandpa.

"Were you with your grandpa when the fires started?"

"Yeah, I stayed with him in the months leading up to the fires. I was gathering supplies for when we would move underground. He's the one who showed me where the cave system started. I knew there were caves throughout the Black Hills, but I wasn't that familiar with the area. Grandpa showed me exactly where we could find shelter."

Lily stumbles, and I catch her by the arm and waist.

"Sorry," I say quickly, letting go of her.

"It's okay. I guess I'm more exhausted than I thought I was."

"Should we find a place to camp?"

Lily nods and reaches for my hand again. I pause a moment, but only a moment, before reaching out and grasping her outstretched hand.

"You said your grandfather helped you find the caves?" We've been walking in silence for what feels like hours, and it's starting to get to me.

"Yeah, he grew up in the area and knew about them. We made for them the day the fires started."

"We did the same. I mean, we moved further into the tunnels when the fires started. Where's your grandpa now?" I ask, afraid that I already know the answer.

"He didn't make it to the caves. When we arrived, there were people already setting up at the entrances. They were charging people to access the tunnels, making hundreds, if not thousands, of dollars off people's desperation."

"Are you serious?" I don't know why I'm shocked, especially given what had just happened at the trading post.

"Yeah, the groups of men with guns wouldn't let us in, so we tried to sneak in. I made it, and grandpa didn't."

"You don't have to tell me about it if you don't want to." I squeeze her hand gently.

"He got hit by the first shot they fired. I somehow managed to sneak in. I hid behind a boulder and then escaped into the cave before the gunmen could catch up. I've been linking up with other groups of survivors since then."

"I'm so sorry, Lily."

"Thanks." Lily's voice cracks, and she clears it, wiping away a stray tear that tracks down her dirt-streaked face.

"Why are you alone now and not with one of those groups?" I ask, not wanting the conversation to be over.

"The other survivors haven't been… nice, I guess. They keep trying to make me stay and want to use me for my medical knowledge, and I don't want that. I can't do that for them."

"I understand," I say quietly, looking down at the outline of our hands in the darkness. They want her to do for them that which she never got to do for her grandfather.

"Do you?" she says, looking sideways at me, as I look at her, illuminating her eyes with my headlamp.

"Every passing day that they made me stay in the group and care for their injured made me despise helping them, ensuring that they stayed alive. I started to hate them. I hated being alive. The only reason I got away was because of the Roamers. They attacked us, killing them while we slept. I was lucky to escape. It wasn't until that moment, when the screaming started, that I realized how badly I still wanted to live, so I ran. I ran until I found you."

We weren't walking anymore, both of us having stopped to look at each other in the dimly lit tunnel. In this moment, I think I finally understand what they mean when they say "bonded by trauma" because I could feel it happening between us. The tightness in my chest wasn't panic this time; it was something else. Something entirely different.

Chapter Twenty
Collapse

November 2030 (maybe)

Lily is more than anything I've ever experienced. She is my anchor, my focal point, and losing sight of her means being adrift in a sea of nothing. She tethers me to reality and keeps me grounded. I think, without her, I would break apart into a million pieces and drift away into nothingness. She gives me meaning, gives me a reason to live.

I look over at Lily's sleeping form and put my journal aside. It's only been a week, but I've never felt closer to someone in my entire life. I know it's stupid and that soulmates aren't real, but what I feel for her, this all-consuming need to keep her safe, is very real. The way my heart feels like it's going to burst when she holds my hand, the flutter of butterflies in my stomach when she looks at me and graces me with a smile, all of these things have so much meaning now.

I think Lily is the first person I've ever been around who doesn't make me feel like I need to fill the emptiness around us. We exist in companionable silence as we walk the tunnels. It's just been the two of us, and I like it this way. I only have to focus on keeping Lily safe, and that has become my sole purpose in life.

As I watch her sleep, I'm reminded of particular animal species that are bonded pairs, and that sometimes, when one of the pair dies, the other soon follows behind. They can't live without their other half. We've become so intertwined that it's hard to tell where she stops and I start. I AM hers, and she is mine.

Leaning forward, I brush an errant strand of hair off Lily's face. She stirs, opening her eyes, looking around before finding mine.

"All right?" she asks sleepily, sitting up slowly.

"Yeah, everything is fine." I smile at her, not breaking eye contact as she stretches and leans forward.

My heart contracts as our lips brush. It's a light kiss, and I'm dying for more, but it's only been a week, and I don't want to rush Lily. Smiling, she sits back, stretching again.

"How long did I sleep for?"

"Only an hour or two. You should go back to sleep." I rub my thumb over the back of her hand as she slips her fingers into mine.

"But I don't think I'm tired," Lily says with a shy smile.

"No?" I say teasingly.

"No." She leans, kissing me lightly again, but lingering this time.

I take my free hand and cup her face gently, reveling in the feel of her lips against mine.

Lily pulls back, her eyes tracking over my face, down to my slightly parted lips.

"I like kissing you."

"I like it when you kiss me," I say back. A small smile plays across her lips, and she leans in again. She's a bit bolder with her kisses.

I'm dying inside, though. I want to pick her up and hold her close to me while I devour her mouth, but I can't do that. I need Lily to make the decisions.

Our heavy breaths mingle as Lily's kisses become more frantic, and my control breaks. I grip the back of her thighs and lift her onto my lap, pulling her close to me. She's never close enough.

Lily grinds against me as she loses control, and I break away to kiss her neck, and the soft sounds she makes in her excitement drive my kisses up her neck and back to capture her mouth.

Lily moans into my mouth as we kiss, before placing her hands on my chest and pushing back from me.

"Wait... wait, I need to pause," she says, pulling back but not moving off my lap.

"Okay, that's fine," I say, leaning my forehead against hers, "that's totally okay."

"Are you sure?"

"Of course, we don't have to do anything you're not comfortable with."

"I'm just . . . I think I'm scared. What if I fall for you and something happens?" Lily's voice hitches.

I rub her back before pulling her in for a hug, holding her close to me. "Nothing is going to happen to me, I promise."

"You shouldn't make promises you can't keep," she whispers back, and I feel wetness on my shoulder as she cries. I hold her until her sobs subside and she falls asleep in my lap.

We set out the next day to find a new cave and possibly meet some people to trade with. I don't know what's going on today, but there's a darkness in my mind that lingers as the day goes on. I keep replaying what happened with Lily and can't seem to get my mind to stop. I'm trapped in my mind with my thoughts spinning around me, and I have no way out. I know the scenarios I'm playing out don't make sense, and they aren't real, but it doesn't matter; I'm caught in the cycle and can't break free.

"Are you all right? You've been quiet today," Lily says after we've been walking for a while.

"Yeah, I'm just in a bad mood today."

"What's going on? Anything you wanna talk about?"

"No, I'm just feeling some way, I don't know how to explain it. My mind is itchy. I can't stop thinking about things I've said and done, and if they were the right things to do. I can't turn my brain off." I huff out a sigh and run my hand through my hair, hating how the short cut has grown out in recent months.

"Hey, stop for a minute. Is this about last night?"

"I don't know, maybe a little bit. Like I'm fine with what happened and what didn't happen, I'm just feeling anxious today, I guess." I run my hand through my hair again.

Lily reaches up and catches my hand before grabbing the other one hanging at my side.

"Look at me, you didn't do anything wrong last night. It was perfect and everything I wanted. I need you to know that. I need you to be okay with going slow and taking our time."

"I'm fine with going slow, I think maybe it's just . . . maybe I feel insecure or something. I really don't know how to put it into words. Maybe you're only with me and like me because it's literally the end of the world."

Lily looks at me before bursting into laughter, "I think if I had met you before the end of the world, I would still like you!" She places a hand on my cheek and goes on her tiptoes to kiss my chapped lips.

I can't keep the smile off my face. "You think so?"

"Definitely. You have nothing to be insecure about. You're my favorite person."

"Right now, I'm the only person," I say teasingly, but still meaning it.

Lily smiles again and gently rubs her thumb over my cheek, "You're my only one."

We continue down the tunnel, the buzzing in my head somewhat quieter. I focus on the feel of her hand in mine and soon forget all about my insecurities.

"Do you hear that?" I asked after we had been traveling for a few hours.

"Yeah, it sounds like voices."

"Maybe it's a group we can trade with." I kiss the back of Lily's hand, and we move slowly forward toward the sounds and dim light coming from around the bend in the tunnel.

As we turn the corner, both of our mouths drop open.

"Holy shit," I whisper in awe.

"No kidding," Lily responds, and we both move forward slowly into the light coming from the massive cavern.

It's like an underground city. They seem to have power for lights, fans, heaters, and coolers; it's fantastic. They've somehow figured out how to power and light the entire cavernous space.

As we walk in, people stop to stare at us, a few children pointing, before a young man steps out of the gathering crowd to greet us.

"Hi there! I'm Mike, welcome to our home. What are your names?"

"I'm Adrian, this is Lily." I look to the young man while also taking in the city that lies deep within the earth.

"How have you managed this?" I turn back to Mike as he steps forward, extending his hand to us.

"We have several engineers who live here. They've done the bulk of the work. The rest of us just populate the place."

I reach for Mike's hand, looking at him properly. He's the typical all-American kid, tall with wavy blonde hair streaked with dust, giving it a look reminiscent of ash. I can tell that at one point, he had the physique of a college athlete, but now, due to malnourishment, he has slimmed down and lost some muscle mass. He's full of charisma; it radiates out of him.

Mike gives me a million-watt smile before turning to Lily. She reaches out her hand, grasping his firmly, before reaching back to take hold of mine.

"You're welcome here. We have some extra space and food if you're hungry," Mike says, turning and pointing in the direction of several tents.

"Oh, you have extra food?" Lily and I look at each other. We're both starving.

"Yup, we're pretty well stocked. Why don't you come in, sit down, and get something to eat? You can then clean up a bit."

"Wait, you have a way to bathe?" I almost can't believe my ears.

"Yeah, we have a way to heat water and use sun showers to dispense the water. It works pretty well."

Lily and I look at each other again, neither of us able to keep the smiles from blooming across our faces.

Nodding, I step forward to follow Mike across the flat cave floor, pulling Lily behind me. She seems a little more cautious than I, but there are too many people around for anything to happen. Or at least that's what I'm telling myself. Honestly, my stomach is driving me. I've been so hungry for days now. The pain pinging through my stomach is almost too much to bear.

I need food, which means Lily needs food, as well. I don't want her to experience hunger pangs like I am.

"Here you go. Take a seat!" Mike points at a little table with several chairs nearby and then disappears into the crowd.

My shoulders tighten with tension as I look around at all of the curious faces. No one is saying anything, but they are all looking at us like we've come from another planet.

Mike pushes back through the crowd, "All right, everyone, give them some room and stop staring!" He starts shooing people away after setting down two plates of what looks like chicken on the table.

"Sit, sit!" he says, looking at us over his broad shoulder.

I sit slowly, and Lily takes the seat next to me, both of us more cautious now than when we first entered the cave town.

I pick a piece of the meat off the bone and eat it. It tastes just like chicken, whether or not that's what it actually is is something I don't want to think about.

Lily picks up her piece and takes a tentative bite. Smiling, she takes another, and together we start to eat the food given to us. As we eat, Mike sits down next to us, watching us with a sad, knowing smile.

"When was the last time you guys had a decent meal?" he asks, looking between us.

"It's... been a while, I'm not actually sure how long it's been," I respond between mouthfuls of food.

"Well, you don't have to worry, we have plenty of food here. Enough for everyone. We do ration it, but it's still enough for folks to have food when they need it."

"Thank you, we needed this," I reply, wiping my greasy hands on my dusty pant legs and going back for more food.

"How did you wind up here, Mike?" Lily asks as she nibbles the meat off the bone.

"It's a long story, but essentially, I was at school, and the government picked my mom to go to space. She was one of the top brain surgeons in the country, so I think that's why they chose her."

"No way, wait. Why didn't you go with her?" I ask, perplexed as to how he's ended up in a cave with the rest of us.

"Well, the way it worked is that they only took the person who was selected. Not their families. So, my dad and I were left behind. My dad tried to go with her, but the military stopped him and prevented us from getting on the truck with her. They beat the shit outta my dad."

"Jesus." It's a whisper from Lily's lips and the only thing on my mind as we listen to Mike tell his story.

"Yeah, my dad didn't take it well. He didn't really recover from his injuries, and then one day I came home and he was gone. I don't know where he went or if he's even still alive."

"I'm sorry to hear that, Mike. That must have been terrible." Lily looks at Mike and gives him a slight smile as he looks at her.

"Thanks. It was rough, but you'll find that everyone has stories like that here. Everyone has lost someone or several people because of the asteroid or the government. We've had a few run-ins with the Roamers as well and have lost a few folks to them."

"We know about the Roamers and have run into them as well. How did you find this group?"

"It started small, and then we found this cavern and started to grow, and just collected more and more people, and I think word spread, and people started looking for us, and we just kept growing. We have over a hundred people now, and I mean, people come and go as they please, but we're pretty consistently around that number."

"It's really amazing that you've been able to build something like this. How do you keep people in line?" My mind is racing as I think about all the logistics involved with so many people in one location.

"It's been rough, honestly. It's taken a lot of trial and error, but we've managed to do so somehow. There are three of us who manage everyone, so if one of us can't figure something out, we have two other people to help us, and that's worked well. I didn't want to be in charge, but we had a town hall, and everyone voted, and that's how I ended up being one of the three." Mike shrugs his shoulders like it's no big deal that he's in charge of keeping roughly a hundred people safe. I couldn't do it; my heart races just thinking about it.

Even though I just met him, it's clear that he's a natural-born leader. His charisma and character draw people to him, making them trust him; even I was letting my guard down around him.

"Why don't you two take your time eating, and when you're ready, come find me, and we'll get you settled so you can rest."

I nod my agreement, taking another bite and looking sideways at Lily next to me. She nods her head slowly, but I can see the trepidation in her eyes.

Mike gets up, shooing away the onlookers as he goes, and soon it's just the two of us enjoying the meal that we've been gifted.

"I don't trust him," Lily says after a moment of silence passes.

"What? Why? He seems nice."

"That's just it, he's too nice. I don't trust it. Something has to be going on."

"Maybe it's legit. There are a lot of people here. If it was something fishy, would they all still be here?" I put down the bone I was picking the meat off of and turn to Lily as she does the same.

"I think they would all stay in line if it were mutually beneficial for them all." She wipes her greasy hands down her pants, leaving dark paths through the dust on them.

Her hands come away dirtier than they were before she wiped them.

She reaches for the rag on the table to clean her hands properly before passing it to me.

"I think you're being a little cynical," I respond, looking around the cavern, looking for anything that set off alarm bells.

"How can you not be? We don't know these people; they could be poisoning us for all we know or waiting for us to fall asleep to kill us." Lily's eyes dart around as she speaks, and for once, it seems like she's the one panicking instead of me.

"Hey, hey," I whisper and brush some of the hair off her face.

"It's going to be fine. I have a good feeling about this place. I think we can relax a bit and consider staying for a day or two. Will you trust me?" I hold out my hand and wait for Lily to take it.

She looks around again before taking my hand. "We don't sleep here, though. We find somewhere outside of the cavern that's nearby. Deal?" Lily looks me in the eye as she says this, and I know that she's serious.

I'd do anything to make her feel safe. "Yes, we sleep somewhere else."

Lily smiles, and I pull her hand up to my mouth, kissing the back of it.

My heart squeezes at the look of uncertainty in her eyes. I would do anything to take that away. I want her to feel safe, loved, and like she doesn't need to worry about anything. It kills me that I'm unable to do that for her. I don't know if I will ever be able to make her feel that way.

December 2030?
We've been with Mike's group for maybe two weeks now, and we're still sleeping in the small cave that we found not five minutes away from the larger

cavern. It makes Lily feel safer, so we sleep here and spend our days getting to know the group and helping where we can. I like the people that we've met so far. Everyone seems friendly and welcoming; they're all an extension of how Mike treats them, which is like treating them like family. Lily doesn't trust them yet, and I think she wants to keep moving. I'm inclined to agree with her because groups only lead to trouble. Eventually, the food will run out, or the Roamers will find them, and when that happens, there will be too many people to take care of. Too many people who can turn on each other, who can turn on you. We should keep moving, but we've agreed to stay for a few more days to gather supplies.

"You're awake?" A sleepy voice whispers up from behind me as I finish my latest journal entry. I've been trying to write every morning, but it doesn't always happen.

"Yeah, I couldn't sleep, so I decided to write for a bit. I didn't wake you, did I?"

"No. It was the weirdest thing, but I swear the ground moved, and it woke me up."

"Hmmm, that is weird." I reach for Lily as she sits up, stretching, and she willingly slides into my arms, wrapping hers around my neck. She's all soft limbs and warmth, and I quickly feel myself relaxing into her body as she wraps herself around me.

"Mmm, you feel good in my arms," I murmur into her neck.

She giggles.

My lips gently graze the soft skin of her throat as she giggles again, tightening her grip around my neck.

Her giggles die on her lips as a low rumble echoes around us.

"Did you hear that?" she breathlessly whispers.

"Yes." I quickly move to place her behind me just in case it's the Roamers.

The rumbling grows louder. The ground shakes under us, the vibrations causing smaller pebbles and rocks to bounce on the surface of the tunnels.

"What's happening?" Lily yells as the roar grows so loud that I can barely hear her.

"I don't know!" I yell back, grabbing her and folding my body over hers as the world vibrates around us. I can feel my teeth shaking in my skull and clench them to keep them from clacking together.

"Adrian!" Lily's scream makes the hair on the back of my neck stand straight, and I pull her impossibly close to my body and clench my eyes shut.

"I love you," I whisper into Lily's hair as the world dissolves into dust, vibrations, and screams from the cavern.

Suddenly, everything stops: the vibrations, the noise, the creaking of my teeth as I clench them together. It's suddenly so quiet I can hear the caves groaning around us.

"Lily, Lily! Are you okay?" I pull myself up and look at her tear-stained face.

She nods, turning in my arms to look out of our small alcove into the tunnel.

There's nothing to see but white dust rushing through the tunnels.

"It must have collapsed," she says quietly.

"What? What collapsed?" I can't wrap my brain around what she's saying.

"The cavern, it must have caved in."

"All those people," I say, and before I can move, Lily is up out of my arms and running down the tunnel toward the cavern.

"Lily! Shit!" I yell as I get up on shaking legs and chase after her.

I can barely see through the cloying dust that seems to be sticking to everything. I've never seen dust like this before. It's thick, so thick it's hard to breathe.

As I near the cavern, I start to hear them: the screams, the cries, the groaning of rocks as they shift. Lily pauses at the mouth of the cavern before running forward. I follow, not because I want to help, but because I need to ensure Lily's safety. I can't let her go alone into whatever fresh hell is waiting for us amongst the collapsed cavern rocks.

The dust is thick but fine, like silt, and clings to everything. It's on my skin, in my eyes, up my nostrils, and down my throat. It makes it impossible to see or breathe, yet Lily moves forward, pulling the collar of her shirt up over her nose and mouth. I follow suit, holding the collar of my shirt up to my face while guiding Lily over the rocks with a hand on her lower back. It doesn't take long for the dust to coat us, making it even harder to keep track of Lily as she moves forward.

The cries of those trapped under the rubble slowly die out, and the cavern is filled with an odd, heavy silence, except for the groaning of rocks as they settle over those they have buried.

Lily and I both pause, overwhelmed with the enormity of what has happened. I can't see anything. I can barely see Lily next to me, but as we inch forward, large boulders take shape. Lily and I push through the thick dust and start climbing over the boulders, working our way toward where we last heard screams. Everything is shifting around us as we scramble through the rockfall, trying to get to anyone that might still be alive.

It's like wandering through the aftermath of an explosion. Everything is covered in the earth, the thick air making it so difficult to breathe.

"We need to split up," Lily says softly to me as I lend her a hand to climb up a larger rock.

"No, we stay together. There could be another collapse."

"We'll cover more ground if we split up. I'm not discussing it, Adrian. You go that way; I'll keep moving toward where the food and tents used to be."

She's gone before I can tell her that I'm not going anywhere and disappearing into the fog of the dust around us.

"Fuck," I whisper, turning and moving in the direction of where many folks would congregate in the mornings.

As I slowly and carefully make my way over to that area, I start to hear it. The whimpers, the quick cries of pain as the rocks shift.

There are still people alive under the rocks.

I try to move quicker, noticing for the first time the dark areas of red painted across dust-covered rocks where the falling stones had smashed people.

This is a futile attempt at saving lives. Even if I find someone, the rock fragments are too large for me to move, too large for either of us to move.

Scrambling over a large boulder, I'm met with a hand sticking up from between two rocks. I drop to my knees and start clawing at the stones, trying to dislodge them to free the person beneath. The flesh on my hands and fingers is torn away as I struggle to free the person beneath me, trapped in their stone tomb.

I can't move the rocks. They're jammed together too tightly, and I can hear the person beneath me crying in pain, calling out for help, and there's nothing I can do.

"Please . . . please help me." It's barely audible.

"I'm trying, I'm trying. I'm sorry, I'm so sorry." It's all I can say over and over again as I move around the area, trying to remove the debris.

Suddenly, the ground shifts beneath me, and the rocks shift, moving, and the hand disappears; so do the faint cries for help. The rocks swallow that person down deeper into the abyss below.

I move on to the next person. My bloody hands leave behind streaks of burning failure on the stones, taunting me with my inability to save anyone from the stone.

I've given up when Lily's cry echoes through the devastated chamber.

"Adrian! Adrian, I need you!"

I scramble over the rocks as quickly as I can toward her voice, my heart in my throat, choking any words I would have called back to her.

I find her crouched on the edge of the rockfall, Mike's head in her lap.

He's partially buried, with a large rock crushing his lower right leg, the ground beneath him soaked with his blood. He's barely breathing, his chest hardly moving, and his pulse so weak I have a hard time finding it.

I stand up, looking down at both Lily and Mike, and wonder if it's even worth trying to save him. We don't have any medical supplies, antibiotics, or a way to move him, and that's if we can even manage to get him free from the rock pinning him to the ground.

We don't even have anything to cover the wounds. Would it not be kinder to let him slip away in his unconscious state rather than force him to suffer from his injuries?

I don't voice the question out loud because I can tell by the look on Lily's face and the set in her jaw that she's determined to save his life.

"What do I need to do?" I ask her, looking from her face to Mike's leg.

"We need to tourniquet his leg and take the rock off slowly."

I reach for my belt, taking it off and using it as a makeshift tourniquet, tightening it above his right knee.

Lily gently lays Mike's head on the ground and gets up to help me move the rock. It seems impossibly heavy, both of us straining, our ragged puffing breaths shifting the layer of dust off the rock.

I'm about to give up when the rock moves, just a little, but enough for both of us to look at each other and to give us a boost.

Doubling our efforts, we push again, the rock moving just an inch or two at a time before it dislodges and rolls away.

Lily immediately moves to Mike's now-exposed leg. I stand back, focusing my head lamp on the wound so Lily can see better.

There's a lot of blood; it's brilliant against the gray of the world around us. The bone sticking through his torn skin is bright white, and the wound is bleeding profusely.

If the world hadn't ended, if we were living our mundane, regular lives, this wouldn't be that big of a deal. They would set his bones in the hospital; he'd get a cast and physical therapy to recover. Maybe he would need surgery, but he would recover. Mike would go back to playing sports and living his life. But out here, now, in the world we live in, this is a death sentence.

Mike might not die today or tomorrow, but he's never going to be the same; his leg isn't going to heal like it's supposed to. I know this as I stand looking down at Lily as she tries to stop the bleeding.

"Adrian, I need you to push the bone back into his leg."

"What?" I ask, looking at her with wide eyes. "Are you nuts! I can't do that! I have no idea how to do that."

"You have to do it, I can't. I need you to do it." Lily's hands are dark with Mike's blood as she holds them just over the area where the bone is sticking out.

"I need you . . . I need you to do it for me, please." She looks up at me, pleading, begging me to do this thing that I have no idea if I can do.

"Lily, I've never done anything like this before. I don't know if I can do it."

"Please, Adrian." A single tear slides down her cheek, leaving a trail of mud behind it.

"Fuck."

I kneel across from her, taking my dirt- and blood-covered hands and wiping them down my equally dirty shirt. If we manage to save him, the likelihood of his dying of an infection is going to be impossibly high.

"Okay, what do I do?"

"You have to push the bone back into his leg, and I'll pull down at the same time, and I think... I think that should work. I've only seen this done a few times."

I'm nodding as Lily talks, taking in everything that she says and trying not to throw up at the same time.

I can do this. I *have to* do this.

Lily moves down to Mike's foot, taking it in her hands, and I position myself over his lower leg, trying not to think about the fact that I'm going to be touching exposed bone.

"On the count of three," I say, looking over at Lily as she grips his scuffed sneaker.

"On three," she echoes back to me.

"One. Two. Three!" I push the bone down and into Mike's leg as Lily pulls his leg, and it disappears into the wound, swallowed into the red goo of tissue, tendons, and muscle.

Mike doesn't move or make a noise, which concerns me, given what we just did. Lily and I look at each other for the briefest of moments.

"We need a splint," I say.

"Right."

Both of us move at the same time, looking around to find something that is flat and long enough for us to splint Mike's leg with.

Lily finds a piece of a broken chair leg, and I find the remains of a wooden palette; both are long enough to use.

Meeting back where Mike lies prone on the ground, we get to work splinting his leg, using scraps of our shirts to tie the wooden pieces in place. We find another scrap of cloth nearby and use it as a bandage, applying pressure to stop the bleeding.

"I think we can try to move him now," Lily says, once the bleeding has slowed significantly.

"Okay, where are we going?"

"I guess back to where we were sleeping, and then we can figure it out from there."

Lily and I both pause, a look passing between us that I understand as both of us agreeing that we're going to take this on. We're going to try to keep Mike alive. I'm not sure if I fully agree with the plan. We don't have a lot of supplies, and we're going to be using a lot of resources to keep one person alive.

I don't voice these concerns, though. I nod to Lily as I lift Mike's upper body, gripping him under his arms and clasping my hands across his chest. Lily grabs both of his legs, trying to keep the broken one as steady as possible.

It takes us hours to navigate the rockfall, and by the time we reach our little cave, we're both exhausted and gasping for air. My hands are raw and bleeding, as are Lily's, and Mike hasn't moved or made a sound since we found him, which doesn't give me much hope.

Lily settles down next to Mike, using some of our water to wash the silt dust off his face, and pours a bit into his mouth. I sit across from them, resting my sweat-soaked back against the cold wall of the cave.

I can't help but wonder what I would have done if it had just been me. Would I have left Mike there and let nature take its course? Would

I have even stopped in the cavern to look for survivors? Was I any better than the monsters that lurked around every dark corner of the caverns?

I couldn't answer those questions right now, but my instincts said to leave him and to focus on Lily's and my survival. Did that make me a bad person, or was I just trying to survive?

Lily and I switch off after a few hours, and while Lily sleeps, I keep watch over Mike. He jerks in his sleep occasionally and cries out once, but other than that, he's quiet, and sometimes it's hard to tell if he's even still breathing.

"How is he?" Lily asks for the hundredth time over the last three days.

"No change. His fever broke, but he hasn't woken up yet or anything."

Lily moves closer to Mike and brushes a piece of his hair off his forehead, and my chest tightens. What am I feeling right now? Is it jealousy?

Lily isn't mine anymore, she's ours. Mike has taken her attention from me, and I'm becoming jealous of an unconscious person. I know it's silly, and I know she's trying to save him, but it doesn't matter. Lily was once solely mine, and now she's not. Where she had once taken care of me, she was now caring for another, and our somewhat carefree life in the caves has become something else. We are now caretakers, taking on the baggage that comes with responsibility—trying to keep someone else alive. I am desperate to go back to how it was before the cave collapsed, to when I was hers and she was mine.

Chapter Twenty-One
New Beginnings

December 2030

I'm riddled with a mix of emotions: fear, anger, jealousy, and resentment. I feel like a darkness has taken hold of me since we rescued Mike. She's with him all the time and rarely pays attention to me. All I think about is her, and how she feels about him.

Huffing, I set my journal down and look across the small alcove in the tunnel wall at where Mike lies, and Lily sits next to him. It's been days, and Mike hasn't so much as flinched in his sleep. I'm beginning to think he sustained some head injury in the cave-in; that, or his leg is infected, and the infection is somehow keeping him from waking up.

"I'm going to check the tunnels," I grunt as I stand up, slipping my journal into my worn pack and slinging it over my shoulders.

"Again? You just got back not too long ago." Lily looks up, finally, her eyebrows furrowed with concern. Surely not for me, though.

"Yeah, I'm going to go back to the cavern and see if I can find any supplies, and I will check out the tunnels around us on the way back. We need everything we can find."

Lily nods, taking Mike's pale hand in hers and looking away from me.

My gut clenches, and I feel anger flare in my chest.

Turning, I stomp down the tunnel toward where Mike's colony was before everything fell apart. It's my third time back here, and I still haven't found any supplies; I doubt I will. But I would rather come here and search through the rubble than sit there and watch her tend to him.

I know it's stupid, and I know it doesn't mean anything, but I can't stop these feelings from surfacing. I can't seem to keep my darkness at bay, and it's getting harder and harder to control as the days go on.

I need Lily; she makes me better.

No. I need to rely solely on myself. That's how I make it out of this unscathed.

This is why I wanted to be alone after my family died. It's easier. There are fewer emotions, fewer responsibilities—less of everything.

I'm at the entrance of the cavern before I know it, having walked the entire distance lost in my thoughts. My headlamp illuminates the immense space, capturing only a fraction of the destruction. The dust still hasn't settled, and the air is full of fragments that clog my lungs when I breathe. I pull out the shirt I've been using as a mask and climb into the cave-in, making my way around the outskirts of the rockfall.

My headlamp does little to light the way, so I use my flashlight as well, hoping to find something, *anything*, that would be of use to us.

"He…Hello?"

I freeze. Did I hear someone?

"Hello?"

The voice is tiny, barely loud enough for me to hear over my heartbeat.

"Hello!" I call out. "Can you hear me? Where are you?"

"Over here." I hear a slight clinking noise from several feet in front of me, and I start toward it without thinking.

A small, blood-and-dirt-caked hand sticks out of a hole in the rocks.

"Jesus Christ!" I don't feel the pain as I drop heavily to my knees at the pocket of darkness in front of me.

"Are you okay? What's your name?" I try to calm my voice and the tremor running through my body.

"Wren. I'm Wren; I'm six years old."

Something inside me clicks into place, and I feel a calmness wash over me. I'm acting without thinking.

"Hi, Wren, I'm Adrian. I'm gonna help you get out of here, okay." Gone are the tremors, and my voice sounds strange to my ears. Calm and soothing.

"Here's some water for you. Are you hurt anywhere?" I hand the water bottle down into the darkness, following it with a beam of light from my flashlight.

Large, luminous hazel eyes look up at me. Her little face is gaunt, not like a child's should look at all. The corners of her eyes are streaked with mud from her tears. There's dried blood on her cheek from a large cut that runs from the bridge of her nose across her cheekbone.

"I think I'm okay. I slept for a long time. I'm hungry."

"Okay, let's get you out of here, and then we can get you something to eat. How does that sound?"

She nods her little head and takes a large gulp of the water I've passed her.

"Don't drink it too fast, or drink too much. It might hurt your stomach."

Standing, I look at the rocks that make up the pocket that she's trapped in. Can I move them? Will it collapse? Should I get Lily?

I climb around the hole and realize that I can remove one of the smaller rocks on top, making the hole big enough to lift Wren out of it.

"Okay, I need you to make yourself as small as possible and to cover your head with your hands. Can you do that?"

Her tiny words of affirmation come back, and I count to three before straining to remove the rock. It's the smallest one, but it's still heavy, and I struggle for a moment before getting a good grip on the dusty surface.

The boulder rolls away, clashing loudly against the surface of the other rocks as it falls down the side of the rockfall.

I reach my hand down into the hole and illuminate Wren with my headlamp.

"Reach up and grab hold of my hand."

Wren reaches up with both of her small hands and grasps mine. Her grip is firmer than I thought it would be, which I take as a good sign.

Lifting, I pull her from the darkness of the hole and immediately pull her in close, clutching her to my chest before holding her back out at arm's length and looking her over as if she were going to sprout wings or something.

"You're okay." It's a question and a statement.

The little girl in front of me is completely caked in dust and blood. Scuffs on her knees, arms, and face show the potential of the injuries that she miraculously escaped.

I carry her down the rockfall to the edge, where the ground is flatter and safe for her to walk.

Crouching in front of her, I hold out my hand, "Nice to meet you, Wren, I'm Adrian."

She gives me a timid smile and shakes my hand.

"Let's get outta here."

Nodding, she lets me pick her up again, and we make our way through the collapsed cavern and back to the tunnel that leads to where Lily and Mike wait.

Once we reach the tunnel's entrance, I put Wren down, and she walks next to me, keeping pace without complaint. At some point, I remember her saying she was hungry and pass her a protein bar, which she consumes quickly before asking for more water.

"I'm taking you to meet my friends; their names are Lily and Mike. Mike got hurt in the cave-in. Do you know Mike?"

Wren shakes her head, "No, I don't remember anyone named Mike."

"That's okay, maybe you'll recognize him when you meet him. He's been asleep for a long time, but maybe he will wake up soon, like you did."

Wren nods her little head, and I watch dust filter through the air as it shakes loose from her knotted hair.

I'm suddenly nervous as I approach the cave where Lily and Mike wait. The feeling sweeps through me and is gone before I can ponder it for too long.

"Lily?" I say softly as I step into the cave. She's in the same place she was when I left earlier. Still holding Mike's hand.

She looks up and surprise flickers across her face.

"Who's this?" she asks, getting up to come over to us.

"This is Wren, she's six years old. I found her buried in the rockfall."

"Hi, Wren. My name's Lily, this is Mike. Wanna sit with us? I can clean up your face and arms a bit."

Wren looks from Lily to me and back again. I put my hand on her back and give her a little push forward. She reaches for Lily's extended hand, and they walk over to the area lit by the lantern next to Mike's prone body. Lily uses our water to clean Wren's wounds, all while talking to her in hushed, soothing tones.

I lean back against the cave wall and watch her as she works, thinking that she would have made a great nurse if she had stuck it out. Lily is so caring and soft. She's everything I'm not.

As I sit relaxing and watching Lily work, Mike surprises us all with a soft moan. He doesn't move much, just a slight movement of his hand, but it's a movement. He moans again before stilling. Lily and I look at each other. That's the most he's moved since his injury. It's a good sign.

2030

I think it's December. The ground seems colder. Maybe that means the surface is no longer on fire? Mike woke up today, and it wasn't a pleasant experience. I've never heard someone scream like that before. It scared the shit out of all of us. We were all resting when he sat up and just started crying. It was like something out of a movie. I've never seen anything like it before in real life.

He is in so much pain, and there isn't anything we can do about it.

Mike woke up yesterday and has been in and out of consciousness since. When he's awake, he's quiet and withdrawn, and he doesn't seem to be fully aware of what's going on. I don't know if it's because of his injuries or if it's more than that, more emotional and mental pain than physical damage. Maybe it's both.

I'd guess it's been about a week since the collapse, and it's clear that Mike's leg is not going to heal right. We did the best we could, but it's still not as straight as it should be, and I wonder if he'll be able to walk on it once he's strong enough. I also wonder how long it will be before he can move. We can't stay in this small cave forever. We need to move. The Roamers could find us at any moment, and the longer we stay in one spot, the higher the likelihood is.

"His leg isn't getting better," I whisper to Lily as she comes over to tuck Wren into the sleeping bag next to me.

"Shhhh…he might hear you, and I know." Lily smiles down at Wren and whispers a soft "goodnight" to her before sitting down next to me.

It's the closest we've been since the collapse.

"I'm worried it won't ever heal. It's weepy, but I don't think it's infected," Lily whispers, her voice so soft I can barely hear her.

"What do we do?" I mutter back, looking past her to where Mike lies, staring at the cave ceiling.

"I'd love to say that we give him time to heal, but we don't have time; we need to get him up and moving soon."

"I agree, but how do we do that?" I ask, looking back toward Mike before looking to Lily again, hoping that she has some answer.

Lily shakes her head, and we sit in silence, neither of us knowing what our next move with Mike should be.

"Let's sleep on it and see what tomorrow brings. He just woke up, maybe he needs a day or two to wrap his mind around what's happened," I say, trying to be hopeful.

Lily nods again and settles in next to me. She hasn't slept near me for a while, and butterflies zing through my stomach. I lift my arm and she snuggles against me as we both lie down on the cave floor, covered in our blankets and sleeping bags. It's been getting colder in the caves, which makes me think that winter has settled over the surface. There's no way to know, though, but if that's true, that means we've been underground for several months. Maybe four to six already.

I wake up to a voice I haven't heard in weeks: Mike. He's talking to someone, and as I rub the sleep from my eyes, I look over to see that he's sitting up and chatting happily with Wren, who couldn't look happier.

Mike may have been broken in some ways, but there seems to be a bit of his former self that stayed intact. His positive attitude and charisma appear to be returning.

Wren laughs wholeheartedly at something Mike says to her, and they both turn and laugh in my direction.

"Are you two making fun of me?" I mutter, still trying to get my bearings.

"Your hair is funny," Wren says, pointing and laughing again.

I lift my hand and feel my hair, which happens to be sticking straight up. "Well, shit," I chuckle and try to soothe the nest of knots.

Lily lies still against my side, and I continue to chuckle, enjoying the feeling and sound of our laughter bouncing around the cave walls.

"How are you two feeling this morning?" I ask, slowly extracting my arm from under Lily and sitting up, stretching my arms out to try to relieve some of the tension between my shoulders.

"Well," Mike says, even though he's wincing as he sits up more and pushes himself back so he's resting against the wall.

"That's really good to hear; like, really good, Mike," I say, looking him in the eyes and nodding.

Mike gives me a million-watt smile and looks down at his leg, "I think I'll need a crutch or something before I can get up and around. Do you think you can find something for me?"

"Absolutely. I'll go to the cavern today and look around to see what I can find. I know there are some wood planks around, so maybe we can use one of those."

Lily continues to sleep as the three of us eat a meager breakfast of half a protein bar each, and I set out for the cavern in search of a crutch for Mike.

It doesn't take me long to find a piece of wood that is long enough to work as a crutch. I know that one of us can shape it into something usable. As I walk back to the cave, I'm struck by how different I'm feeling today, like maybe this will all work out, like maybe my darkness isn't as consuming as I thought it was just a few days ago. I think I'm feeling hopeful, and believing in it, for the first time in a long time.

I can hear our small group before I'm close to the cave. Their laughter and the light of their voices bouncing around the tunnel welcome me as I near the place we've been calling home.

I walk into the cave and am greeted by three smiling faces, and I can't help but smile back.

"Look what I found." I hold out the piece of wood that I'm so proud of and receive a round of applause from Mike, Wren, and Lily.

"I think we can use a knife to whittle it into a cane or crutch. What do you think?" I hold the wood out for Mike and Lily to look over.

Mike holds it and rolls the already slightly rounded piece of wood in his hands, nodding his head, "I think we can make this into a crutch or cane. Who has a knife?"

I go over to my pack and grab my hunting knife, the one that I took from Garrett's pack after he died, and hand it over to Mike.

I'm glad that it's being used for something good.

I watch as Mike begins to whittle away at the top of the piece of wood and sit down. The amount of satisfaction I feel knowing that I've helped him makes me happy. I'm overcome with happiness, and Lily comes over and cuddles next to me.

"Hi," she says softly, leaning into me.

"Hey, there," I say back, smiling down at her. My smile only grows as Wren comes over and sits on my other side, taking my hand in her small hand.

I'm overwhelmed with so many different feelings that I don't know what to do or say, so I sit back and let the sound of Mike's whittling lull me to sleep.

Chapter Twenty-Two
Elle

January or February 2031

I've lost track of time and haven't been keeping up with my journal. So much has happened since I last wrote that I don't even know where to start. I suppose I'll start by mentioning that our group has grown from four to six. We keep stumbling upon abandoned and half-finished camps that have left people behind, and we're just collecting them as we go. Some of them are half-feral from fear, staring at us like we're a trick their mind invented to survive the loneliness. Some of them are too quiet, too careful, like they've already learned what happens when you trust the wrong people. Taking them in is a risk every single time—food is tighter, sleep is lighter, and nobody wants to admit how easily desperation can turn into violence. But leaving them behind feels worse. It feels like choosing to become the kind of people the surface made. So, we keep gathering survivors, one trembling body at a time, building a family out of strangers because the alternative is walking away and pretending we didn't hear them calling after us in the dark.

We've been walking for hours already today, and I can tell that we will need to stop soon. Mike and the kids are getting tired, and I can only carry one little one at a time.

"We should stop soon," I say to the group and hear a murmur of "yeses" in response.

We walk for a bit longer before finding a small alcove in the tunnel wall that's going to be a tight fit now that we are six, but the kids are all so small that I think it will work.

"Let's stop here for the night," I say, putting Rachel down and looking for Wren and Oliver, the other two littles, to get them settled. Oliver is in Lily's arms, and Wren is holding Mike's hand as he limps over, bringing up the rear of the group.

His leg is doing unbelievably well, I mean, really well, given what he's been through. I can tell it hurts, and it still weeps from time to time, but it seems to be healing okay, given the situation. And Mike is always in high spirits, which we need in the group, especially since we added two more kids whom we found left behind at an abandoned camp. He knows how to connect with them and entertain them. I'm awkward as hell, and Lily seems distant, so without Mike, I think we would all be in trouble.

I take off my pack and look around at our small group, and a feeling of protectiveness rolls through me. I'm torn, as always: I want to keep them all safe, but I'm terrified that I won't be able to. What if something happens and we start losing people? What if I can't save any of them?

The tiny creature in my chest claws at my sternum before reaching for my lungs, tightening its grip on them for the briefest moment before I draw a strangled breath and force it back out.

Relax. Everything is fine.

I repeat this to myself over and over as I look over the group. Lily is dishing up some canned peaches for the kids, and Mike is eating cold soup from a can. We've been able to gather more supplies as we go. Finding things that others have left behind. We've been fortunate.

I keep waiting for our luck to run out.

"I'm going to take a quick look around. Mike, or Lily, do one of you wanna come with me?" I ask, looking at each of them.

"I'll join ya," Mike says, getting back to his feet.

"You sure?"

"Yeah, I'm all good." He pats his leg and the wooden crutch, and I nod in satisfaction. I know he wants to push himself, but I don't want him to feel like he has to. I also appreciate that he's willing to put in effort and help out even though he's injured.

"We will be back soon, Lily," I call as Mike and I walk away down the tunnel, heading in the opposite direction that we just came from.

It has become standard protocol to scout the tunnels ahead after we find a place to make camp, ensuring that the tunnels are safe. It also helps us see more supplies.

As we round the curve in the tunnel, we both freeze in place.

Huddled against the wall of the cave is a young woman. She appears to be holding the body of another young woman, but it's hard to tell in the dim light of our headlamps.

"Hello?" Mike calls out softly. The figure doesn't move.

Mike and I look at each other before we start forward slowly. Not knowing if this is a trap or if this person needs help.

My heart beats so loudly in my chest, I'm sure everyone in the tunnels can hear its thundering.

We draw closer, and that's when the smell hits us.

I put my hand over my mouth and nose and have to turn away as I start to gag.

I've smelled death before, but this is something I can't even describe. I don't have the words for it. The stench is coming from the woman and the corpse that she clings to.

Mike keeps moving forward as I hang back, pulling my shirt collar up over my mouth and nose.

"Hi, are you all right?" Mike's voice is soft and gentle, as if he were speaking to a scared animal.

"My name's Mike. What's yours?"

She doesn't respond, doesn't move, doesn't look up; there isn't even a flinch as she stares unblinkingly ahead at the darkness.

It's evident by the state of decomposition that they've been sitting there for quite some time. The flesh has started to slough off the bones slowly, and there are all kinds of insects on the body, as well as what appear to be rodent teeth marks left behind on the flesh.

Mike reaches his hand out slowly and gently shakes the woman's shoulder.

Nothing.

"Help me move her," Mike says, standing up and looking over to me.

Nodding, I take a breath through my mouth and move forward.

We slowly extract the woman from the corpse; she neither stops us nor helps us. She just is. Mike holds her by the elbow to steady her once we have her up and standing.

We all look down at the corpse, not the woman.

"Do we bury her?" I ask.

"Let's come back and take care of her later," Mike says.

"Okay. Let's go back to camp. I'm Adrian. What's your name?" I ask again, looking at the young woman in front of me. She appears to be in her 20s, maybe a bit younger, but it's hard to tell.

At first, she says nothing, but as we walk back toward camp, she seems to snap out of it.

"My . . . name is. . . Elle." It's forced and quiet, but she speaks, and I can tell that she hasn't spoken in a while by the hoarseness of her voice. It's raspy as her vocal cords warm up.

"Nice to meet you, Elle," Mike says. He still has a grip on her arm and seems to be supporting her as they walk.

Before long, we're at camp and introducing Elle to the rest of the group. We're seven: me, Lily, Mike, Wren, Oliver, Rachel, and now Elle.

Lily immediately starts tending to Elle, pulling out some water and a cloth to wipe her down, and also finds some fresh clothes for her, as Elle's are spoiled with remains.

Elle doesn't say anything; she lets Lily care for her, her eyes drifting shut now and again as she begins to relax. She's soon clean and, almost immediately, she passes out.

"Mike and I will be back. We need to take care of the body. Are you all right here alone?" I pull Lily aside, gently swiping some hair from her face.

"Yes, I'll be fine, we—we'll be fine."

My hand lingers on her face, and I desperately want to kiss her, but since the kids and everyone else have joined us, Lily has been distant. I'm not sure why, and I haven't had a chance to talk to her about it, but I will. I need for us to be okay, I need for her to still be with me. She's the reason that I'm still going; without her, I would have given up long ago.

"I love you," I whisper, still stroking the side of her face.

She doesn't say it back. She smiles and gently places her hand over mine before turning away and going back into the small alcove in the tunnel.

"Everything all right?" Mike asks as he joins me.

"Yeah, it's all good." I don't sound very convincing, even to myself.

"Let's go," I mutter, and we start down the tunnel back to where the body awaits us.

"I wonder how she died," I say as we stand over the corpse.

"Who knows. I feel like down here it could be anything."

We gather rocks of all sizes as we make our way back to the body. The walls are too unstable to dig into and the ground too solid. Neither of us says anything, and we work in silence, covering the body with the rocks we've collected, before walking back to join the group.

Lily's whispers fill the tunnel before we arrive back, and I find myself picking up the pace. Even though things have been off with us, I'm desperate to get back to her. I always miss her, even if I'm only gone for a few minutes. I'd spend every moment with her if I could.

To our surprise, Elle is sitting up and talking to Lily in hushed tones.

"You're up," Mike says, stepping forward.

I look to Lily, and she gives us both a smile.

"Elle was just telling me about herself. She grew up in a small town in rural Iowa. Her father was an Aerospace Engineer and taught at Iowa State University."

"I visited Iowa State University when I was looking at schools," Mike says, settling down on the ground next to Elle.

Elle looks at him, and I take note that she has long, brown hair and large, brown eyes; they're the color of a murky river, like what you see after a heavy rain.

"Did you go there as well?" Mike asks, leaning in to hear her response.

"No, I never got the chance. My dad died two years ago from cancer, and I've been taking care of my family since then."

"Oh, I'm sorry to hear that. That must have been tough."

Lily gets up and joins me where I've settled on the floor of the cave, and soon Wren joins us as well, sitting against me and falling asleep. The other two littles have already dozed off and are fast asleep on the far side of the camp.

"Do you mind sharing more about yourself?" Mike asks.

"I'm the middle child of three, and when my dad died, he told me that it was my responsibility to take care of everyone, including my mom.

She wasn't much of a mom." Elle's voice breaks and gets softer as she continues.

"Mom was always quick to get angry and relied so much on me to take care of my older sister and younger brother. I did everything. I cooked, cleaned, did the laundry, and made sure everyone had what they needed for school or their jobs. Everything."

"That must have been hard."

"It was. It was so hard." Elle starts to cry softly, and Mike reaches out to rub her arm gently, careful not to push her too far.

"My brother, Darren, was killed when people came to our house and tried to loot it. They stole all of our supplies, and he ran after them, and they shot him in the street." Mike pulls Elle in for a hug, and she goes willingly into his arms, sobs wracking her body as she continues.

"My mom went crazy after that and ran off into the night. I couldn't find her anywhere. I looked for a long time and eventually had to give up. My older sister and I made it to the caves, but my sister wasn't the same; something broke in her mind. She would yell and scream and push me around for no reason. She kept telling me it was all my fault, everything that was happening was all my fault!"

I almost get up to go to Elle, but Mike holds up a hand to stop me and holds Elle closer, making soothing noises as he rocks her back and forth.

"She was so mean all the time, I couldn't take it anymore; I couldn't take all the screaming. I snapped. I don't know what happened. One minute she was screaming at me, and the next she was dead, and I had a rock in my hand. I think I killed my sister!"

Mike, Lily, and I all look at each other in silence as Elle's admission hangs in the air between us.

Chapter Twenty-Three
Daylight

"The loneliest moment in someone's life is when they are watching their whole world fall apart, and all they can do is stare blankly." — F. Scott Fitzgerald

After Elle admitted to killing her sister, she sobbed herself to sleep in Mike's arms. None of us spoke until she was asleep.

"What do we do?" Lily asked.

"What do you mean?" Mike looked from the sleeping woman in his arms back to Lily. "What is there to do?"

"We can't take her with us, she's a murderer." Lily's voice climbs an octave.

"Shhh…I think we don't do anything. I mean, Elle had some mental breakdown because of how she was being treated. Or at least that's how I see it," I say, looking between Lily and Mike.

"Are you serious?" Lily gets up and walks a few steps from me, looking down at me as I sit on the cave floor.

"Yes, I think she was pushed to her limits and snapped. I don't think it was a planned-out thing, and I don't think it's something that she will do again."

"You can't be sure of that, though. She could kill us all in our sleep."

"Lily, please, I think that's a bit much."

"You and Mike are wrong about this. She's not safe, and we're not safe with her."

I look to Mike for help as Lily storms out of the cave and into the tunnels. Mike shrugs his shoulders and shakes his head.

"I think it'll be fine. But I also think that we never bring up the fact that Elle killed her sister. It might trigger her. Don't you think?"

"I agree. I'll go tell Lily and try to calm her down some."

"Good luck."

I follow the direction Lily went when she stormed off and find her a short distance away, leaning against the tunnel wall with her head in her hands.

I slow as I approach. "Hey," I say quietly. "Talk to me. What's going on?"

She doesn't look up. "I just… I needed you to be on my side." Her voice wavers. "It feels like you chose a stranger over me, and I don't understand how you don't see why that scares me."

I stop a few feet away, giving her space. "I do see it," I say. "I understand why you're worried. But I also understand why Elle did what she did. She didn't think she had a choice, and we don't know how bad things were with her sister." I hesitate, then add, "Leaving her behind would be a death sentence."

Lily lets out a sharp breath. "Maybe that's just how it goes now. Maybe we're not meant to keep saving everyone. We can't keep collecting people and hoping it works out."

Something in her tone makes my chest tighten. "That doesn't sound like you," I say gently. "You've always been the one fighting to help. So, what changed?"

She swallows hard and finally turns away from me. "It's not just this." Her voice drops. "I feel like I'm losing you. Like you're always somewhere else, too busy to even notice."

I step closer. "Lily," I say softly, "you could never lose me. I'm here because of you. I stay because of you." I wait until she looks at me. "I love you. Completely."

She turns back, tears tracking down her cheeks. "You really do?"

"Yes," I say, without hesitation. "Everything I'm doing, holding this together, making these calls, I'm doing it because I love you. Because I want us to survive this."

I reach for her, and she grips my arm, pulling me into a hug that knocks the air from my lungs. She cries against me, and I hold on, grounding us both.

When she pulls back, she presses messy, desperate kisses to my cheek, my mouth. "I love you too," she whispers. "I'm sorry. I didn't mean to shut you out."

"It's okay," I say, resting my forehead against hers. "Just...talk to me when it feels like this. Don't carry it alone."

She nods. "I will."

"Promise?"

"Promise."

We seal our promise with a kiss and start back toward the camp and the rest of the group.

Mike is still holding Elle as she sleeps in his arms. She must have been exhausted. I know this will slow us down some, waiting for her to recover, but it seems like she and Mike have already formed some bond.

"We should keep moving tomorrow, if Elle is up for it."

"What's the hurry? Where are we going?" Mike asks, shifting under the unconscious woman's weight and stretching out his injured leg.

"I think it's time that we start looking for a way out instead of just wandering around from empty camp to empty camp. I mean, why are all the camps empty? Where did all the people go? They have to be going somewhere, right?" I search Mike and Lily's faces as if they have the answers.

"We can't live underground forever, and our supplies are running low. We're lucky that the hollows run along the aquifer and we have water."

"I mean, I guess it makes sense that people are going somewhere, but maybe it's like with the cavern, maybe there's a large colony somewhere." Mike shrugs his shoulders as if that explains everything.

"Wouldn't you like to find out if that's the case?" I shoot back, my frustration growing.

"Do you guys *want* to stay underground forever?" I can hear my voice pitching upward and know I'm getting worked up, but I can't understand why they would want that.

Lily places her hand on my upper arm, "I don't think anyone is saying that. I think what Mike is saying, and I know what I'm thinking, is that the surface might be in worse shape than the underground. What if we emerge and there's nothing there, or worse, it's complete chaos?"

"I'm sorry, but I can't think like that right now. The 'what-ifs' are what's going to kill us, the doubt. We need to keep moving and keep searching for a way out." I place my hand over Lily's and squeeze gently, letting a breath out when she squeezes my arm back.

"Okay, we'll plan to start looking for a way out then," Lily says, looking over to Mike, who nods his agreement.

"Tomorrow," I say.

"Tomorrow," they echo back in unison.

I sit down and Wren and Lily join me, and soon we're lying on the floor, cuddled up and drifting to sleep. Or at least they are. I'm too wound up to sleep. I have been thinking about the surface a lot lately and know it's the only way for us to survive. We can't stay underground any longer. We're all weak, malnourished, and becoming weaker with every passing day that we're down here.

There must be a way out; it's the only thing that makes sense. We haven't seen another group in ages, which worries me.

"I can hear you thinking." Lily's sleepy voice drifts through the darkness, finding its way to my ears.

"Sorry."

"What're you thinking about?"

"Finding a way out. I'm worried we won't, and I'm worried we will."

"I thought you said not to think about the 'what-ifs.'" She stirs against my chest before settling back down, her head a comforting weight in the space between my neck and shoulder.

"Yeah, I did say that, didn't I. Maybe I should take my advice." I chuckle softly and let the tension slide from my body. I take a breath, and then another, and feel sleep tugging at my consciousness before too long.

"Adrian!"

The shout wakes me. I have no idea how long I've been asleep or what's happening, but I bolt upright, reaching for my flashlight all in one motion.

I hear chuckling, giggles, and my mind cannot compute what is going on.

"You should see your face!" Mike says, smiling and pointing at me, giggling at the shock I'm sure is on my face.

"What the hell is going on?" I ask, looking around, searching for something out of place.

"You've been sleeping like the dead, and it's time to get up and get moving," Lily says, smiling at me. "Mike thought it would be fun to play with you a bit."

"Oh, well. . . You got me." I can't keep the dryness out of my voice as I rub the sleep from my eyes. I forget that Mike is still so young, only nineteen or twenty years old. He still has moments of being boyish, and that's okay. It's important.

I force a smile to my face and give him a gentle push as I gather myself.

Looking around the camp, it's already packed up, and Elle stands off to the side with some of our gear already packed and on her back.

"Wow, I slept through all of this?"

"You were out, man, you were even snoring and talking in your sleep! It was hilarious," Mike says, turning and limping over to his pack.

I turn and start rolling up my sleeping bag and blankets, and Lily helps me pack our bags.

"Sorry, but Mike wanted to wake you up like that," she whispers while smiling at me, and it's a full, genuine smile.

"It's really okay, it's good to have moments of laughter."

We're packed before too long and are moving down the tunnel in under ten minutes from the time that they woke me up. I feel anxious today. I want to find a way out, but I know it will take us some time.

March? 2031

I'm feeling a lot of pressure to keep the group's spirits high. We've been looking for a way out for weeks now and haven't found anything. Mike and Elle are growing closer with every passing day, which is good for them both, I think. Lily has up days and down days just like I do, but I can tell it's getting harder for both of us to maintain our positive outlook. We need to find a way out.

I can feel myself getting weaker, my bones sticking out from under my thin, pale skin. I feel like my skin will tear away from my bones with the lightest touch.

Putting my journal down, I look at the group. We've stopped for the day, and everyone is exhausted. It's another day of nothing.

"I'm going to keep going for a bit; check out the tunnels ahead of us and see if I can find anything." I'm exhausted as well, but my anxiety is fueling me to keep going.

"I'll come with," Elle whispers, standing up and letting go of Mike's hand in the process.

"Okay, let's go."

Elle and I walk out of the camp and head toward a part in the tunnels that has multiple branches. We'll have to choose which direction to go tomorrow, and if we pick the wrong one, we could just be going deeper into the caves.

We walk in silence until we reach the fork in the tunnel.

"Which way do you think we should go?" I ask Elle.

She shakes her head, shrugging.

"Maybe we can go down each tunnel a little way and see if we find anything?" I ask.

She shrugs again.

"Okay, let's do that. Let's go to the left first." I head to the left, and Elle follows closely behind.

We walk for long enough that I start getting hungry, and my legs start to hurt, which may mean we're walking uphill.

"Do you smell that?" Elle asks suddenly.

"Smell what?"

"It's. . . it's raining!" Elle exclaims.

I pause, steadying my heart and breathing, and take a deep breath through my nose.

Holy shit. It *is* raining.

It's carried through the tunnel on the slightest of breezes, and is the lightest touch of a smell, like lovers caressing one another.

"Elle, run back and get everyone. I'll wait at the entrance to the tunnel."

She nods, turns, and races off into the darkness, leaving me alone.

The scent of rain rides on the back of the wind like a leaf drifting through the breeze. It sends a shiver down my spine as memories flood through me. Rain. I haven't seen, heard, felt, or thought of rain in so long. I almost sink to my knees at the rush of emotions and overwhelming sensations that the smell invokes throughout my body. I'm suddenly overcome with hope, which pushes fear to the outskirts of my mind, where it still lingers.

I jog back to the tunnel entrance and wait for the rest of the group to arrive. As I wait, the glee and hope suddenly give way to anxiety as my mind races ahead of my heart. What will be waiting for us on the surface? What if we don't find anything on the surface?

It's my responsibility to ensure that the group stays safe, including Lily and Wren. I need to keep them safe, motivated, and moving. What if we go down this tunnel and there's nothing there? What if this is a false lead?

Everyone would be devastated; I would be the killer of hope. This small thing, a hint of a smell on the breeze, could be the thing that undoes all of us.

Before I can disappear into my thoughts, I hear the thudding of feet coming my direction, along with lights bouncing off the tunnel walls, and I know it's my small group.

Elle leads the way as they round the corner, and the smile on Lily's face steals the breath from my lungs. Her eyes are luminous with happiness, and it's like a dagger to my heart, making my heart skip a beat and my breath catch.

It will kill her if this isn't the way out.

Lily wraps me in a hug, and none of us says anything. We turn as one and keep moving down the tunnel, Elle pulling Mike along and me pulling Lily, who is carrying Oliver. Wren holds tightly to my other hand, and Rachel walks between all of us, managing to keep pace just fine on her tiny legs.

We pause often to catch our breath; we're definitely hiking uphill, and I can feel it in my calves. It reminds me of the days I used to hike for work and pleasure. The burn is a welcome feeling.

The smell of rain and fresh air gets stronger the further we walk.

"Do you think we're close?" Mike asks as he limps next to Elle.

I know his leg must be killing him, but he keeps going.

"I don't know, we've been walking for a long time. Should we stop and rest for the night?" I pause, pulling the group to a complete stop. I look around at the kids and can see the fatigue.

"We have to keep going. Just a little further," Lily says, pulling my hand.

"We have to be close," Elle says, lifting her chin and smelling the air like an animal would.

"Okay, we keep going, but we will have to stop eventually, especially for the littles."

"Just a bit farther," Elle says again, and we all set out following her up the tunnel.

The tunnel begins to widen as the incline steepens, and the smell of rain becomes more pronounced, tingling my senses with the scent of freedom.

I almost run into Mike when he stops abruptly as the tunnel gives way to a massive cavern. I squint past him into the murky gray light filtering in from the small opening at the top of the cavern where the ceiling has caved in. There's a massive rockfall leading up to the hole. It's not big, but it's there—a path to the surface.

Chapter Twenty-Four
Surface Level

March (maybe) 2031

*It's been two weeks since we found the cavern with the path to the surface.
With sunlight streaming through the hole, we could now tell time and get
our circadian rhythms back in order. That's how I know it's been two weeks
already. We're close, though. We have a singular focus, and it's to get to the
surface. We should manage that tomorrow.*

Placing the journal next to me, I stand up slowly; my body is tense and sore from clearing rocks away from the entrance. I feel physically and emotionally raw and battered—older than my actual age. It's incredible what living underground does to the body. I'm nothing close to who I was when I entered the caves, and that goes for both my physical and mental state.

I'm not sure who I am anymore; I don't know what I've become or what the outside world will turn me into. I am aware that I will do everything to ensure that our little group survives. This group is now my family; they're my responsibility.

I stand on the edge of filmy sunlight that is filtering into the cave and watch the others. I can't help but let my brain spin as I watch. What will we find out there? People, a new society, or worse... nothing? My anxiety intensifies with every passing thought. What if we're doing all of this work only to find that a place once our home is nothing but barren land devoid of everything?

To stop my brain from spinning out of control, I step into the circle of light, immediately feeling the old comforting warmth from so long ago. Instinctively, I close my eyes and raise my face toward the light that struggles to break through our stone barrier.

I stand there for several moments, taking it in, feeling the sun, and letting it take me back to better days. It reminds me of summer, simpler times, being a child, and everything that had once been good. The sun is comforting.

I want to stand in the sun for hours, but we have to be careful now. We haven't been in the sunlight for who knows how many months, and our skin is so pale that we need to be cautious about getting sunburnt.

After a few minutes soaking in the sun, I can feel the warmth becoming too intense on my thin, fragile skin. I turn around slowly, open my eyes, and take everything in.

The littles are all playing together in the patchy sunlight, raising their dirty little faces to the rays breaking through the dusty air. Elle, Lily, and Mike are all relaxing after a long morning of moving rocks from the opening. Mike has been doing what he can, but it's hard with his leg, so the rest of us have been picking up the slack. Hauling larger rocks away from the entrance and passing smaller ones to Mike for him to toss aside. We've all lived in the bowels of the Earth for as long as we can, and it's time for us to claw and kick our way to the surface, no matter how terrified we may be.

The more I watch the group, the more tense I get. I'm terrified for all of us and have my doubts about the surface.

Mike notices my tense stance and limps over.

"Ya all right?" he asks, his brow furrowing in concern. Nodding, I avoid eye contact with him; his genuine sense of worry for me makes my chest tight, and I hate it. I hate feeling weak and out of control.

"Yeah, I'm fine. Just thinking about tomorrow."

Mike nods in understanding, following my gaze as I look around the cavern.

"We don't have any other choice; this is our only option, but that doesn't make me feel any better about it," I whisper.

Mike pats me on the back, "Try not to think about it too much. We'll know more tomorrow once we reach the surface. Until then, don't overthink it." He smiles at me and goes off to join Elle, who is sitting on a rock, soaking up the sunlight like a lizard.

Elle has opened up significantly in the last two weeks since we discovered the cavern. She seems so happy, it's like what happened to her in the tunnels never actually occurred.

No one seems to be as scared as I am, and I'm having a hard time understanding why they aren't. I am absolutely terrified. There's no telling what's out there, but instead of being scared, a tangible feeling of excitement fills the air, electrifying the entire cavern.

I know Mike and Elle are looking at this as a new adventure, but I see it as another hurdle to overcome without knowing the horrors that await us on the other side. I'm so exhausted from constantly worrying and caring for everyone that I think I'm on the brink of a mental breakdown. I'm burned out and barely functioning.

We are bringing down our safety net, yet it's something that has to be done. I know that getting out is the only option; we're out of food and water. This is it, our last chance for survival, and we have to return to a world that we left to die. We have to brave the wide-open space of Earth's pillaged and raped body or die inside of her, buried under her flesh, weak and in the dark that we have grown so fond of. I'm terrified and know that what lies ahead of us is going to be the biggest challenge we have yet to face.

"We should get back to moving rocks," Lily says as she walks toward me.

"Sounds good," I mutter, still lost in my thoughts.

"Everything will be fine," she whispers as she takes my bruised hands in hers and looks into my eyes.

"I hope so."

Lily pulls me in for a quick hug, then moves away and starts toward the rock pile.

"Mike! Elle! Let's go," I shout, and soon the four of us are back to clearing a path to the surface.

It takes us the rest of the day, and by the time we finish, the outside light has faded, and we are all exhausted, our hands bruised and bloodied from the rocks. We've left pieces of us behind as we push and shove the stones out of the way. We're almost there.

Tomorrow, at first light, we will leave the underground.

We all sit down, getting comfortable and ready for the night, enjoying the air flowing into the cavern, stirring the dust, and making it dance through the dim lights of our flashlights and headlamps.

Fresh air mixes with the stagnant, breathing life back into a place that has been dead for so long. It's terrific and makes me forget about all of the uncertainty for a moment, and the fear slips away as Lily reaches out for my hand.

Holding her hand tightly, she lays her head on my shoulder, taking comfort in the closeness and the familiarity. Tomorrow will bring all new things, but tonight it's about embracing what I know and what I love.

We melt into each other, becoming one in our comfort. Lily gives me everything I cannot provide myself: confidence, love, strength, and affection. Lily makes me into someone I never thought I could be; she makes me into a leader, into someone reliable. I'm worried that without her, I won't be anything.

Everyone settles into their bedding, and soon the quiet air of the cavern is filled with the sounds of steady breathing.

I can't sleep.

The fear of tomorrow keeps me awake. My swirling thoughts make my mind race so fast I can't keep up with them. Memories mix with worries, all of them cascading through my mind every time I close my eyes, overwhelming me. The darkness is suffocating me. It haunts me, the dark; I can hear the memories of those I've buried with the tunnels, their bodies screaming as they are returned to the soil that we have survived on for so long.

After all this time in the dark, the feeling of absolute fear is over-whelming. I can feel my chest tightening with every forced breath that escapes between my tightly clenched teeth.

I'm having a panic attack.

I can feel myself shaking with the force of it. I'm trapped, constricted in every way, a prisoner in my body, and my mind is the warden.

I sit up, putting my arms over my head, desperately gasping for air. Lily wakes up beside me, immediately sitting up, saying my name in concern.

She knows not to hold me; I'm already in a prison of my own making, and adding more restrictions will send me over the edge. Instead, Lily begins to rub my back, slowly, in circles, while speaking to me in a soft tone.

I manage to draw in a few stuttered breaths, and as I do, Lily slowly puts both hands on the side of my face, lifting it. She looks me right in the eyes as she continues to soothe and talk to me.

It calms me enough that my muscles release their grip on my lungs, which fill with the torpid air of the cave. Lily smiles softly, pushing the hair off my forehead. Leaning in, she kisses me gently on the lips. I can feel the light smile on her lips as she pulls away. Lily anchors me back to the ground, holds me in place.

"Tomorrow. will be amazing," she says, still holding my face in her hands, "stop worrying about things you can't control. We will all be there together, and we will figure it out together."

Nodding, I try to believe what she's saying, and I repeat her words over and over in my mind. If I focus on her, I'll focus less on the "what-ifs."

"Come on. Let's lie back down, close our eyes, and think of something wonderful." Her soft voice lures me to a calm place like a sailor to a siren's song. My thoughts slow their wandering and soon sleep blissfully closes my eyes, calming my tumultuous mind.

Chapter Twenty-Five
The Man in Black

"Civilization is like a thin layer of ice upon a deep ocean of chaos and darkness." — Werner Herzog

We emerge into the grumbling, groggy morning light the next morning after little sleep, and what we find is what I was scared of. The land on the surface is bare and as emaciated as we are. There are no rolling hills of green grass with herds of cattle grazing leisurely over them, no people waiting to welcome us into the husky light of morning. The sky itself is as unwelcoming as the dark that stared back at us as we considered retreating into the obscurity of the Earth.

There is no blue upon blue of the sky going on for as far as the eye could see. The sky is a grubby color of gray, and the sun barely punctures the impermeable film covering every inch of the air. Everything is covered in fog or smoke. It's hard to see and even harder to breathe. Maybe it was better underground, after all?

As we stand outside of the hole we had just dug through her skin, my mind screams at me to go back. Whatever happened on the surface, it's destroyed, and at least we know the devils that wanted for us in the darkness.

My body shakes with the force of the sob ripping at my throat, and my eyes sting with tears as they struggle to force themselves out of my already stinging eyes. I can feel my shoulders slumping and my battered body struggles to stay upright under the immensity of our failure. All that hope for the surface was misplaced; there isn't anything here for us. It isn't any better than the underground.

"Do you think it's always like this?"

I force my sobs into my chest, swallowing and burying them deep inside.

"Yeah, Elle, I think this is how it will be out here. It explains why there isn't any grass or plants... or life." My voice breaks as I finish my thought, and I bow my head, refusing to look at anyone. I've let us all down, and I think we all know that our struggle isn't over yet. We're going to have to continue to push forward, even though we're all exhausted. We have to keep fighting. The moment we stop trying is the moment we die, and I'm not sure I'm willing to give up just yet.

The nothingness and vastness of the surface are stifling. The desolate land gives us nothing. I turn to look at our little group, taking in everyone's appearances. We're all haggard, worn, bloodied, and exhausted from our escape. We are covered in dust, which clings to our sweat-covered bodies from the exertion of digging and clawing our way to the surface.

I'm not sure how long we've been standing here, but I know we need to get moving. We have to do something; we can't just stay here, staring at each other.

"What do we do?" My body clenches as the doubt behind those words is whispered into existence, knowing that it will continue to grow and consume every bit of my brain and body with more and more anxiety. The monster is already increasing and slowly clawing its way from the small of my back and up my spine. Consuming all my confidence as it goes.

I can feel my anxiety and paralysis starting; the weight of everything is almost too much for me to handle. I don't think I should be the one making the decisions, yet here we are. I look at Mike, searching his dirt-stained face, asking for help without saying a thing.

"I guess we head out. We can't stay here unless we want to go back into the hollows. I say we pick a direction and start walking," Mike says, picking up on my panic.

I nod in agreement; it's the best, and only, solution that has been suggested. We don't have any other plan; I don't think any of us thought much past the effort it was going to take to get out, and what we would do if we didn't find anything upon our exit. Now we're here, exposed, with no plan, not knowing what to do. We're vulnerable.

Elle, Mike, and I look at each other, none of us willing to make the final decision. Lily steps forward, looking into the grimy sun, and points.

"We follow the sun; it's the easiest way to keep track of our direction. We'll keep it in front of us during the morning and behind us in the afternoon. We go East." She's so confident, her voice steady, leaving no room for doubt.

It makes sense that we use the sun to navigate; otherwise, we would be aimlessly wandering through the barren hellscape that awaits us. We need the structure.

"I agree," I say, looking to Elle and Mike for their consensus.

"Sounds good to me," Mike says as Elle nods beside him.

"It's settled; we go East," I say, looking at Lily and reaching for Wren's hand. Elle and Lily reach for Rachel and Oliver, and the seven of us turn into the sun and set out, hoping that it will lead us to something better.

I can't help but hope that over the next hill there will be something, that this is just the beginning of our time on the surface, and that it will only get better. We were born again from the Earth, and this is our second chance at life. I choose to believe in that, and with every step away from the sanctuary of our caves, I cling to that hope.

We let the sun lead us to something better, or so we hope. We've been walking for hours, and the sun is above us now, and so far, we haven't seen anything. The surface is bleak and sterile. There aren't any animals, or signs of any animals, and very little vegetation. I keep my eyes on the horizon, looking for any structure that we might be able to use for shelter. From the looks of everything around us, I have a feeling we're going to have a difficult time finding anything that will work as shelter. It seems like food and water will be even harder to come by—everything is burnt and dead.

I don't know how many miles we've gone, but the sun is quickly moving through the sky, and the group is exhausted. The littles wore out fast, and those of us carrying them are quickly running out of energy. Even Mike is holding one of them, and I can't help but keep an eye on him as his limp grows increasingly more pronounced with every step.

I'm proud of how we've kept moving throughout the day, plodding on with a sort of grim determination to find somewhere that we can rest. I can't help but feel that every step we take is taking us farther away from the known and into the terrifying.

As we crest yet another hill, we're greeted by a large species of pine tree in the valley below. It's the only thing that we've seen since leaving the depths, and it seems to be the only thing that exists in this strange new world. It's the first sign of life we've seen all day. There are even small tufts of grass around it; the grass is dead or in the process of dying, but it's a good sign.

Right?

We move toward the tree, no one saying a word, but all of us moving as one. The sun is low and behind us, a sign for us to stop for the night. It's the best we can do for shelter and maybe even food. I know that some pine tree bark can be consumed, although not the bark itself, but rather the inner layer, which I think we can eat.

"Let's stop here for the night," I announce, standing under the tree, one hand resting on it, while looking up at its bare branches.

Mike sighs and slumps to the ground, leaning back against the trunk of the pine. Elle follows soon after; the little ones immediately find places to lie down. All of them except for Wren, who clings to my other hand, looking up at the tree, mimicking me.

Lily stands at my side, her hand on my lower back.

"It's weird, isn't it?"

"What?" I ask, looking from the branches to Lily, who's looking around slowly.

"That we haven't seen any signs of life, that there's nothing out here. Why haven't we seen any signs of animals, not even tracks or droppings? There's nothing out here." She turns a slow circle, dropping her hand from my back before looking at me. Her eyes are forlorn, desperate, searching.

I wish I had something to say to her to ease her doubt, but I don't have any answers.

"I don't know. Maybe we're just in a remote part of the country and people have all moved to the cities or something?"

"But the wildlife, Adrian. There should be some." She's whispering, the desperation in her eyes growing as unshed tears cling to her dark lashes.

"It'll be okay, Lily. I don't know how, but it will be; we'll find a way to make it work."

I know that what I'm saying doesn't soothe her worry, but she nods, taking Wren's hand and coaxing the small child to come with her to lie down for a bit.

I watch as they settle next to Mike, Elle, Oliver, and Rachel. As they all rest, I take the knife out of my pack and start to cut and shave off the bark of the tree, taking the inner, softer layer of bark and setting it aside for them to eat when they wake up. It will provide us with some much-needed nutrition and hydration and lessen the unbearable hunger that continuously gnaws at our hollow bellies.

We spend our first night on the surface huddled together under the pine tree, consuming its flesh and trying to see if we can find the stars in the cloudy sky.

I wait until everyone is asleep before I get up again and start carving more bark off the tree. We're going to need more food, and this is the best we have right now. I still have a few protein bars and cans of fruit in my bag, but with so many of us, and the fact that we're burning a lot of energy walking, we'll need more food. Tree bark is going to have to suffice.

I stay awake for as long as I can, listening to the pine-less branches above us groaning in the wind. There aren't any insect noises, there aren't any crickets, there's just absolute silence that envelops me and makes my head hurt. I close my eyes only for a second, and the next thing I know, I'm being shaken awake by Lily.

"Good morning," she whispers, "did you sleep much?"

I sit up, stretching slowly, wincing at my sore, stiff muscles.

"A little. I tried to keep watch for most of the night." I smile at her, rubbing her arms gently to warm her in the chilled air of early morning.

"We should get everyone up and get moving soon," Lily says, standing and slowly moving around to wake Wren up.

Our small group is soon up, stretching and chewing on some of the bark. We have to ration it just like everything else. There's no telling how long it could be before we find more food.

"Where are we going?" Oliver asks, looking around at each of us adults, searching for an answer that none of us knows.

"Somewhere new and better," I say with a smile, hoping that it will be enough to satisfy his curiosity.

"When will we get there?" Rachel chimes in from her spot next to Mike, where she clings to his hand.

"We don't know, but we will know it when we get there. It'll be wonderful." I try to lighten and infuse my statement with some energy, but it sounds dull in my ears—a blatant lie to everyone but the children.

Lily gives me a forced smile. "Come on, kids, let's get moving!" She walks forward, and the littles follow her like she's the pied piper. They love her more than the rest of us, and I think it's her kind nature. They are instinctively drawn to it.

Wren gives me a look, searching for permission before letting go of my hand and running after the others and Lily.

Mike, Elle, and I follow behind them. As we move away from our tree and travel further from the cave, the ground starts to rise and fall as we enter the foothills. We begin to move more slowly as the landscape becomes increasingly hilly, taking our time and resting frequently.

We're not used to climbing hills, even this gentle and rolling one, and it takes a lot out of our malnourished bodies.

At the crest of every hill, I hold my breath waiting, hoping to see something on the other side, but there's nothing there.

It's a little after midday when we crest the top of another hill and look down into the valley.

"What's that?" Mike says, pointing into the valley.

"It looks like a man," I say slowly, straining my eyes to see farther in the murky light.

"He's not moving or anything. Let's go closer," Mike says and starts moving before any of us can oppose him.

The man stands in the valley, stooped slightly, with his dark cloak billowing in the wind that whistles through the low area.

He's odd-looking, but I can't quite figure out why. He has long, black hair, streaked with gray, tied at the base of his neck with a piece of cloth that appears to have been torn from his cloak. He's an illusion of a man. He looks real from a distance, but as we get closer, it's as if the fantasy begins to unravel, and he becomes a wisp of a man. Maybe that's why I can't wrap my mind around him being real.

We move closer and hunker down behind some rocks, watching him for several minutes. He hasn't moved once since we first saw him. Not a twitch of a finger or tilt of the head. Nothing, and I have a sinking feeling that he's not a man at all, but more of a scarecrow, existing to scare off those who travel in this valley.

The wind picks up and shifts the placement of his hair, and I can make out what looks like scars on his face, or maybe burns. I'm too far away to see what exactly is going on with this figure in black.

The sun is getting lower in the sky, and it's going to be dark soon. The last thing I want is for our small group to get caught out in the open at night with a strange man in the valley. Everything about this feels wrong.

"What do we do?" Elle's question echoes in the silence that follows as we look at each other for an answer.

My heart skips a beat, my breathing speeds up, and my brain spins. "Stay here. I'm going to see what's up with this guy."

I try to say it with as much confidence as I can muster. I need the group to believe in me, that I know what I'm doing, and that everything will be okay. They rely on me, and I need to ensure that they know they can trust me.

Lily grabs my arm as I stand up from behind the rocks. Her small hand slides down my arm slowly before interlocking with my fingers. Lily grips both of my hands in hers, staring into my eyes. "Be careful and come back… please come back." Leaning in, we kiss, our lips pressing together, my hand on her cheek, holding her to me for as long as possible. I'm pretty sure she can feel my heart beating as we kiss. I can feel it in my chest, ready to burst free.

Pulling away, I look down at her, seeing her as if for the very first time. Her hair blowing across her face in the howling wind, her hazel eyes flecked with shocking green. She's fuller of life than anything I've seen on the surface.

Looking into her eyes, feeling my breath catch in my throat, I try to muster a small smile for her. "Don't worry, I'll be back, I promise." I know this isn't the place for promises, but I have to say it for her and myself. I have to believe it. I get up and begin to walk cautiously down the hill toward the man in black.

As I near the man in black, I catch a faint scent that seems to emanate from him. I can't quite place it, but it seems somehow familiar to me. It's clear to me, the closer I get to him, that he's not moving, which gives me a little boost in confidence. However, what I see when I can see his face steals my breath, and I know exactly what I'm smelling. Death.

This man has been dead for a while now, and not just that; it looks like he had been burned. What I was smelling was rotted, burned flesh. The bile immediately begins to rise in the back of my throat as I pause before moving closer.

The illusion of a man is cracking as I peer at the figure. His body is mostly burned, and it appears he had been impaled on the stake pinning him to the ground. It's almost like he had been burned at the stake, like a witch. It's strange and makes the hair on the back of my neck rise.

Why would someone do this? Is it a signal or a warning of some kind?

None of this makes sense. Why would someone go through the effort to do this to a corpse? It doesn't look like he was killed out of need for food or survival. It seems like it was done to make a point.

My head starts to spin as I try to walk closer to the man; there are too many possibilities. I feel the same tension rising through my body that I had felt in the cave. It slowly creeps up my spine to my chest. My little monster that has been growing since the caves rears its ugly head. My anxiety becomes its own entity with a mind of its own, and it has plans for me. It tiptoes up my spine, consuming every inch of bravado I have with every one of its tingling steps. It moves up my spine until it reaches my chest, where it slithers into my lungs, and without a second's thought, it steals what air I have left in my heaving chest.

The tiptoeing beast on my back has now worked its way to my chest, and I feel my knees growing weak as I stand looking at the man's burned corpse. The dead man's eyes stare blankly back at me. He may be gone, but it seems as if his eyes know what is happening to me and that he's welcoming me to the darkness that awaits.

The beast continues to pilfer the air from my lungs, turning them into solid, unmoving cages that imprison me. Blackness swirls throughout my vision—tiny black dots dancing on the edges of my sight. A darkness all my own, pulling me under.

I gasp for air, desperate for relief from the tightening in my chest as the thieving beast rears its dreadful head. The darkness increases, spreading throughout my vision, driving me to my knees; my hand on my chest doesn't feel like my own as I grow numb. Somewhere in the distance, I hear Lily and Wren calling my name. It seems so far away, though; it's as if she's a million miles away, screaming my name into the abyss. I need Lily close; I need her to hold me so the darkness disappears.

I fall to my back and lie there for a moment, my panicked brain stopping its spinning, as the only thought that lights up my brain is that at least I'm not dying in complete darkness underground. At least we made it to the surface. I got to see the sky again, to feel the sun on my skin.

I'm lying there on my back, staring at the darkening sky, trying desperately to breathe around the panic and to stop the monster from digging its claws deeper into my chest, but nothing is helping. My throat constricts, and it becomes increasingly difficult to breathe. I'm fully aware that I'm doing this to myself, that if I can focus and calm down, I can stop all of this, but nothing seems to be working.

The dusky gray sky swirls above me as if a tornado were forming, and the dancing black dots turn into a tunnel, leading me into nothingness. Everything grows fuzzy and narrows, the gray sky turning black and fading away. As I slowly slip into unconsciousness, my last thought is that I'm breaking all of my promises to Lily. I've never been great at keeping promises, so why would it change now?

The darkness carries me away like a leaf in a stream being whisked away by the current. I'm sinking down into the water, into the darkness. It takes away any resolve I have left to survive; the darkness overtakes me, and the only thing waiting for me there is Death. He stands at the end of a hallway of doors, hands outstretched, waiting.

Chapter Twenty-Six
Poison

"The capacity for passion is both cruel and divine." —George Sand, Intimate Journal 1834

Pounding. Relentless. It starts in my chest and tears outward, up my neck and into my skull, until my temples throb and fireworks burst behind my eyelids, white light against black. I surface through it, half-aware, dragged back into my body.

I lie there in silence, stunned to still be breathing. It takes a moment to register that the panic attack has passed, that I've survived it. My brain feels split open, burning, every thought a blade. The idea of opening my eyes is unbearable. The rest of me is numb, slowly rebooting: lips tingling, jaw aching from where I clenched too hard. The headache remains, brutal and unyielding, the last thing to loosen its grip.

I slowly crack my eyelids open, just the slightest bit, and a hiss escapes from my dry and cracked lips.

Fuck.

I tentatively open my eyes the rest of the way. The pain that ripples through my head is intense and reminds me of a migraine. I feel nauseated as waves of pain roll through my head. Turning to my side, I rest my head on the cold ground and take deep breaths to ease the queasiness. Lily and Wren immediately come over, and Lily gently touches my back.

"Are you all right?" Lily asks. I can hear the concern in her voice, and it tightens my chest. It feels like my heart is pulling in on itself. I hate making her worry, showing weakness, and having feelings more than anything. I don't want anyone to know how much I need Lily and how weak I am. Lily's concern makes me feel loved, which makes me feel vulnerable. I don't like feeling vulnerable. My thoughts swirl, confusing me.

"I'm okay; my head is pounding, but I'm all right." I manage to squeeze the words out through gritted teeth. I'm fighting back tears not only due to the pain but because Lily is too sweet, too good for me. I'm a bad person, and it's only a matter of time before she realizes it and leaves me. I don't want these emotions; I don't want to feel right now.

I roll over slowly and sit up, keeping my eyes closed and resting my forehead on my knees, trying to fight the deep-seated pain rattling through my brain. Lily moves with me, kneeling in front of me; Wren stands, worried, by her side. Lily places both hands on my shoulders and sits with me as I try to sort my body and my mind out. She gives me a soft squeeze before rising, "I'll grab you some water."

As Lily leaves, Wren steps forward, placing her tiny hands on my shoulders, mimicking how Lily had held me. Wren doesn't say anything; she gently rubs her small hands over my shoulders, and I find it oddly comforting.

I lift my head, smiling weakly at Wren and watching as Lily walks away, swaying a bit as dizziness washes over me. I immediately close my eyes again, putting my head back on my knees. I need to fight through this. There isn't any medication to help me deal with the pain; I need to suck it up and overcome the migraine. I can do this. I need to stop focusing so much on the pain.

Think happy thoughts.

I lift my head again as Lily walks back to me. The rest of the group stays a few feet away, watching, giving me space to recover. Lily hands me a small canteen that only has a few drops of water left in it, as Wren moves back. I take a small sip, aware that this is the only water we have left for the whole group. I don't want to drink it all, but I desperately need it. I take another small sip before handing it back to her.

I focus on the water and try to think less about the searing pain in my brain. I look over at the group and count heads. It's become a habit over time, a habit I can't kick. I need to ensure we're all here and that everyone is all right. Counting seems to calm me, and some of the tension leaves my shoulders. We haven't lost anyone, despite my weakness and inability to control my body.

I lock eyes with Mike across the short distance between us. "All right?" he asks. I give him a weak smile and a slight nod that sends lightning through my brain. "Yeah, I'm all right," I say, speaking and moving slowly as not to jar myself. Mike nods in return and goes back to whispering something to Elle. The littles, Rachel, Oliver, and Wren, have all settled near Mike and Elle, sleepily listening to us.

For the briefest moment, I think about trying to stand up but decide against it. My head is still spinning, and I'm worried that I'll fall over or throw up if I try to stand. Maybe both.

"Where are we?" I ask, looking at Lily as I look around slowly. There aren't any landmarks, and it doesn't look like the exact spot where the man in black was.

"Not far away. We carried you as far as we could, but it was just Elle and me, so we didn't make it very far."

Going against everything I'm thinking, I reach for her hand. I can't fight the longing I have to feel her soft, warm skin. "Was I out long?" Lily's fingers lock with mine. "No, you were only out for maybe an hour. I was worried about you. You weren't breathing when we got to you."

I look down, ashamed of my weakness. "I'm sorry, I'll do better next time," I say softly. My weakness disgusts me, and I can't understand how someone could love me when I find myself so despicable.

Lily doesn't say anything back for a moment before squeezing my hand in reassurance, "You have nothing to be sorry for. You can't control how your body reacts in scary situations like this one. You understand that, right?" I nod, looking at our locked fingers, focusing on feeling the warmth spread from the tips of our fingers up my arms and into my chest. I look up at her, nodding again, and taking a deep breath.

"Should we try to move further away? I don't know how that man got there or who did that to him, but maybe we shouldn't stay here." I look back toward the valley where we found the corpse.

"Let's just stay here for the night. Everyone is exhausted, and we need to rest to get far away from here tomorrow," Lily says, brushing the hair away from my somewhat clammy forehead.

I give her hand another squeeze and let myself sink down onto my back. My body and mind are utterly exhausted, and I think I could lie here forever. I don't know what keeps driving our small group forward; maybe hope? I'm beginning to doubt everything, and I have a feeling that we're all going to be pushed beyond our limits in the upcoming days. We will be tested, and something tells me that not all of us will make it.

We're going to have to make decisions that no person should ever have to make, and we will have to live with those decisions for the rest of our lives.

I try not to think about the possibilities coming our way, but I can't shut my brain off until Lily settles in next to me. She runs her hand over my flat chest, resting it on my scars and running her thumb back and forth over the scar under my left pectoral muscle. It's soothing, and before I know it, I'm drifting to sleep.

I sleep like the dead that night: no dreams, just endless darkness. As I wake up this morning, I know I slept so well because my body needed it. I was exhausted, and my body was so tired it couldn't even muster up a nightmare.

We start off almost immediately, the seven of us eating the last of our protein bars in the early morning light. We don't look back at the man in black; no one mentions him, and we pretend as if yesterday never happened.

The man in black was our first encounter with another human outside of our caves, and I think that's what we have to look forward to. I'm deeply concerned for our group's well-being.

We've been on the surface for five days now, and he's the only being we've encountered. I don't know precisely what that means for us, but it doesn't bode well. I understand that the group doesn't want to think or plan for what the man in black means for us, but I can't stop thinking about him as we walk away from his place of death.

I'm still thinking about him when we come to the forest. There's no inkling that it exists until we look down into the valley and see it. It's a vast, sprawling forest and goes on for as far as we can see. It's beautiful and majestic, evoking memories of years past, when I was an archaeologist in such places, cutting my way through vines and foliage to dig for ancient artifacts.

My heart clenches as I remember those times. I feel tears rising as we stand at the top of the hill, looking out at the green world before us. Live trees mean food and possibly wildlife, AND WATER! It means hope. This is a place where we could maybe find shelter and live. We can hunt. My heart swells with the possibilities as I look at the green canopies stretching into the horizon. There is a physical lightness and happiness in the air around us as we all start running down the hill into the trees.

This place could be our home. I'm still thinking this as we reach the edge of the forest and start into the woods. Luckily, it's easy to navigate through the underbrush, which isn't too thick, and we're soon well into the forest.

It's cooler, and the world is alive. There are sounds all around us, bugs and birds chittering as we disturb their quiet space. I turn a slow circle, taking in this new world that we've found, and can't keep the massive smile off my face. I look around at the group and see my hope and happiness mirrored in their faces.

"We should stay here for the night," I say, looking to each of them.

"I think that's a great idea," Mike says, wrapping his arm around Elle's waist and giving her a quick kiss on the lips. Her pale cheeks flush from the excitement and Mike's show of affection.

I reach for Lily and Wren's hands, and we move off into the trees to find a place to settle for the night, which is swiftly approaching.

We walk for a few minutes before finding a massive tree with huge, exposed roots that create hollow spaces. It's the perfect place to rest for the night.

"Mike, will you come with me to find some food?" I ask, and he quickly joins me. It doesn't take us long to find some edible berries and grubs. Using knowledge I picked up from camping and being a nerdy hiker, I identify them as safe to eat, and we bring our finds back to the group.

"I don't think I can eat those," Elle says, looking at the large grubs we collected.

"It's eat the grubs or go hungry; it's up to you," I say with a shrug of my shoulders.

Elle looks from me with a frown to Mike before grabbing one of the squirming grubs and slowly pushing it into her mouth. Wincing, she starts to chew, and the rest of us watch as she slowly and painfully consumes the grub.

I grab a grub next to some berries and throw them all into my mouth without thinking too much about it, chewing fast and swallowing even quicker. I don't want to feel the texture of the grub too much before I eat it. Otherwise, I know I won't be able to do it.

The kids, Mike, and Lily follow suit, and soon we've all been fed and settle back into our makeshift home. I'm feeling calm and comfortable, and then the fog starts to roll in with the dusk.

It rolls in and slowly settles over the land. The fog coats everything, wrapping the world in a blanket of cold wetness. With the fog and mist comes the wind; it whistles through the trees, singing along with the rattling of their bone–like branches. Standing in the thick fog is like walking in a different world. It makes everything seem enchanted.

Not knowing if we are alone in the forest does little to dampen our fear when the mist settles over us. All the lines are blurred; the trees seem to meld into one and blot out the world around and above us. It consumes everything yet seemingly sharpens the world around us. It amplifies sounds yet also somehow dampens them. Small shadows become monsters in the fog.

We all hope that nothing is out there, but fear is our biggest enemy right now. Fear of the unknown makes us overly cautious and anxious, causing us to jump at every sound as we sit in our new shelter. The trees come alive around us as the fog thickens. Their branches sway with the wind, reaching for us before pulling away and intertwining with each other in a beautiful, skeletal, seductive dance.

Time is weird in the fog. I lose track of how many hours have passed, and soon it's too dark to see anything. We settle in, sleeping in a puddle of arms and legs, hoping that we'll make it through the night.

Sleep doesn't come easily or quickly. I lie awake, listening to the sounds of the trees, insects, and animals. Eventually, I begin to feel the tug of sleep and close my eyes, letting my dreams take me far away.

I come awake as everyone starts to stir. But what I find when I open my eyes is not what I'm expecting. I'm hoping to see the sun, see the green of the forest around us, but that's not what's waiting. It's just gray: it's fog and mist and cold winds. The sun seems to be lost in the trees and mist. It's not the paradise I thought it would be.

I stand up, stretching and picking at my damp clothes, shivering as the wind shifts and tugs at my garments, making them chill against my skin.

"What is this?" Elle asks, looking out into the mist.

"Maybe a storm or something?" Mike supplies, looking around.

"We should maybe keep moving? Try to find a better shelter," I say, turning to Mike, Elle, and Lily, while also looking at the little ones, who are all shivering in their damp clothes.

Seeing nothing but nods, we eat some of the berries that we have left over and start walking. We no longer know which direction we're heading in, as there is no sun, but we keep walking, realizing that the forest may not be the godsend we initially thought it was. I feel like we've been trapped in some magical world where time doesn't exist. The fog seems to feed off our hope, dining on it as it grows thicker around us.

The day seems to creep by until there's no light at all, signaling nightfall. I don't like this, and I know that this routine of slow, blurred days will wear us all down quickly.

That's precisely what happens: the next day, we get up, we walk, we rest, we walk some more, we sleep, and we start over. This continues for several days. At least, I think it's been several days. Without the full sun, it's hard to tell.

Endless walking lulls us into a trance of sorts. We only stop when someone can no longer walk, and we all slowly begin to realize that we might be alone out here, that there isn't anyone coming to save us, and that we may not get out of the forest. The fear of being utterly alone on the surface is as stifling as the darkness of the caves.

Our lives have become a monotonous daily struggle to survive. Is there no end to this? Would we ever be able to stop, relax, sleep in a bed, have an authentic meal, feel safe?

My brain is going a mile a minute as we walk in silence, surrounded by cold gray, haunted by the skeletons above us, whispering in the wind.

It must be at least three days like this when the first signs of illness start to show. A tickle in the back of the throat, a stuffy nose, little things that typically wouldn't mean much. But out here, without care, those small things are deadly.

Rachel is the first to get sick. It starts as a sniffle, then a cough, and then she can't breathe. We slow down, taking our time, making sure we move at her pace, carrying her when needed, and resting as often as she needs it.

"What are we going to do about Rachel?" I ask Lily as we walk in front of the rest of the group.

"What do you mean?" she asks, looking behind her to Elle, who carries Rachel on her back.

"I mean, what if she doesn't get better. What do we do?"

"She'll get better; she has to." Lily gives me a look that makes me drop the topic.

Rachel is getting worse. I can hear her breath rattling through her lungs as she struggles to draw every single breath. Her face is pale and sunken, the dark circles under her eyes only accentuating the pallor of her skin. We all know that she's getting worse, that she may die, I think even she knows. It's hard to see a child so sickly and not be able to do anything about it. There's no way to ease her pain and suffering. I can see the resignation in her eyes.

I watch Rachel struggle to draw in every single breath. It is a battle of wills. It's painful for her, and there are many times when I've had the thought to help her with her struggle. To relieve her of the pain. Wouldn't that be the right thing to do? To help her into the darkness? Why do we want to keep her here so that she can continue to suffer? I feel like if Rachel could talk, she would tell us to end it for her, maybe even beg us. She's in so much pain, and it's written across her face.

Rachel is slowly drowning. Her own body is killing her, and all we are doing is watching it happen. It's so slow, dragging out her suffering. Every day is filled with her rasping breaths, and the nights are filled with nonstop coughing and gasping for air. They echo through the trees as we walk on, hoping to find help, for the forest to end, for anything.

"Let's make a stretcher to carry Rachel on," I suggest one day after carrying her for several hours. "It'll make it easier and probably be more comfortable for her."

Mike and I gather branches and ferns, lashing them together with vines. Elle and I pick up the stretcher once it's finished, and we all keep moving, only stopping when Lily asks us to so she can check on Rachel and give her some water.

I don't know what day it is, but we've stopped for the night, and as the littles sleep, I turn to Mike, Elle, and Lily.

"Should we help Rachel on her way?" I ask, looking at each of them. "Wouldn't it be kinder to put her out of her misery?"

It's the first time I've voiced my thoughts to the whole group, and their instant reactions tell me all I need to know. They are appalled, especially Lily. I know immediately that I've made a mistake in asking.

"How could you even ask that?" Lily angrily whispers at me. She's visibly shaking with anger, and her words are whispered yet hurled in my direction.

I flinch as if they were darts thrown at my heart.

"Don't you think it's the humane thing to do?" I say back, looking around the group. "She's in a lot of pain. Every breath is probably like fire for her. Don't you think it's cruel to keep subjecting her to that pain?" I pause, but only briefly. "Are we keeping her alive for ourselves? What would she want?" I ask, pushing on, past their looks of disgust.

"Rachel is a CHILD. She doesn't know what's good for her. I can't believe you would say something like this. What you're suggesting is MURDER!" Lily's voice rises with every word, and she moves to stand in front of me, punctuating every word with a finger in my chest. Her eyes are full of something I've never seen before. Her light brown, green-flecked eyes are dark and murky and so alive. It's rage, anger, and hate that I'm seeing.

Fear grips me. I've taken it too far; I've revealed myself as the bad person I am, and Lily is finally realizing it. The fear seizes hold of my heart and starts to squeeze. If I'm not careful, I'll lose her. She's finally realizing that I'm no good; they always do. Lily is doing the same, recognizing me for what I am. A terrible, cold human being. She'll leave me soon; everyone always does, eventually.

Mike and Elle watch our exchange before coming and standing behind Lily. It's the group against me, and I look down at the ground. I know I'm right; I know that maybe Mike feels the same way as me but is too afraid to say anything. What I'm saying goes against everything we know. It isn't what's supposed to happen toward the end of someone's life; we aren't the ones who are supposed to make those decisions. But maybe, in this new world, we need to be.

"Sorry, sorry, guys. I think I'm just tired. I didn't mean any of it. We've been in the forest too long. I think I'm losing my mind." I give a little chuckle, tucking a strand of loose hair behind my ear and trying to lighten the mood a bit. Maybe they will think I wasn't serious.

Lily glares at me, and Elle and Mike give me a similar look. "It's not funny. You're talking about killing someone, and not just anyone: Rachel, a child. How could you?"

I can't take the judgment, the criticism, the hate, especially not from Lily. We're supposed to be a team, always a team.

"I'm sorry. I didn't mean it, I promise." It's all I can think to say as I try to smooth over the tension that is electrifying the air around us like lightning about to strike.

Lily looks at me with disgust written across her face as she turns and walks away, Elle and Mike following close behind her as they walk back to where the three littles are sleeping.

I decide to sleep off by myself, not wanting to push my luck with the rest of the group. Curling up amongst some ferns, I let sleep take me, but it isn't restful; it's a night haunted with dreams of choking children, hacking coughs, mouths full of blood, and death.

I wake up to hands grabbing my shoulders and roughly shaking me awake. "Wake up, wake up! How could you do it?" Lily's screaming jerks me awake. My brain is cloudy with sleep; visions of Wren coughing up blood haunt me, and I have no idea what Lily is screaming about. That is, until I look over and see Mike carrying the limp body of Rachel.

Elle, Oliver, and Wren are all quietly crying.

I push Lily off of me and stumble over to where Mike is standing. Rachel is white, her lips slightly blue, cracked, and flecked with bright red blood. Rachel died in her sleep, choking silently on her blood as it filled her lungs. Rachel was killed by her own body.

They all turn to look at me. I don't understand what's going on immediately until I look at Lily again. "Did you do this?" she asks between sobs. I'm stunned into silence; it takes me several heartbeats before I can respond, "What?"

"Did you kill her?" Mike clarifies, laying Rachel's body down on the makeshift stretcher. I turn, looking at each of them, searching their faces and seeing nothing but sadness, fear, and anger. Anger directed at me. My heart is pounding; my mouth is dry. I know I can't defend myself; it will only make me look more guilty. I know in that very moment that I've lost all of them. I've lost my family for a second time. Trust is what has kept us together, and now that trust has been broken.

I look around at Mike and Elle; my eyes linger on Lily. She can't even look me in the eyes. "You guys, I didn't do this. I swear, I swear! I didn't do this. You have to believe me, I could never." I search desperately for any sign that they believe me. I'm met with flickering eyes and doubtful looks. Lily turns and starts walking away.

"Lily, wait, please!" I reach out, grabbing her arm as she walks away. Turning abruptly, she slaps me. It rings through the trees, echoing back to us before returning. The slap splits my lip and leaves my ear and face ringing. But it does more than just that. It breaks me. Shatters my insides, tearing loose the anchor and breaking the bond.

"Don't EVER touch me again, you MURDERER." She's cold and calm as she spits the words at me, turning on her heel and walking off into the woods.

I'm too stunned to move, and the sounds of Elle's sniffles and sobs mixed with Mike's calming whispers as he soothes her fill the deafening silence that encompasses me. The remaining little ones are quiet, no doubt confused by everything that is happening around them. None of this is correct; none of it makes sense. The one person I trust and love the most in the entire universe has turned on me. She betrayed me in a few moments without giving me the benefit of the doubt. Lily has left me.

A deep sadness buries itself at the base of my sternum. Burrowing, eating away at my insides until nothing is left where my heart once was. Now there's nothing but darkness.

I move through the rest of the day in a daze— shutting my brain off is the best way to cope with what is happening. Mike and I bury Rachel under rocks and leaves on the forest floor. It's not the best grave, but it's the best we can do.

Lily has disappeared into the woods, only appearing after Rachel's body has been buried. She won't look at me, won't come near me. The anger and hate in her eyes have been replaced by something much worse. Fear.

I'm the reason for her anxiety, and it's only a matter of time before the others in the group begin to fear me as well. Fear is a poison; it can spread from person to person, just like a virus.

I spend the rest of the day alone, walking behind the group as we continue our trek through the woods. There are moments when I think about leaving them. Maybe it would be easier for everyone if I just went out on my own. I think about this for the rest of the day, but at night I'm still with the group and I can't bring myself to leave them.

I curl up alone, making myself as small as possible to keep warm. I notice that Mike stays up and keeps an eye on me throughout the night. The fear is already spreading. They think I'm a killer and that I'm willing to kill others.

My mind goes numb with this knowledge. I can't understand how they can all turn on me so quickly. Wren won't even come near me, and she's like my child. I've kept them safe for so long, and they turned on me in minutes. They won't even hear me out. I didn't kill Rachel; I didn't do it, I don't think I could have, even though I mentioned it.

I tell myself this repeatedly as I lie in the cold, wet leaves under a large tree. I know if things don't change in the next couple of days, I'll have to leave the group.

The next day, everyone is exhausted, and it seems that the fear has subsided somewhat. I approach Mike and try to defend myself one more time before deciding to stay or go.

"Mike, you know I couldn't have done that to Rachel, right?" I look searchingly at his face. Mike looks at me, actually looks at me.

"I honestly don't know. We're all capable of things we never thought we could do. This world has made us into monsters," he says pointedly, looking directly into my eyes. I'm taken aback. Am I a monster? Had I become something that I fear the most?

"I didn't do it, Mike. I can only say this so many times. I'll leave the group if that's what you guys want, but I didn't do it." Elle walks over, followed closely by Lily. Elle looks from Mike to me, then to Lily.

"Listen, we talked and decided that you can stay with the group, but you should know that none of us trusts you. We don't feel safe with you, and we're all keeping an eye on you." Elle looks over to Lily for verification of her statement. Lily still won't look at me; instead, she nods to Elle before staring at the ground in front of my feet.

"You heard her. Don't come near any of us, especially me." Lily's words are like a dagger in my chest; they steal the air from my lungs, deepening the darkness growing in my chest.

I look at each of them slowly, nodding. "I understand," I say softly. I'm resigned to my fate. I know deep down I will have to leave the group. The trust is gone; if they feel unsafe around me, the only right thing to do is to go. I will wait for the right time, and then I will disappear.

Chapter Twenty-Seven
Betrayal

"Yet each man kills the thing he loves.
By each, let this be heard.
Some do it with a bitter look.
Some with a flattering word.
The coward does it with a kiss.
The brave man with a sword."
— Oscar Wilde, The Ballad of Reading Gaol

It's been a week since Rachel died, and I'm still with the group. I'm not sure why, since they treat me like I'm a murderer, but I can't bring myself to leave. I'm following a few steps behind them, making myself small, and staying out of the way. I don't want to ruffle feathers or give them a reason to kick me out. Maybe if I keep my head down, they'll let me stay.

It is hard; I miss them, especially Lily and Wren. I need her now more than ever, and she's terrified of me. I need her even though she hates me. Being away from her and unable to talk to or touch her is slowly killing me inside.

As I trudge behind them, my mind runs wild. I'm not aware of where we are, where I'm walking. I barely know if it's night or day. I'm just walking mindlessly behind the group as they keep going, hoping to find someone, something. I start playing a game to keep my mind sharp;

it's not a fun game, but a necessary one instead. I start looking at how everyone is doing, who in the group is falling behind, who's doing well, and how the kids are holding up. I can't stop myself from keeping an eye on them even though they despise me.

Elle is doing well enough; she's a little unsteady on her feet now and then, but then again, we all are. She occasionally stumbles around a bit, but overall, she is doing well. Elle stepped up after my downfall and has taken over the group's leadership. There's a weird mix of anger and jealousy that comes from her that I don't understand, yet the feeling is somewhat mutual. I hate that she's taken over the leadership role, even though I've always fought against it. I want to make sure that they are all safe. It is my responsibility to keep them safe, and it's been taken away from me. Now I'm the one they are trying to stay safe from.

Mike, on the other hand, is not doing well at all. His broken leg is visibly swollen, and his limp is more pronounced now than before. It's blatantly apparent that he is unwell. His face, pale from the lack of sunlight, is even paler now, with bouts of being flushed as his fever spikes. His leg, which never quite healed, is infected, leaking, oozing with every step that he takes. It needs to be drained; it's red, swollen, and seeping. I can almost smell the infection from here.

Mike won't last much longer if his leg keeps getting worse. Everyone is ignoring it, though. They ignore that he can barely put any weight on it now, that his pants are covered in pus from the open wound. No one wants to address it, which is the worst possible thing to do.

I look from Mike to Oliver and Wren. I'm surprised at how remarkably resilient the littles are. They're doing better than all of us adults, helping one another over larger obstacles and keeping up with us. When they get tired, they ask for piggyback rides or to be carried. Amazingly, they are keeping up with us.

I seek Lily out next. She's walking behind everyone, only a few feet in front of me, and she's not paying close attention to what she's doing. I feel a slight twinge of anger toward her, but it's mostly sadness and confusion. I can't understand how someone you love, like she said she loved me, could cut me off so quickly, as if I never existed. Nothing makes sense anymore. From what I can tell, Lily is doing fine. She's keeping up with the group. I can tell she's sad, but this is the decision she made; this was her choice. She was the one who decided that we were no longer a bonded pair; she was the one who broke us.

As I watch, she stumbles and falls to her knees. I run forward and grab her arm to help her up without thinking. I act. It's what I would do with anyone. I don't think twice about it; I don't realize that she may not want my help or for me to touch her.

Lily recoils from my touch as if I were a flame. Snatching her arm to her chest, she backs away from me; the fear oozing off her. I can feel it radiating from her. I can almost smell it.

How can she be so afraid of me? How can she do this?

I hold up both of my hands and back away. I don't want to hurt her; I don't want to make her uncomfortable, and I don't want to scare anyone else in the group.

Lily looks away from me and then runs. She runs away to where Elle and Mike are waiting for her.

I turn away for a moment to gather myself before I move to follow the group. My anger rising quickly, I need to remain calm. I don't want them to see me affected. I feel like I'm swimming in mud, breathing it in, and choking on it.

I'm so confused; I don't understand how she could be afraid of me.

She knows me... right? Was everything in the caves a lie?

I keep my head down, submissive, and wait for them to start walking again before I move. I know that I need to stay with them just a little longer, mainly for Wren and Oliver. I want the kids to be safe, and I know that Mike's leg is going to become an issue, and someone is going to have to make the hard decisions.

It might as well be me. I'm already an outcast, feared and hated.

I plod behind the group, halting when they stop, and keeping my distance. I'm so lost in my thoughts that I don't realize we've stopped or that we've broken through the trees until I hear Elle's heavy sigh.

Looking up, the trees have thinned out, revealing more of our nightmare. There's nothing on the other side but gray, dead earth. It's the same as before, still no rolling hills or wildlife. This forest seems to be the only living thing remotely close to us.

Do we stay in it? Or do we risk it back out in the open?

Walking through the forest for so long has taken a toll on us; we're exhausted, but it's a different kind of exhaustion. Tiredness that comes from being emotionally drained, always on high alert, and never being able to let your guard down. It's mental exhaustion. It's palpable, and it's what broke our group into pieces.

Elle, now the leader of our ragtag group, steps forward.

"Let's rest here on the edge of the forest for the night." She looks to Lily and Mike, glancing down at his leg quickly but not saying anything. The remnants of his torn pant leg are stuck to his leg with pus and blood that is weeping from the wound where the bone punctured the skin. The wound itself is dark red, angry, and swollen.

As the group settles in for the night, I wander off in search of some bark and maybe some water and berries. We should take the time now to gather as much as possible before we head back out into the wasteland.

A few weeks ago, I would have been riddled with anxiety about leaving the group, but now, that anxiety is replaced with anger and jealousy. I guess now the only one that I need to worry about is myself.

That makes everything easier. If I keep telling myself this, it'll come true, won't it? It's just like it was in the caves when I was by myself; it was always more manageable when it was just me. I need to focus on keeping myself alive; that's how I need to start thinking. It's the only way I think I can cope with the complete and utter betrayal of Lily and the group turning against me.

Turning back to the group, I feel a tug in my stomach. What if I just left now? I look down at the berries and bark in my hands. Would they be all right? Why do I still care about them when they've given up on me?

Tucking the bark and berries into my pockets, I head back to the group. They all turn expectantly, looking for food, but I don't give them any. If they want to treat me like a murderer, they can fend for themselves.

A wave of shame and guilt washes through me, and I turn away again and find a place nearby where I can sleep for the night. Rolling over so my back is to the group, I settle in. The nights are always the hardest for me. The absolute darkness reminds me of the tunnels, and while there is a bit of comfort in that, often it feels like I am being suffocated by the weight of the rocks bearing down on me from above. My mind is always racing at night; it's too quiet, and it's the perfect time for my mind to wander and race off into thinking about all the "what-ifs."

Tonight, though, all I can think about is how Lily has given up on me and how she's taken Wren away from me. Lying in the dark, all I see is the look of fear on her face. I am so wholly hurt by what has happened that I can feel it numbing me from the inside out.

Eventually, I drift off to sleep, Lily's face haunting my unsettling dreams. Morning couldn't have come sooner, and I'm already awake by the time the sun starts to break through the fog. I'm desperate for it, begging for it.

I'm the first one up, and I disappear into the woods again to gather more berries and bark, chewing on a piece as I walk back toward the group. I fill my two canteens with as much water as I can find before returning to our camp.

As I walk back through the trees, a moment of peace washes over me. This used to be one of my favorite things to do: hiking and being in nature. Now it felt dangerous in a weird way, foreign. I pause, looking up at the trees gently swaying above me and listening to the birds. Maybe I'll stay here. The thought comes and goes quickly, and I find my feet moving back to the group before I can fully process all of my emotions.

By the time I get back to the group, they're already on the move. They didn't wait for me. Maybe they thought I left them? Maybe I should? Would it make a difference if I left now or waited a few more days? I stand there on the edge of the forest watching them climb the next hill, contemplating whether now is the time to leave them. But I can't seem to convince myself to do it, and I don't know why. I know it's for the best, and if I leave now, it might prevent Lily from hating me more than she already does. But no matter how hard I try to convince myself to walk away, I can't do it. Yet another sign of my weakness; I need them more than they need me, and we all know it.

Picking up my supplies, I start after them, moving quickly to catch them. They've already crested the hill in front of me, so I pick up the pace, not wanting to lose sight of them. I'm out of breath by the time I reach the top of the hill and, looking down, I see that they are already taking a break. I know it's because of Mike's leg, but I'm not going to say anything about it. I slowly descend from the top of the hill, not wanting to get too close to them. My new spot in the group is to be a shadow.

Standing at a distance, I rest and catch my breath as I wait for them to start moving again. Elle must have found a stick for Mike to use as a walking stick before they left the forest this morning. He's sitting on the ground now with it resting next to his infected leg. His leg is foul, so infected that it looks like it's rotting from the inside out. I know that once it gets to a certain point, there will be no helping him, and I feel like he's almost to that point.

Elle and Lily help Mike to his feet, and I stand back. The kids look between them and me, unsure where to go or who to trust. Wren catches my eye and gives me a sad smile, accompanied by a small wave. I know this has to be hard on her, but I don't go to her. I don't want Wren to get in trouble for talking to me, so I nod to her and give her a small smile back.

Once Mike is up and balanced on his crutch, the group moves forward slowly, walking as if in a trance. I assume my position behind them, walking in their wake.

Time stops as it does when everything looks and feels the same. It becomes monotonous. It doesn't matter anymore. Maybe time never really matters at all. As we walk, we blend with the landscape, becoming one with it, ash- and soot-covered and ragged. We look like a small band of zombies wandering through the wasteland, stumbling and kicking up dust in our wake.

There's no talking as the group walks. Lily and Elle are now carrying Oliver and Wren, as the littles have grown tired of walking. I've slowed down considerably to keep behind Mike, who is forever falling behind. The only sound as we walk is the crunch of the brittle earth beneath our battered and uncovered feet, punctuated by a cough or our heavy breathing. All I can hear is the beating of my heart in my ears. It fills everything with a rhythmic thrumming.

The terrain begins to undulate with small rolling hills, and the sun approaches midday. It's hot and there aren't any trees around for shelter. It's weird, because I can barely see the sun, but it feels like it's boiling my skin; it's excruciating. I can see small blisters forming on my exposed skin. My lips are cracked and bleeding, and my tongue feels like it's made of sandpaper.

I only have my two small canteens of water, and I don't know how much the group has with them, but if it's going to be this hot the whole time, I know it won't be enough. We need significantly more water than what we have available to us to survive this. I look back and wonder if it's too late to turn around and go back to the forest. I miss the trees, the stillness, the coolness. Right now, all of that sounds like a godsend.

Elle stops the group in one of the shallow valleys between hills to rest again. They are all red-faced and sweating. The kids are hot, maybe too hot. I start to worry about Oliver and Wren getting heatstroke and then realize that it doesn't matter if they do or not; there's no way to help them. No way to cool them down. We don't have shade, and we don't have a lot of water; there's nothing we can do about it.

I try to hand my canteen to Lily so she can share it with Wren, but she won't look at me or take it from my hand. I toss it on the ground near where Wren and Oliver are sitting. Even now, when they need help, Lily doesn't want me; she wants absolutely nothing to do with me.

We won't be going any further today, as everyone starts to settle into the valley, finding comfort in the little shade provided by the hills. Mike uses the canteen I gave them to dab water on the kids' faces, trying to cool them down. The shadows grow longer as the sun moves through the sky, offering a brief respite from the heat. I walk down the valley away from the group, not wanting to impose or make them feel uncomfortable. I pull some bark out and chew it slowly, savoring the small amount of fluid it provides.

As I sit there, all I can think about is that our small group is in a difficult situation. There are six of us, and the kids and Mike can barely move. That leaves Lily, Elle, and me to manage everything, and that's only if they let me help them. What happens if we can't get everyone up and on their feet tomorrow? Will we get stuck here? I don't think that's a situation we want to find ourselves in. We need to keep moving, even if we have no idea what we're walking into. Movement means we're still alive, and that's a good thing, right?

As the sun begins to set, the little ones liven up a bit in the cool evening air. Perhaps we should consider moving at night rather than during the day. It's too hot during the day, and our bodies are not ready to be in the sun and the heat, so moving at night seems like the way to go. I turn to the group to bring this up but stop short. Elle, Mike, and Lily are all asleep, and the kids are starting to settle in for bed as well.

It looks like we'll be here for another day if we want to travel at night, or maybe they'll prefer to keep walking in the heat. I'll bring up my suggestion tomorrow and let them decide for themselves what they think is best.

Lying down on my back, I look up at the darkening sky. I haven't seen a single star since we came to the surface. I know they're out there; I know that stars exist, but no matter how hard I look, I can't see them. The moon, like the sun, seems further away than before, duller and, I don't know, it just doesn't seem the same as it did before the event. Perhaps Earth was shifted or altered in some way during the impacts?

Our world is different now. I haven't seen a single animal, except for hearing birds and bugs. The only human we saw was the man in black. Where are all the people and the animals? Some of them had to have survived. My brain swirls with questions until exhaustion wins over and I doze off.

"HELP!"

The scream tears through the night, jerking me awake. I bolt upright, unsure of what is happening, but instinctively, I know it's something terrible. Oliver is screaming, screaming, screaming, shattering the surrounding night air.

His screams are enough to wake the dead, and they shake all of us to our cores as we scramble up from our makeshift beds in the valley.

Oliver never had a chance. He was taken from us as we all slept, only waking when he awoke to his doom. The sound of his screams will forever be with me; they were worse than death itself. They were terror embodied and released into the air.

Oliver's screams unleash chaos and hell upon us and are followed by an unearthly sound that I recognize as someone screaming in terror.

I can't see anything as I run toward the cries for help. It's pitch dark, and I don't know the area well enough to know where I'm going. All I know is that Oliver is being attacked, and someone else is screaming. Where are the others?

Running full speed through the darkness, I finally see them. They look human, but it's clear that they are not. They're dressed in dark clothing, covered in what looks like Spanish moss, with hand-carved wooden masks pulled over their faces. Whatever these things are, they have no humanity.

I stop in my tracks as I try to figure out what the fuck is going on in all the chaos. I'm unsure of what to do; I don't have a weapon, and the dark figures are enormous compared to me. Oliver screams again, and I look over to see him being carried away by one of the creatures. His screams intensify as they carry him away; it's as if I can hear his vocal cords tearing with the exertion behind his screams. I put my head down and run full tilt into the nearest intruder, hitting him low around his waist and driving up with my legs, hoping to throw him off balance. It doesn't work. But it does cause enough of a distraction that the other creatures that have grabbed Elle and Wren are surprised. Mike takes this distraction and drives into the thing holding Elle, knocking them both to the ground. Mike pounds his fists repeatedly into the creature's face, knocking the mask off to reveal that they aren't creatures. They're just men.

Mike knocks the man out and then grabs the closest thing to him that he can use as a weapon, a rock. He slams it down into the man's face, killing him.

As Mike fights, Wren, Elle, and Lily make a run for it. Sprinting away from the men in masks toward the direction that I came from. As they run past me, the man I ran into grabs me by the throat, lifting me off the ground. I try to remember how to break someone's hold from self-defense classes I took ages ago. But everything I may have remembered disappears from my brain as he squeezes, cutting off my oxygen. I struggle, kicking and hitting his arms, but it's as if he is built of stone. Nothing seems to faze him. I'm burning valuable air and energy with every kick and hit and am quickly running out of fight.

Small black dots start to dance throughout my vision, and something surges through my body moments before I pass out, giving me the will to keep fighting. I bring both of my legs up, placing them on his chest, and push with everything I have left in my body. The man-creature flies backward, his clenched hands ripping from my throat as my body is propelled in the opposite direction. The last thing I see before I black out as I hit the ground is the starless sky spinning above me, then nothing but darkness.

Chapter Twenty-Eight
Man

There it is again. Pain. It ricochets through my brain, making me wince before I'm conscious enough to know how badly I'm hurt. I moan as I swallow, and there are hands on me suddenly, helping me into a sitting position.

"Hey, can you open your eyes?" It's Lily's voice cutting through the fog. She sounds concerned, but that can't be right, though—she hates me. It must be my oxygen-deprived brain making things up. She'll hate me forever.

Another moan escapes from my chapped lips before I can stop it; my head feels like it weighs a million pounds and my throat is killing me. Making just these slightest noises makes my throat light on fire. I open my eyes slowly and reach for my throat as if I could ease the pain by touching it.

My eyes try to focus on the face peering down at me, and Lily slowly comes into focus, then behind her Mike and Elle. Lily reaches for my arm and helps me sit the rest of the way up. I try to swallow and wince in pain. My throat must really be bruised; it's almost hard to breathe around the swelling. I try to ask what happened but can't get any words out. Instead, I cough, which causes me to double over with pain.

"Don't try to talk. Your throat is pretty much crushed; it's going to need time to heal." Lily is in full doctor mode, speaking very matter-of-factly, almost emotionlessly, which I would believe if it weren't for the look of concern written across her face. I can see the internal battle happening behind her troubled eyes. Is she struggling with her desire to care for me and her fear of me? Maybe now she will realize that there are many worse things out here on the surface than me. I think I should be the least of her worries.

I nod to indicate that I understand it's a no-go, but even that makes my head and neck hurt. Closing my eyes, I try not to focus on the fact that everything is throbbing, and if I move too quickly, it feels like my head might rip off my body. I open my eyes again and look around, trying to see how we all made out.

Everyone is here except for Oliver. Poor Oliver. His screams echo through my head, filling every space. Wren looks like a terrified animal cornered by a predator, her eyes wide and her body shaking.

I look in the direction of where the attack happened and can see the remains of the attacker Mike killed and the splash of bright red across the dead grass. The red is brilliant against the brown-and-gray world around us. It's both oddly beautiful and disturbing at the same time.

I look at Mike. "What happened?" I rasp.

"I don't know, it all happened so fast. I heard something, like scuffing over the ground. I thought it was you coming to join us, so I didn't think anything of it. Then the screaming started."

"How many?" I manage.

"I don't know; they were shadows, they moved so quickly and quietly."

I nod; whoever they were, they had perfected the art of stealing lives. I wonder if they had been tracking or watching us for a while. They seem to have known when we would be sleeping, how many of us there were, and how to approach the group.

"They're like the Roamers," Lily whispered from beside Mike, a distant look in her eyes.

I reach for her hand, stretching my fingers out before curling them back into my palm. She doesn't meet my gaze but continues to stare at the ground.

"They took Oliver." She still doesn't look up, stares at her dirt-covered feet.

"I know," I rasp back, trying to draw her out of her shell.

"They tried to take all of us," Elle says, walking up with Wren in tow.

"What do you think they were planning to do to us?" Lily asks, finally looking up, her eyes still slightly glazed over.

"Nothing good," Mike says, sitting down roughly.

"We shouldn't stay here," I say, sitting up a little straighter. Whatever ounce of safety we thought we would find on the surface was a lie, a hope borne of ignorance. It's just as brutal here on the surface as it was underground.

"You're right, we need to keep moving; get as far away from here as possible."

I get up, thinking about what Mike had just said. What if we didn't run, though? What if we went after them? What if we tried to get Oliver back?

There's a part of me that wants to see if I can find them, to get Oliver back, dead or alive. I'm torn, but only for the briefest of moments. As the rest of the group starts to move off, I turn and follow behind them, rubbing my sore, swollen throat as I walk. I know I have nothing to lose, but my fear far outweighs my bravery.

I'm a coward. I always have been and always will be.

Hanging our heads, we walk away from the site where Oliver was taken and don't stop until it's physically impossible for Mike to continue.

I'm not faring much better. My throat is so swollen it hurts to breathe and swallow. Our group is exhausted, mentally, emotionally, and physically—in every way possible.

As we stop to catch our breath and get our bearings, I look down and realize that we've been subconsciously following a trail the entire time.

"You guys... this is a trail," I grit out.

Lily, Elle, and Mike all look around as if coming out of a stupor. Wren is looking to each of us, trying to figure out if she should be scared or not.

"Where do you think it leads?" Lily asks, looking at the small dirt path that continues out in front of us.

"Do we follow it?" Elle asks, glancing around at each of us before looking at me.

My eyebrows shoot up, even though I'm trying to keep my face passive.

"I don't think we should."

"I think we should do it, should follow it," Mike says, almost simultaneously. We glance at each other before looking back at Lily and Elle.

Elle nods, looking between us, "We follow it."

Shaking my head back and forth, I start to protest, "I don't think—"

"I've made up my mind, Adrian. You can come with us or not, I don't care."

Harsh.

I snap my mouth shut so fast my teeth click.

I take my place at the back of the pack and let them get ahead of me a few steps before I follow.

As we crest the hill in front of us, we see something that we haven't seen since we got to the surface. Fire.

They have fire, and in the glow, we can see what they've done to Oliver. They've slit his throat and have hung him upside down with small bowls placed under him to collect the blood. It reminds me of how you clean a deer.

Upon seeing the scene unfolding below us, we drop to the ground. My heart is immediately beating out of my chest. Panic, fear, and anger are all angling for a spot at the forefront of my mind.

Elle turns away from the gory display and grabs Wren's hand, pulling her away as well, sparing her from seeing her friend in that state. Lily follows them as they slide on their butts down the hills a bit.

Mike and I watch. I'm somewhat transfixed by what I'm seeing, almost hypnotized by the dancing firelight. As I watch, my mind drifts to how abnormal this is, even for the new world we're living in, but perhaps this is the new normal?

I was stunned into inaction, like when a car crash happens in front of you. You know you should look away, but for some reason, you just can't. You have to know what's going to happen.

Mike and I continue to watch as the strangers disembowel Oliver's small body. Cutting from the base of the throat toward the waist. Just like how you would dress a deer. Maybe that's how I'm rationalizing this in my brain, thinking of Oliver as an animal rather than a child. What does that make me? Am I a monster just like them?

The men are meticulous about how they remove Oliver's organs, taking each without damaging them. They've done this many times before. It's evident in the way they cut and how they cut.

The shock is starting to wear off, and I begin to feel queasy watching them continue to dismember Oliver's corpse.

The sounds, smells, and what I'm watching force their way into my brain. The sounds of Wren, Elle, and Lily all sobbing quietly behind me; the sound of the dull knives cutting through flesh; the smell of campfire mixed with the smell of death and cooking flesh. All of it assaulting my senses.

I turn just as Mike does, and we both become ill.

My world trembles and shifts on its axis before turning upside down. My stomach turns with the world, and I continue to be violently sick next to Mike. Trying to be quiet while the bile burns its way up through my stomach, into my injured and raw throat, before expelling what little contents I hold onto the ground in front of me.

My body doesn't have much to give and is emptied quickly, but the heaving continues. The vomiting becomes painful, every convulsion a new form of punishment. Yet I'm thankful for the pain. It reminds me that I'm still alive, that I can feel, that I'm human.

I gather myself slowly off the ground, body shaking with the effort it takes to sit back on my heels. I shake my head, a cold sweat snaking its way down my face and the back of my neck. I'm still trying to process what's going on; I feel like I'm in a fog. Nothing wants to click over into action. I know it's my body's way of trying to protect me and that I might be going into shock. I also know that I need to break out of it, that I need to get us the fuck out of here. I need my body and mind to start working together so we can leave.

"We... have to go," I say, still breathless from throwing up.

"Now."

Mike is moving next to me, crawling toward the others to get them moving. I stay where I am just a little longer to catch my breath.

I risk one more glance over the hilltop and almost heave again. The men are eating Oliver's remains and don't seem to think anything of it. They all seem so normal, except for the part where they're consuming a child. I watch as they finish their meal, pack up their camp, and start to head off down the valley with their torches.

They've taken every last scrap with them, leaving nothing but smudges of red on the blackened ground. They left the fire burning, and I'm mesmerized again by how it dances, casting shadows across the tree, now splashed with brilliant red. It's almost pretty. Red is the first real color I've seen since coming to the surface. Everything has been so dull and gray, and red is so vibrant. The color has become a living, breathing thing in my mind; it's beautiful. I am lost in the sight of the fire and the red tree before shaking myself free of it.

I crawl backward down the hill a way before turning and jogging to catch up to Mike, Lily, Elle, and Wren.

We're one less now.

That could have been any of us.

When the thought flees through my mind, it makes me pause; my limbs start to shake.

No, not now. I need to keep moving.

There's an overwhelming feeling of being unable to control my limbs, and tunnel vision starts as if I'm about to pass out. I take another step, forcing my body to move past the fear: another one, and another. I focus on each step and put one foot in front of the other.

Movement is life.

I manage to stave off the panic attack and catch up with the rest of the group. They're waiting for me. I look at them as I approach. They all wear the same tear-stained, shocked, haunted look.

As I walk up to them, the panic starts gnawing at the base of my skull and tries to claw its way into my mind. I force it back, looking at each of them before settling on Lily. Her sad eyes tug at my soul. There's still fear there, but the sorrow in her eyes far outweighs the fear.

I stand before them, pleading with them to take me back just by standing there, body shaking from the exhaustion of getting to them.

Lily reaches for me first, then Wren, taking my shaking hands and welcoming me back to the group. I pause before reaching for her. I glide my fingers down Lily's before connecting our palms and intertwining our fingers.

I take Wren's hand in my other one and look down at all of our hands, now together again.

Can I trust Lily?

She abandoned me so quickly, and I don't know if I can fully trust her again. I know that I need to stick with the group, but I'm not sure if I'm ready to forgive her, to forgive any of them.

Lily squeezes my hand, her gaze seeking mine, and I look into her eyes. I love her, I still love her despite everything; she is mine, and I am hers, even though I'm incredibly hurt at the same time. I still need her, still want her, and will always need her.

As I look at Lily, my heart clenches, and I feel my resolve leaving me. At this moment, I'm willing to forget and forgive. But will I regret it?

Lily smiles, looking from me to Wren and then to Elle and Mike. They don't smile back.

Turning, we all set out again without a word. The sun is starting to rise to our left as we decide to continue in the direction we're going rather than keeping the sun in front of us. There's nothing good for us from that direction.

Anywhere is better than where we had just been.

We've been walking all morning, and the sun is now high above us, beating down through the haze above us. It's only when Mike stumbles that we huddle together for a break.

"We should have someone on lookout," I say, turning around to look at the landscape around us.

"I'll take first watch," I continue, and walk up to the top of a nearby hill, giving me a better vantage point.

I stand there, watching the group rest. Turning in a slow circle, I'm struck by how alien the world seems now. How it's nothing like it was before, yet the evil of man still persists. I don't understand it. I struggle to comprehend how a world-ending event can occur, and yet people continue to inflict terrible things upon one another. It just doesn't make sense.

I make a slow circle, gasping as a cold hand slides cautiously into my own.

"Fuck! Jesus, Lily, you almost gave me a heart attack."

"Sorry." It's all she says, but it speaks volumes. She links her fingers with mine and lowers her head to my shoulder. Everything in my body is drawn to her. No matter how hard I resist, I just can't. We don't need to say anything. Being close brings me a small amount of comfort, even if it's fleeting.

"Mike, if you're up for it, it's your turn on watch."

He nods, slowly getting to his feet, crutch in hand. As he moves, I catch a whiff of his leg. Rotten.

I notice the pallor of his skin and how he avoids my gaze.

"We need to keep moving, and it would be wise to find somewhere on higher ground so we can have a better line of sight," I say softly to him, not wanting to push too much.

"I think we should stay here for the night. I don't think Wren can go any further." I feel a slight surge of frustration as I turn to look at him, knowing that this is the worst possible choice we can make.

"Listen, we need to keep moving. We should try to get as far away as possible and keep walking until nightfall to find a better place." I say it with a confidence I don't feel, sweeping my arms out wide to drive the point home that we have zero coverage here.

"We're in the same situation as we were last night if we stay here!"

From behind me, Lily softly agrees. "I think we should keep moving for a little longer. It's like Adrian says, we need more coverage." I fight the urge to give her a massive hug and smile, but I hold back. I'm suddenly entirely in love with her again. However, I also need to be cautious and look out for myself. After what happened with Lily turning on me so quickly, there's a part of me that knows that I'm expendable, and that if she could discard me so quickly, she can do it again.

Mike and Elle exchange glances before agreeing, and Elle drags herself up, reaching down for Wren's hand. I don't like how close Elle and Wren have become. Wren used to be the closest to me, and now I rarely have a moment with her.

I push that thought to the side. Now is not the time.

"We need to find somewhere on the top of a hill with some coverage. That will allow us to see more than if we sleep in a valley," I say, and my chest expands with happiness as everyone nods in agreement. We only have a few hours of daylight left, and I want to make the most of it.

The sun is setting by the time we find somewhere that is perfect for what I had in mind. Before us lies a small rocky outcrop that we can use as a safe place to sleep; it's just big enough for three to four people to fit under the overhang of the rock slabs. It's perfect, and we set up camp around it.

"We need to take turns keeping an eye out so we can all get some sleep," I say, gazing out at the valley directly below us. "I'll take the first watch." I get up and go to sit on top of the outcrop, where I have a 360-degree view of the surrounding area.

The others all lay down, forming a barrier between Wren and the outside world. If only it were that easy to keep them safe. We are so ill-prepared for the surface, and I'm beginning to doubt that we can even survive out here. What's our plan? Do we keep walking until we eventually all drop from hunger or dehydration?

We can't keep going like this. We need to take action before it's too late for all of us. It's only a short matter of time before we lose someone else.

Standing on top of the outcropping and looking around, I can see a considerable distance. If I close my eyes, I can envision a beautiful view, filled with trees and lush, rolling hills. But now, everything is brown or gray, dead or dying. It's a sad, lonely place.

Looking up, I still can't see any stars in the sky, but the moon is full and just perceivable through the fog. I look at it; it doesn't look the same after the asteroid as it did before. It seems far away and less bright, just like everything else. Thankfully, it gives me just enough light to see the world around us. I can make out shadows in the night, enough to feel relatively safe. I know I'm not—none of us are.

I'm not sure how long I'm up here, just sitting, watching, lost in my thoughts. It's peaceful. I don't understand how the world is so cruel yet so beautiful at the same time. Full of small, peaceful moments. I'm so lost in thought that when a noise comes from my left, I almost fall off the outcrop. I turn quickly, expecting to see killers emerge from the shadows, but instead I see Lily.

She doesn't say anything. She walks forward, wrapping her arms around my waist and snuggling close. I pause; she looks so lost and forlorn, the embodiment of what life on the surface is. I tell myself not to, but her soft sniffling tugs at my heart, and I pull my arms up and around her.

I hold her close as her sniffles grow into sobs. I don't have any words to make any of it better. I can't do anything but keep her pressed to my chest until it passes. I wish I could make everything better, wish I could find a place where we could all be safe, where we didn't have to worry about killers coming out of the darkness.

I want all of these things so much that it physically hurts me, I can't give them to everyone, especially Lily and Wren. I want to provide them with everything they need. Even though Lily broke our trust, our bond, I still want her with every fiber of my being.

I sit down slowly, taking Lily with me. Holding her in my arms only reminds me of the time before we came to the surface. I wish I could turn back time and go back to when life made more sense, to when we were all young, living our care-free lives, completely unaware that the end of the world was hurtling toward us. I want a simple life, free from constant worry and pain.

I want all of these things for all of us, and the impossibility and immensity of it all hits me full in the chest and catches in my throat.

I struggle to hold my sobs in as the feeling of hopelessness surges over me.

As Lily nestles into my lap, laying her head down, her sobs become muffled, and she soon falls back asleep. I watch as clouds roll in, blocking the scant moonlight. The feeling of hopelessness deepens as it grows darker and darker, dragging me down into a dark hole. The darkness is overpowering as I sit here, letting every ounce of hope I have mustered slowly slip away.

I'm sitting with my heart curled and sleeping soundly in my lap. This all seems so pointless. Why are we even trying? There's nothing out here, no cities full of people welcoming us with open arms; none of that exists out here. It's a wasteland and, eventually, it's going to consume us like it has consumed everything before us.

Chapter Twenty-Nine
Jagged

"Decision is a risk rooted in the courage of being free." — *Paul Tillich*

The one small comfort I have in this world is asleep on my lap. Lily's breathing lulls me into a light sleep, and I forget to get Mike for his watch.

I'm jerked awake by rough hands dragging me down off the outcrop. I unconsciously fling my hands out, trying to fight whoever has a hold of me, while also trying to find where Lily is.

"Hey! Hey! It's Mike." The yelling and shaking rattle me into full consciousness, and I slowly become aware of what's going on around me.

It's. . . raining.

This is the first time it has rained since we reached the surface. We've seen fog, but never rain.

"Is it safe?" Mike asks, looking up at the rain as he tries to drag Lily and me under the outcrop.

I flinch as the first drop hits my upturned face, expecting it to burn and melt my skin. The coolness of the rain fully wakes me up, and I scramble with Mike and Lily under the protection of the outcrop. I curl around Wren and reach for Lily, folding her into myself and waiting for the pain to begin.

Only it doesn't.

My skin isn't melting from my bones. I don't feel any pain. Slowly, I hold my hand out from under the rock outcrop and look up at the darkened sky. Nothing happens.

"I…I think it's okay," I say, turning to look at the others as I step out into the rain.

Ignoring the reaching hands, I step fully out into the rain. If I'm going to go out, let it be the rain that takes me. I want to feel it on my skin, want it to wash away everything: my despair, pain, darkness, and fear. I want to return to my childhood, when I could smell the rain in the air and wasn't scared of it.

It feels like this is my baptism; I'm being given a clean slate. We all are.

"Adrian, please come back!" Lily cries after me as I move farther away from our cover.

"Join me," I say, turning to her with a huge grin plastered across my face. I reach my hand out for her.

Lily pauses, then rushes forward, arms outstretched, her fingers grasping mine. I pull her to me, spinning her in the rain as our bodies collide.

Her laughter is music. It lights my soul on fire. I kiss the side of her wet neck as she continues to turn her face upward.

Mike, Elle, and Wren join us in the rain. Wearing huge smiles of our own, we dance around, wiping the grime off our bodies.

The rain sweeps through our downtrodden group, washing the ash and dirt from our skin, our dreaded hair, and what remains of our clothing. This is what we need to keep us going. This will provide us with the hope and strength we need to keep moving forward.

As the rain falls, it begins to transform the ash on the ground into a strange paste, washing some of it away from the world around us. With the rain comes a breeze, and dancing on it is the smell of fresh rain. It's different than what I remember, but it still brings back memories from my childhood of sitting on the porch with my mother and enjoying the way the air comes alive with the smell of rain. I can almost hear her voice as I sit here with Lily in my arms, can practically hear the creaking of the rocking chair, and taste the green of the rain-covered grass. I can feel the rain just as I could when the world was right. Everything has changed, but the rain has stayed the same. It tastes the same, smells the same, and makes me feel the same…alive.

I'm so caught up in the rain and let it wash the grime from my body; I'm consumed by the rain and the sensation of it on my skin. I know we should be collecting it in our canteens, but I can't bring myself to leave where I'm standing. It's such a relief, this feeling of being clean and having a fresh start.

I finally return to my senses as my body begins to shake violently. It's not due to the rain; it's because I'm freezing. The relief I feel quickly turns to panic. How stupid could we be? We are wet, in the dark, with no heat and nothing to change into or curl up under. We're all so caught up in the rain that none of us has thought about what we're doing.

"Shit," I whisper. I was careless, and out here that will get us all killed.

"What?" Lily asks with blue lips and chattering teeth.

I turn, looking at all of us, completely soaked to the bone. What have I done? This stupid mistake could be the one that kills us all, and that would be my decision to *enjoy the rain*. Mike catches the look in my eye and glances around, immediately knowing what I am thinking.

He knows it, too. This could end us all.

"Hey, everyone, I think that's enough time outside. Let's go back under the outcrop," Mike says, keeping his voice calm. Wren turns in a circle, still oblivious and enjoying the rain. Her little lips are blue, and her skin is pale, almost translucent, in the dark of night.

I don't know what to do; I don't know how to deal with the cold when we're all cold and wet. We don't have a fire, we don't have blankets, and we don't have a change of clothes.

"Mike, what do we do? How do we get warm?" I ask him softly as we push Lily, Wren, and Elle back toward our small cave.

"I don't know. It's still raining, so I think we'll stay wet. I don't think we can walk for warmth because of that. We'll just be cold, wet, and walking. It doesn't look like it's going to stop anytime soon, either." He's glancing up at the sky.

"I guess we wait until it's done raining and then we move. Until then, we'll need to huddle together to stay warm." I look at him, following Mike's gaze up to the sky.

We squeeze into our tiny shelter, our bodies uncontrollably shaking as they struggle to cope with the cold.

I huddle closer and closer to the rest of the group, pulling Wren and Lily to me, trying to keep us warm through our soaking wet clothes. It's been raining for hours, and none of us has been able to sleep. Our bodies are shaking too hard for us to rest.

I'm wide awake when the rain stops and the sun starts to rise, peaking through the murkiness of the atmosphere and providing little light, but enough to chase the rain away.

My body hurts from shaking, and my muscles feel like rocks from being taut for so long. I can barely move as I try to stand. I almost laugh watching Elle and Mike try to stand up. Maybe I'm losing my mind, but they look so funny trying to straighten up and walk. The slight smile on my face slips away as I watch Mike, who can't seem to put any weight on his bad leg now.

Lily is slow to get up as well, stretching slowly, like a cat, her body coming alive with the rising sun. Wren is even slower to get up, her little body not handling the cold well. It's still chilly, but hopefully it will start to warm up a bit now that the sun is trying to chase away some of the clouds.

"We should get moving, I think that will help our bodies warm up some," I say to Elle and Lily. "We might have to carry Wren, though. I'm not sure if she's up for walking just yet."

I glance at Mike, trying to assess the state of his leg without being too obvious, before I give up trying to be discreet.

"Hey, Mike, why don't you take it easy today, and the three of us will worry about Wren and keeping watch?"

I try to keep emotion out of my voice. I don't want him to think that I'm judging him or that I don't think he's capable of helping us. I want him to focus on his well-being today.

The truth is, though, that if Mike can't keep up with us, and we slow down to match his pace, it's going to take us forever to get anywhere. Even worse is if he can't walk. That puts us in danger.

We can't afford to sit and wait for Mike's leg to get better because the reality is that it's never going to get better. I know this, and I think Mike does too. Elle, on the other hand, refuses to see the truth. She's going to have to deal with it sooner or later, though, because the time to do something about his leg is coming sooner rather than later.

Mike looks up from his leg and catches my eye. Wren, Elle, and Lily are already on the move. I can see it in his eyes; he knows exactly what I'm thinking about, and my sadness and regret are reflected there, looking back at me. He knows that things are going to get worse for him soon and that someone will have to make the tough decisions. I give him a sad half-smile and a nod and move off to catch up with the others.

Catching up with the group, we all pause, waiting for Mike to join us. When he does, he's winded and his face is blanched in pain.

Elle reaches over, touching his face gently and kissing him. "Just hold on a little longer," she says softly, her hand trailing down his sweaty cheek before dropping to her side.

Elle turns quickly and takes off, walking at a brisk pace. But she doesn't turn fast enough. There are tears in her eyes, and I know now that she is aware of what's coming.

Elle turns quickly, finding me watching her, and narrows her eyes at me; her face goes red, as if she's embarrassed or angry.

I'm not sure what that means; why is she angry with me? Am I still the monster in her eyes?

Elle continues to glare at me as Mike reaches her. "Let's get moving," she says, throwing another glare in my direction. I meet her gaze, refusing to give way to her unfounded emotions. I thought that perhaps we had moved on from what happened to Rachel, but apparently, Elle hadn't. Or maybe I'm too apparent in my ponderings about what will become of Mike.

Elle's not wrong. I have been thinking about what will happen to Mike since the day we rescued him from the collapsed cavern. I'm always thinking about Mike; I'm always thinking about everyone in the group.

I want Mike to be fine and for his leg to get better, but I'm worried that we've passed that point. I can't bring up my concerns, though, because I'm afraid that I'll be exiled again. Kicked out and abandoned. I need to be mindful of everything I say and do. I know that Elle, Mike, and maybe even Lily will betray me at a moment's notice.

The sun moves through the sky as we slowly make our way through the plains, our blood pumping through our bodies, warming us from within. My sore muscles loosen with every step, making walking more manageable. Wren warms up quickly and is soon walking alongside us.

Elle and Lily seem to perk up as we walk and get warmer, even though we still have no idea where we're going or what we will find. The act of moving seems to have reinvigorated everyone. Everyone except Mike. He's lagging, and his slow pace from this morning has gotten slower; it's evident that he's in a tremendous amount of pain. It's etched across his face.

Whatever drive he had at the beginning of the day, whether it was adrenaline or just the need to move to get warm, has worn off. My heart aches as I watch him trying to keep up with us; he's practically dragging his leg. Even though we stop about every ten minutes for him, it doesn't seem to matter. I want to ask him if I can take a look at his leg, but I'm scared. I don't like the group to think that I'm planning his demise or something.

As I stand waiting for Mike to catch up with us once again, I find my thoughts wandering to the dark part of me. I can't help but think about how much easier it would be without Mike. Traveling would be faster if he were just gone. I don't know where these thoughts come from or why I have them, but it just seems logical to me, and it would be better for the group.

I watch Mike as he makes his way to where we are all waiting for him. Elle has come up beside me, with Wren holding her hand, her brow is furrowed, creating worry lines across her forehead and between her eyebrows.

"We need to stop for Mike, his leg is getting bad, and I'm scared he's hurting himself trying to keep up."

I know it's taken a lot for her to say this to me, and I glance from her to Mike. I can see that his pant leg is covered in blood and pus; his face is white and etched in pain.

"I agree. Let's rest here for a bit." I say it softly, almost as if I am speaking to a frightened animal. I hope that it shows that I care. I want Elle to know that I'm not a monster, a killer.

"We should try to find some shelter before nightfall, though," I follow up, looking around to see if there is anything nearby that would work as a shelter.

"Right. I got it. I wouldn't want to hold you up for too long, would I?" Elle snaps, rolling her eyes as she drops back to meet Mike where he is.

"Lily! We're stopping for a bit!" I shout to her from where I'm standing as she plays with Wren several yards away.

Guilt tugs at the pit of my stomach; I feel like Elle knows what I've been thinking about and knows that I've been watching Mike. I know I can't do anything for Mike, or to Mike. Elle would be devastated, and I would have blood on my hands. I would be just like the others who attacked us earlier. Lily would hate me. Wren would be scared of me. The reality is that I need them just as much as they need me, and I need to keep them alive, even if it means slowing down and risking our overall safety.

As Elle and Mike get settled, I watch as Lily takes Wren over to a small tree nearby to see if they can get any bark from it. I've shown everyone in the group how to collect the bark so that we can all find food if we come across any trees.

I want to give Elle and Mike some time before I venture over. I want to give them time to relax. After ten minutes, Elle gets up and joins Lily and Wren over by the tree. As I watch her walk away, I decide that now is as good a time as any to check in with Mike.

As I get closer to where Mike is sitting in a reclined position, his back resting on a rock, I'm appalled by what I see. His leg, from the knee down, has a black tinge to it, and I can see black veins racing up his leg to just above his exposed knee. I try to mask my reaction, but don't manage to turn away fast enough. I know that he's seen the surprise and disgust on my face. I tilt my head down, hiding my face as I crouch down for a closer look.

"It's fine, I'm fine," Mike says through gritted teeth. His skin is tight, cold, and clammy. He looks like shit. No, like death.

"Mike, I'm sorry that I have to say this, but you are not fine. Your leg is massively infected. Why didn't you say something earlier? We could have tried to clean it or rebandage it, something?" I'm speaking softly again, pleading with him, or maybe to some higher power. I look up and see something pass across his face, perhaps pain or anger?

"I have eyes, Adrian. I can see you trudging along, looking at me, measuring me, and calculating how long I have. You don't think I haven't noticed how you look at me like I'm a burden, expendable?" Mike's voice rises as he speaks, and his face flushes red with anger.

"Mike, that's…that's not true! I'm just trying to keep everyone safe and ensure that we consider the group's well-being. I don't want anyone to get hurt or to be in pain." I can hear the pleading tone in my voice. I know he won't understand, and I can feel myself being dragged back to what happened with Rachel in the forest.

I'd broken their trust once and had never truly regained it. It would be so much easier for them to throw me out this time because they'd already done it once before.

"Right, right, because you know what's best for all of us, is that it? If you had it your way, anyone that slowed us down or showed any weakness would be dead by now, wouldn't they?" He hisses the words out at me through his teeth, with pure hatred in his eyes. I reach for him to do something, maybe comfort him, to drive the point home that I'm here to help him, not hurt him.

"Do not touch me!" Mike screams it, and I see it then—the switch from hate to fear. I pull my hand back as if I'd been burned, shocked by his reaction.

Lily and Elle turn to see what the commotion is, and Elle springs to her feet, running over to where I'm crouched before I can move away. She runs up to me quickly, pushing me hard and knocking me backward.

"Leave him alone," she snarls, standing over me. I put both of my hands out, raising them, palms up in surrender.

"Elle, if we don't do something about Mike's leg, it's going to get worse, and it will kill him." It's a matter of fact, and I say it in such a way that my voice is devoid of any emotion. Looking her dead in the eyes, I continue, "This is a fact, Elle. He will die because of his leg, especially if we don't do anything about it, which, if we do something, will only prolong his pain and suffering." It's a cold approach, and I know that, but I don't have any other options. They aren't going to listen to me anyway, so what does it matter how I deliver the message?

"What do you suggest? That we kill him instead?" Elle is severe, almost snarling, as she throws the words at me. She seriously thinks that's what I want. She doesn't believe that I didn't kill Rachel and now she thinks I want to kill Mike.

"No, Elle, I don't want to kill Mike. What I'm saying is that something needs to be done about his leg, and it needs to be done soon, or we won't have to decide because he'll be dead." I'm speaking calmly, but no matter what I say, I can see that it's just escalating things. Elle is getting more and more worked up, pacing now in front of me. Lily stands off to the side with Wren, not saying a word, and it's starting to piss me off. She's had medical training, she knows what this means for Mike, and could help me talk to Elle about it. Why won't she speak up?

Maybe Elle would understand what I'm saying if Lily helped me explain it.

Something snaps in me, and I turn back to watch Elle pace the space between Mike and me. "Elle, you and I both know that there's only one killer between the two of us, and it's not me." I know bringing up her sister's death is a low blow, and I don't know why I'm saying it, but I need something to throw her off, to get her away from me.

Elle freezes, everyone does, and it's as if the air around us is sucked away. It's silent for a beat as Elle turns to look at me and, for a moment, I wonder if she'll kill me, too.

"Fuck you." She quietly spits the words in my face as I lie on my back with my hands still raised.

"If you come near either of us again, I'll fucking kill you." Elle turns and crouches next to Mike, brushing the hair off his clammy forehead.

I believe her. I think that Elle would do whatever it took to protect Mike. But who will protect Mike from Elle?

Nodding from the ground, I look to Lily again for backup, but she won't even look in my direction. Her gaze is fixed on Mike and Elle.

"Lily? What do you think?" I'm not quite ready to let this go. Lily looks at me for the first time since the argument with Elle kicked off and then looks back to Mike's leg.

"Adrian is right. If we don't do something for Mike's leg, it won't matter for much longer. I'm sorry, Elle, but that's the truth." She speaks so softly that I almost miss what she says. Sitting up slowly, I watch as Elle turns on Lily.

"How could you? How can you agree with that… that…monster?" Elle is almost hysterical as she points a shaking finger in my direction. She's in a complete panic, knowing that if Lily agrees, it must be true. Elle is fighting back against reality right now, and it's only a matter of time before she loses.

I don't say anything; this decision is Mike's and Mike's alone. But that doesn't stop me from running through the options in my mind. Elle is back on her feet, pacing, chewing her nails, and glaring at Lily and me. Mike has sat up, but he looks almost confused, mainly in pain. I'm not sure if he has fully registered what we're talking about. Someone is going to have to make the hard decision about his leg, and I feel like whatever decision is made, I'll be the one to carry it out.

"I feel like we have two options," I start quietly, "We clean the wound and leg as best we can, rebandage it, and see how it turns out. Or we try to amputate the leg and stop the spread of the infection." Pausing, I look around. Elle is next to Mike now, whispering words I can't make out, and Lily is standing off to the side, her arms wrapped around her mid-section. Only Wren stands next to me, her small hand on my shoulder as I sit on the ground, waiting for someone to make a move.

If it were up to me, I would cut the leg off at the knee and hope to stop the infection. But it's not up to me. This decision is Mike's to make. Mike is likely either going to die of a massive infection or possibly die from blood loss if we remove the leg. I don't really see either of these choices improving his chances of survival.

Is it even worth trying to amputate the leg?

Perhaps it would be better to help him along the way. Isn't it cruel to keep him here in so much pain?

As I consider the options, I shoot a glance at Lily and see her shaking her head slightly, as if she's warning me to keep my thoughts to myself. I lower my head between my legs, suddenly feeling sick, knowing what is likely going to happen.

"Listen, how about we try to cut his leg open a bit and get some of the fluid out so it can drain a little and see how it is in the morning?" I pose the question to the group softly, attempting to ease myself back into the conversation. I need them to get on board with the idea that Mike might have to lose his leg to survive, but I need to do it in increments to lessen the shock of it.

Mike and Elle stare at me as they mull over the suggestion. I think both of them know that this is a good option, but are scared, as they should be. I'm terrified. I don't want to do this, but we need to do something. None of us can continue like this, especially Mike.

I can't imagine the amount of pain he is in. I stay where I am on the ground next to them. Watching as Mike looks at his leg and Elle glares at me. Elle doesn't trust me, and I understand that, but it's not like I'm going to pull a butcher's knife out of my back pocket and cut his leg off while they all sleep. I want this to be Mike's decision, and I want to do whatever I can to help him.

"Look. Maybe if we just cut it open a bit and relieve some pressure, it will help with the pain. Please, Elle. Mike, it may make it less painful." I look between them, holding my hands out in front of me again, almost as if I'm begging. Which I guess I am; I'm asking them to give me a chance to make what remains of his life a little better.

Elle and Mike look at each other, then at Lily. "I think we need a few minutes to talk this over," she says softly, still looking at Lily, unwilling to address me directly.

Taking the hint, I get up and walk away. I've done everything I can to try to convince Mike and Elle that this is the path that we need to take. I know I'm alone in this battle; Lily is picking and choosing her side carefully, and it doesn't seem like I'm on the winning side. Lily takes Wren's hand and leads her over to Mike and Elle, speaking softly to the group as I walk away.

I don't know what to do with myself as the group discusses next steps, so I start looking around for something sharp enough to use as a cutting tool. My knife was lost somewhere in the forest, and I'm wishing I still had it. It would be dull, but maybe I could have sharpened it.

The truth is that I have no idea what I'm doing. Lily is the one who should be doing this. She has the most medical training out of all of us, and yet she's choosing to be a spectator instead of taking action.

I'm infuriated with how Lily has become so unwilling to take action. She was never like this in the caves; she would make decisions, take action, and now it's like she's lost her voice. It's as if she's willing to make me the bad guy to save herself. Lily's inaction is damning us all, and I need her almost more now than I have ever before. I need her to step up and help me figure this out. I'm worried that without some guidance, I'll do more harm to Mike's leg than good, and that's the last thing I want.

My mind is racing at full speed as I search for anything that I can use as a knife. I've found several rocks that I think I can sharpen enough to do the job, but what I wish is I had my knife. I need something that allows me to make a careful, clean incision, rather than a jagged cut.

I know this is a terrible idea, and my gut tells me it won't end well, but what other options do we have?

I've gathered several rocks at this point and am sitting on the ground, shaping one of them into a harsh cutting tool. I took flint-knapping in college as part of my archaeology studies, but I never thought I would need to use these skills to create a knife capable of cutting through flesh. I hold one rock in my left hand, bringing the rock in my right hand down to smash it into the other, causing portions to flake off. It's taken me a few tries to remember the proper technique, but eventually I get it and can start shaping the rock into a crude cutting tool.

The edges are jagged, which I think may help cut through flesh and tendon, so I leave them like that. Perhaps I should try to make the edges serrated to aid with cutting, but I'm unsure if I can achieve that. I don't have the skill to do it.

I glance over my shoulder, wondering if a decision has been made, and decide to join the rest of the group. I slide my makeshift knife into my back pocket, not wanting to scare anyone.

"Have you decided on what you'd like to do?" I ask them, crouching in front of Mike and looking from him to Elle. Lily takes a step back, disappearing out of my line of sight. It doesn't seem like she's going to take part in this discussion, either.

"Yeah, I think we're good with just cutting into his leg and trying to clean it out," Elle says, looking from Mike to Lily to me.

Nodding, I look at Mike's leg again, "I think that's a perfect choice, you guys. I think that will help you feel more comfortable. Mike, it might even help with some of the pain." I speak in a soft tone and make no sudden movements.

They're just like a scared animal, I keep thinking to myself over and over again. I need to gain their trust, and I need them to trust me so that I can help them.

"Elle, do you have anything that we can use as bandages? I'll also need some water to rinse the wound out once it's open."

To my surprise, Elle listens, getting up immediately and going to where we've dropped our packs. I watch as she leaves, turning back to Mike.

"Are you okay with this?"

I can't read what's on his face; maybe it's the pain, anger, fear, or a mix of all of them. That look on his face, though, will haunt me for the rest of my life, and I know that as I look at him, I am too transfixed to look away.

It's the look of someone who knows that they're going to die.

"We have to do it, right?" he says, dryly staring straight into my eyes.

"This is up to you, Mike. You are the one who needs to decide if this is what you want. If it's not, we don't have to do this." I want to look away so badly, but I can't look away from the haunted look on his face.

"No, I'm good. Cut it open and I guess we'll see what happens." It's almost as if Mike's will to live has broken with those words. He looks away, turning his head to the side, and slumps farther down against the rock he's propped up against. I don't have any words for him. I don't have anything inspiring or hopeful to tell him. Watching him slump in defeat breaks something inside of me. I feel it slipping free and disappearing along with Mike's will to live. Maybe it was what little I had left of my humanity. Perhaps it is how I'm protecting what little sanity I have left.

Elle returns with a few scraps of cloth and one of the small canteens of water. I look around for Lily. I really need her to help me with this. I can't see her anywhere.

"She doesn't want to be here for this, and she doesn't want Wren to see it," Elle says, reading the look in my eyes.

Looking at Mike's leg, all I can think about is that I'm about to cut into it. How am I supposed to do this? What's the best way to do it? Where should I cut?

I have all of these questions, and no one is here to help me answer them. I'm terrified.

My breathing is shallow and rapid, almost to the point of inducing panic. My hand is shaking with the rock in it, and even though I'm cold, my hands are sweating. I can feel a bead of sweat rolling down my forehead. So many questions running through my head: What if I cut too deeply and slice into a vein, muscle, or even tendon? What if he can't walk afterward? Or, worse yet, what happens if he starts bleeding and I can't stop it?

"I don't know if I can do this." I can't stop the words from leaving my mouth on a stuttered breath, and there's no way to take them back. I breathed them to life and gave voice to my terror.

Elle and Mike look at me, shocked, then down at my shaking hands.

"You have to, you said this was the best choice. You pushed us here, and you can't back out now," Elle says coldly. "You don't get to back out now, you will do this. You have to."

I feel nothing but panic and the prickle of tears in my eyes. "I need a minute," I manage.

Shaking my head, I put the rock down and walk away. I put my hands on top of my head and walk in a circle, trying to steady my breathing and my hands. I'm not sure if I can do this. I don't want to be responsible for whatever is about to happen. But Elle is right; I did recommend this. Did I push them to do it? I don't think so, but maybe I did. Either way, I'm trapped. If I say no and he dies, it's my fault; if I say yes and he dies, it's still my fault. There is no winning for me, and if this goes wrong, we all lose. My panic worsens, and I'm unable to control it.

My body is going into fight-or-flight mode, and right now, I just want to take flight and get the fuck out of here. I don't want to do this, I don't.

"Stop pacing, and let's get this over with, dammit!" Mike yells at me from where he's propped up. I know I'm just making the situation worse by freaking out, but I'm cutting into someone's leg! I'm not prepared for this, none of us are. The only person who has any idea about what is happening has decided not to be of any use.

Walking back over to Mike, I rub my hands together, trying to psych myself up. I can do this, it's just a small incision, that's all. I can do this. I start to repeat this to myself, trying to drown out the other voices in my head telling me that this is a terrible idea and that Mike is going to die.

I'm going to kill Mike. This is the loudest voice, yelling at me and shouting in the brightest colors against the backs of my eyelids.

I take a deep breath, steadying myself. Crouching over Mike, I look up at his pale face and slightly blue lips; they are trembling harder than my hands.

"You ready, Mike?"

"Yeah, just get it over with."

Kneeling next to his leg, I pick up my stone knife and make the first cut.

Chapter Thirty
Two Ghosts

"If two people love each other, there can be no happy end to it." — *Ernest Hemingway*

This isn't working, I need to try something else. I press the makeshift knife against his blackened skin again, using my body weight to press the dull stone into his flesh. I can't get it through his skin, and pushing on his infected leg is just causing him more pain.

As I try to find a different place to cut, I look over the original wound that never quite healed right and decide that it might be the best place to make an incision. If I can get my knife through the thinner flesh on that part of his leg, maybe I can open the old wound and use that to drain the infection.

I reposition myself lower on his leg and glance up quickly at Mike's face before looking back down at his leg that I am sure to mangle.

Tears begin to fill my eyes as my panic grows and I try to find the best place to make my first cut along the old wound. I finally find a spot that already has an open wound and unceremoniously jam the rock knife into it. Mike's scream scares the shit out of me, causing me to jerk my hand back, leaving the rock knife jutting from his mottled skin.

Damn it, that was stupid of me. I knew he was going to scream, had thought to prepare myself, and wasn't expecting it to be so loud and jarring. His screams remind me of a rabbit caught in a snare, screaming for its life.

"Don't stop! You have to keep cutting!" Elle is screaming at me through her tears as she holds Mike's head to her chest, trying to calm him and hush him at the same time. His teeth are clenched so tightly that I'm worried he's going to chip them.

We should have put something in his mouth.

I look around for something that he can bite on, settling for a piece of bark discarded nearby. I hand it to Elle, motioning for her to put it in his mouth.

"For his mouth," I say, barely able to get the words out or steady my hand enough for her to snatch it away.

Mike bites down on the bark as Elle strokes the sweat and hair off of his clammy brow.

Taking a deep breath, I press the knife deeper into his leg and drag it down, opening the old wound more. The soft, infected skin is like cutting into rotting fruit. It parts quickly, curling back as I push the knife down the line of the wound.

Now that it's open, I can see how bad it is. I can also smell it. Mike has gone silent in the last couple of minutes and has stopped trying to pull his leg away from me. He's probably in shock, or maybe it's the sight of the black ooze and pus coming from his leg that has stunned him into silence.

Bracing myself, I press gently on his leg, starting just below the knee and running my hands down toward the opening. I barely make it out of the way as a spout of greenish-black pus shoots out of the cut. Gasping, I look away as the smell overwhelms me, causing me to gag and cover my nose and mouth with my forearm.

The smell is more than I can handle, and my stomach turns on me, drawing dry heaves through my rail-thin body. If I had anything to throw up, it would have been over. I put the knife down and stand, walking away a short distance with my hands on my hips and my head tilted back to look up at the sky.

Breathing through my mouth, I look back at Mike's leg; the smell is indescribable and follows me as I walk away. It's in my skin, on my hands, forever staining me. I'll be marked forever by what I've just done, and everyone will know. The stench is a mix of every foul-smelling thing possible. I've never experienced the smell of someone's body rotting from the inside out, and it's something I hope never to experience again. It smells as if his muscles, nerves, and bones have been pureed and left to sit in the hot sun. It's the smell of death.

The stench makes me reconsider what I'm doing, and I take a few more steps away, trying to gather myself and figure out if I can keep going.

"Wha…what is that?" Mike's voice is an inhumanly high pitch, and so soft it's hard to catch what he's saying. He looks like he's about to pass out with every achingly painful breath that his poisoned body is pushing out. He's terrified, and I can see it written across his face, smell it on him like the infection.

My fear is reflected in his eyes. This is fucked. I don't know what to do; I've never seen anything like what's oozing from his body. It's like some dark creature is slowly crawling its way out of him through the cut that I made.

"Mike, I don't know how to tell you this or what to say, but your leg is really bad. You've got a nasty infection, and it will kill you." I don't know what else to say or how to say it gently. I turn away again, running my hand through my matted hair and trying to think of any options that we might have.

As I pace, trying to figure something out, Elle sits with Mike, holding him silently as he weeps. Her eyes are closed, as if that will save her from what's unfolding in front of her. The most disturbing part is her silence; it's almost scarier than what's coming out of Mike's leg.

"What do we do now?" she says, finally opening her eyes and looking at me. There's a calmness about her that is unexpected, and it forces me to take a breath and calm my racing mind. Elle is stoic and resigned, and it's exactly what I need to help me focus.

"I'll cut it open a little more and try to push as much of the infection out as I can. Then we can clean it with some water and go from there." I sound more confident than I feel and can't believe that's my voice sounding that way.

I look down at my dirty hands, collecting my thoughts one last time and taking a few breaths of fresh air before the stench of his leg fills my nostrils again.

I can do this. We've come this far; I need to get through this, and Mike needs to get through this.

Letting out a deep breath, I walk over to Mike, kneeling in the black-ooze covered grass, and press my rock knife back into his rotting flesh. Cutting it open just a little more with every push and drag of the stone. I thought the first cut was going to be the worst, but I'm so wrong, so very wrong.

The second incision widens and makes the first cut longer, and the infection springs from Mike's leg as if it is a living thing. It flies from his leg, splashing across my arms and chest. I sit back, heaving and gagging as the pus soaks into my skin and clothes. I'm trying to hold it together, but it's impossible not to gag at the smell emanating from the ooze.

Sitting back on my heels for a moment, a weird feeling of disconnection flows through me. I stare at my hands, now covered in fluid, and can't seem to pull my gaze away from them. This is all wrong, and I can't seem to make any sense of what I'm doing. I feel as if I'm going into shock; my brain can't seem to comprehend what is happening and what I'm looking at.

I need to sit for a moment and let my brain catch up.

"You have to keep going," Elle says, breaking through the fog rolling across my brain.

Nodding, I return to Mike's leg and begin massaging the flesh downward from his knee to help move the infection toward the incision. I'm still unsteady and feel like I can't catch my breath, but I keep going. I know I need a hot compress to draw out the infection, but I don't have one, and my mind continues to race as I try to remember anything I've read or seen somewhere that could be helpful. I'm grasping at straws and struggling; I don't know what else to do.

Looking around, my desperation for Lily spikes. She can help us. She's the one who should be doing this, not me.

"Lily!" I shout, cracking the still air around us with my panic.

"Lily, please. Mike needs you, please come help!" I call out, my voice sounding shrill and thin in my ears.

I continue to push the infection out of Mike's leg as I wait for Lily to come. He squirms in pain every time I touch his leg. Every push is excruciating. I stop for a second, sitting back on my heels again and trying to catch my breath. I might pass out; the panic crawling its way up my spine, working its way into my lungs, and forming a cage around my heart.

What if the oozing never stops? What if there is no end to the infection?

I put my hands on Mike's leg again and push, watching as more of the dark liquid splashes out, across my hands and the earth. It doesn't look like it's getting any lighter. I'm expecting it to start looking red or maybe a mix of red and black as more of his clean blood mixes in with the infection, but all I see is the poison leaking from his body.

Lily doesn't come. She's abandoning me again, and in a moment when I need her the most. Not just me, but all of us, especially Mike, need her, and she's nowhere to be found.

As I continue to massage Mike's leg, his breathing becomes increasingly labored. I know that we've pushed him too far in one session and that he needs to rest. He needs time to recover from the pain and shock before we try anything else. He's not even fully conscious at this point, and I don't think that's a good sign.

Elle looks up at me, and my heart skips a beat. The look in her eyes makes the tears that have been riding on the rims of my eyes spill over and run down my cheeks, leaving streaks of clean flesh behind them. I don't have the words to make this better for her. I don't have any words of comfort or hope that will help ease the pain. I shake my head slightly and shrug my shoulders in hopelessness and a pathetic attempt to apologize for what's about to happen.

I think we both know in this moment that Mike is going to die. I can see every inch of her heart and soul in her brown pleading eyes and feel a tiny part of myself die. She's silently pleading with me to find a way to save his life, and I am powerless to tell them that everything is going to be okay. That I can fix this.

Elle slowly lowers her forehead to Mike's as she sits with his head in her lap, as he fades in and out of consciousness. I use a little water to wash my hands and then pour some over the wound in a pathetic attempt to clean it. Handing the water to Elle, she pours a few drops into Mike's mouth. I stay where I am, kneeling next to them and watching the wound continue to ooze.

"We should take a break and let Mike recover for a bit," I say, running my black-stained forearm across my sweaty forehead. The sun is about to set, meaning we've been at this for several hours.

"I'll leave it uncovered and let it seep throughout the night. We can check on him every couple of hours to see how he's doing."

Elle doesn't look up; she nods before gently placing Mike's head on the ground, curling up next to him, and closing her eyes. She has to be just as exhausted as I am. Before I leave them, I take a scrap of cloth and pour some water on it, and as I walk away, I try to wipe the sickness from my flesh. It seems to cling to me, seeping in and staining me. I can't get it off, as if it's a badge of shame I'll carry with me forever.

I need to find Lily.

Tossing the scrap of cloth to the side, I go in search of Lily. It doesn't take me long to find her behind one of the larger boulders nearby. She's cuddling Wren tightly and sitting silently, looking out at the valley below us. She turns to look at me as I walk up to her.

"Is he dead?" Lily asks softly, her eyes puffy from crying, her voice raspy.

"No. Mike is still alive. Barely." I'm so fucking angry that I almost can't stand to look at her. "I needed you back there. I have no clue what I'm doing, and I could have used your help." I'm trying to hold back the anger, but it comes out, making me sound stern as I hiss the words at her.

"I couldn't. I couldn't watch another person die."

"And you think that I can! Do you think that I'm so soulless that I don't mind watching another person die? If you had helped, maybe Mike would be in better shape than he is in right now."

"I tried, I really did. When you called for me, I got up, but I couldn't move. I couldn't make myself move. I tried." Her voice cracks, and for a moment, my anger wavers before flaming to life again.

"I don't believe you, Lily. We needed you." I'm the one turning my back this time and walking away as her sobs follow me through the dusk.

I don't think I'll be able to sleep tonight. I should probably keep an eye on both Elle and Mike. There's a good chance that Mike won't make it through the night, and I want him to; I so desperately want him to make it. I need him to stay alive. If Mike dies, Elle will never forgive me. She'll blame me for his death, and that will be the end of the group. I know it's selfish, and the guilt is a constant companion, but this is the reality. I need Mike to survive so that I can stay with the only family I have left in the world.

Glancing over my shoulder, I pick a boulder to sit against and settle down next to it. Trying to ready myself for what the night will bring. I don't see Lily again, and neither Elle nor Mike moves.

Soon, the hazy sun sets and darkness falls. An eerie silence settles over our camp.

The first scream makes every hair on my body stand up, and I rush over to Mike. He's woken up and is reaching for his leg, frantically trying to claw at the open wound. He isn't making any sense, and as I grab his arm to stop him from peeling his skin from his leg, I can feel the heat coming off his body.

Shit.

Not only is his pain getting worse, but he now has a fever. That can't be a good sign.

I take our small canteen and another cloth scrap and wet it. I keep the cold compress on his forehead throughout the night. Trying to calm him in his fever dreams and whispering to him as he tosses and turns.

Elle doesn't wake. She must be so mentally and physically exhausted that even Mike's screams of pain and thrashing can't wake her.

Just as I start to doze, Mike sits straight up, thrashing his arms around and screaming at the top of his lungs.

"Mike! Mike! Calm down, you're fine, we're right here." I try to talk him down, but it's not working this time. Luckily, Elle wakes up and immediately jumps into action, wrapping her arms around him and holding him to her body. Rocking him as if he were a little child and talking to him in soothing tones. It takes about five minutes, but eventually he calms down and slips into unconsciousness.

Elle looks at me in this moment, pleading for me to save him, and I'm powerless to help her, to help him. I put my head on my knees and wrap my arms around my legs, rocking myself slowly back and forth to self-soothe. I let my tears freely fall down my cheeks at that moment and let the hopelessness wash over me.

I'm still curled in on myself when the morning comes, and with it, the hazy world around us gets just a little brighter. I look at Mike, and the realization that he will likely not make it to see another sunrise sets in. His face is pale, his lips white, tinged with blue. His body is shaking from shock and fever.

The morning also brings a change in Elle's demeanor. Yesterday, she was pleading with me to save his life, and maybe a small amount of trust had been restored between us, but today, I am met with eyes full of accusations and betrayal. I'm shocked at how quickly she has turned against me again.

I am now the enemy.

This is my fault.

I am the one to be blamed for this, and I am suddenly overwhelmed with shame, guilt, and sadness. I quickly look away and turn back to Mike's leg, avoiding Elle's accusatory looks. The ground around Mike's leg is soaked with the infection, but his leg doesn't look any better. His breathing is quick and shallow, and his body is on fire, so warm from the fever, and I don't have a way to cool him down.

"I…I think he's septic," I stutter; what little confidence I had is now gone. "I don't know what to do now, Elle. What do you want me to do?" I can't bring myself to look at her.

I'm pleading with her to take the burden of decisions from me; I don't want the responsibility. Never, in my mind, have I considered taking charge. It has been forced on me by the others, and now I'm pleading with the one person who can ease my heart and soul by taking the weight of this decision off my shoulders. Please take this burden from my soul.

Elle doesn't respond.

We sit next to Mike for hours this morning, staring at him as if that will magically make him recover. I know that Elle won't decide, and that she'll blame me for all of this. It's easier to blame someone and take your anger and pain out of them than to blame yourself. If you hate enough, sadness can't creep in.

Elle's sniffles are the only sounds around us as the morning transitions to the afternoon.

The longer I sit here, the more certain I am that this is my fault, and I let the guilt and shame press me down, shrinking me until there's nothing left but a husk of who I was.

I move slowly, my body protesting as I unfurl myself and crawl over to Mike to flip the cloth on his forehead.

He stirs, fighting to open his blue eyes against his pain-laden lids. We lock eyes, and all I can feel and see is his pain and confusion.

"Mike? How are you feeling? Can you hear me?" I swallow back my built-up panic and lean forward over him, trying to hear his response.

"I need you to end it. I need the pain to stop… please." Mike means what he says, and the words may be whispered from his dry, chapped, pale lips, but there is force behind them.

"Mike, no! No, we can't do that!" Elle shouts, shaking him slightly as his head rests on her lap, ignoring his wince of pain as she does so.

"Mike. Are you sure? We could bandage your leg and try to keep it clean to see how it works out. Or maybe we try to amputate it?" I hate that I'm suggesting an amputation, but I don't want to give up on Mike yet. I want him to keep fighting.

"Just make the pain stop. Please. I can't deal with the pain anymore. You have to help me with the pain." His plea is slow, every word forced out from behind clenched teeth, ending on a sob. He grabs at my arms.

I inch closer still, letting him grab onto me as I nod slowly, clasping his hands in mine. I understand what he's asking of me.

"Just. Make. It. Stop," he says again. I grip his hands tighter in mine and keep nodding. It's the only thing my body is capable of doing in this moment. My heart is beating so fast that I might burst into a million pieces and scatter in the wind.

Elle is sobbing quietly next to Mike, "Don't you do it. He doesn't know what he's saying, don't do it."

There isn't a correct answer.

I'm torn between two evils and don't know what to do. I can help Mike end his pain and do what he's asking me to, or I can listen to Elle and let him continue to suffer. He is likely to worsen throughout the next couple of hours. Maybe he'll last another day before dying of his infection and pain.

"We amputate it. We'll take the leg off, and then it'll be better, right?" Elle asks, frantically looking from me to Mike and sobbing. Mike shakes his head on her lap.

"No, no, you can't do that to me. Please don't do that to me. Please, I can't take any more pain." He tosses his head from side to side, moaning.

"I can't make the decision, you do it, Elle." I can't catch my breath. My heartbeat is roaring in my ears, and I feel the darkness creeping in on the edges of my vision. My chest hurts from the force of my heart, and my panic paralyzes me.

"We take the leg, and that's it. Mike doesn't know what he wants; he has a fever and he can't make this decision." As Elle says this, Mike looks up at her in shock, the weight of the situation settling over all of us.

"Elle, you can't. Please don't do this," he whispers to her.

The pain in my chest grows with my panic as it becomes clear that Elle is making this decision for herself and not for Mike.

"Mike, I'm sorry, but I don't know what to do," I say, gripping his hands tighter.

"You can't do this, Adrian. You can't listen to her. Please."

"Cut his leg off." Elle's voice is stern and authoritative, leaving no room for negotiation. The conversation is over; the decision has been made.

I'm going to cut off Mike's leg.

Should I do what Elle is asking of me, or should I listen to Mike?

I look around for Lily. I need her to walk me through this decision and how to amputate a leg. I don't even know where to start.

Mike's grip on my hands tightens as he stares into my eyes, pleading with me.

"Please..." a last whispered prayer as I pull my hands away from his and back away slowly, determined to find Lily.

She's where I left her last, still huddled with Wren by the large boulder.

"Lily, I need you to help me amputate Mike's leg. Elle has made the decision, and I'm going to do what she wants. Please could you walk me through it?"

Lily looks up from where she sits, Wren mimicking her movements to look up at me. I manage a smile for Wren before turning my focus back to Lily.

"I don't think I can help. I don't know how to do it either," she says, looking down at her hands, before looking back to me. I see it now.

I know the shame and guilt written all over her face. We are similar in many ways, this being one of them. We are creatures driven by our guilt, shame, and fear. The difference between us is that I'm willing to push through it and do what needs to be done, and she stopped trying at some point.

"Lily, please. I need you to help me with this. Even if it's just walking me through the basics. I need you there with me to help me. Please," I plead with her, trying to coax her into action. "Don't do it for me, do it for them," I hiss to her, pointing behind me at Mike and Elle. "Stop thinking about yourself for one minute and think about them."

"That's rich, coming from you," she hisses back, glaring at me momentarily before looking away.

Huffing, I walk away from her. I know I'm being harsh, and I know that Lily is the last person that I could call selfish, but we need her now, and she needs to step up.

I walk back to Elle and Mike, noticing that Elle looks as shellshocked as I feel.

"Are we doing this?" I ask her, reaching forward to feel Mike's throat for a pulse. It's there, but it's weak and a little hard to find. His breathing is labored, as if it takes all his effort to draw air into his lungs and then push it back out again.

"Yes, we have to save him. I can't let him die here. We have to try."

"Elle, there's another option; you know that, right? It's what Mike wants." I don't say it out loud, but I need to make sure that she has considered all the options.

"Do not mention it again. I will not let you kill Mike."

I don't have the heart to tell her that we are already doing that. We are just going to cause him more pain before the end. Shaking my head, I pick up my blunt stone knife and look for something I can use to tie off his leg above where I'm going to cut.

Lily walks up, handing me her tattered jacket.

"I'll help as much as I can. You were right."

I slowly take the jacket from her, our hands brushing briefly, and our eyes seeking each other out. There's comfort there, safety in the known.

I crouch down, head swimming, and tie the jacket above Mike's knee as tightly as I can. I've decided to cut just below the knee. I know I need to break the leg where his tibia and fibula meet his knee joint. I also know my stone knife is not sharp enough to go through bone, tendon, or muscle. It barely got through the skin. If I break the leg I'll be severing some of those ties—at least, I hope so.

I quickly run through my plan with Lily as I finish tying off the jacket, looking up at her once I'm done.

"I think that will work," she says, "you have to make sure you break everything, though, and then you'll have to cut through the rest of the muscles, tendons, and nerves."

"Right, tendons and nerves." I gulp in a huge breath, holding it for a moment, before letting it out slowly. Looking around, I spot a large rock to my left.

"Lily, help me get that rock." Pointing it out to her, we both start walking toward it.

As I pick up the large stone, I look over to Lily, looking for her approval. Nodding, she gives it.

"That should work. You'll want to use the sharpest edge of it. You'll bring it up high and then smash it down with as much force as possible. You can't just drop it. You have to smash through everything. It might take a few tries." Lily talks quickly and quietly, providing me with as much information as possible before we begin.

I don't say anything; I don't know what to say, I don't have the words for what we are about to do. I'm afraid that if I open my mouth to speak,

I might throw up. My hands start to shake so badly that there's a real chance that I might drop the rock before I can even use it.

"Take a deep breath before you do it. Calm your nerves, and then do it—try not to think about it too much."

"Lily. You have to promise me that you'll forgive me for what I'm about to do." I look directly into her eyes.

"I don't know if I'll be able to do that." She looks away.

"I don't have a choice, Lily. I have to do something, and Elle is the one deciding."

"That doesn't mean that you have to do what she says. You could walk away. We all could. We could leave Mike and Elle here. Why don't we do that? You, me, and Wren. Let's go. Start over somewhere new."

I can't believe what I'm hearing. I grab her arm, turning her toward me.

"We could just leave right now, walk away from this," she continues, grabbing my hand, "please let's run away from this."

This sounds too good to be true. Is Lily fucking with me? I want to leave; I want to run, to not look back, but I can't do that. I can't just leave them here for Mike to die slowly and for Elle to watch.

"I can't do that, Lily, and you know that. I could never do that. Elle and Mike need us right now, and we can't leave them to do this on their own."

"I hope you're ready to live with the choices that you're making today. Once you do this, there won't be any going back. Elle will never forgive you, and I don't know if I will be able to, either."

"How is my choice any different from yours? You would choose to leave them to suffer and die on their own, and yet I'm the bad guy? I don't understand your thinking; it doesn't make any sense."

Lily doesn't say anything back; she knows that inaction is still an action. Yet she sees this as if I were the one doing the killing. I know she will never forgive me, and that this will be the end of everything we've built. That is the end of our family.

I won't be able to earn her forgiveness, and she will always fear me. I put the rock down and reach out slowly, pulling her toward me and cupping her cheek with my other hand. My heart is already breaking, but when I look at her, all I see is fear, and that's enough to shatter what's left of my heart into a million pieces.

"You know I'll always love you, right?" I say softly, choking on every word as I force them out. "You brought me back to life." I give her a weak, lopsided grin, knowing that this will likely be the last time that I get to touch her, to hold her.

"We were just two ghosts in the tunnels, weren't we?" She snuck up on me, holding onto my forearms as we look at each other. I want to kiss her so badly, just one last time. Resisting, I run my thumb lightly over her cracked lips, knowing that she also longs for the kiss.

Dropping my hands, I turn around, pick up the rock, and walk to Mike and Elle without looking back.

Chapter Thirty-One
Cruelty

"Man is the cruelest animal." — Friedrich Nietzsche

"**A**re you ready?" I pose the question into the open air, asking more to myself than anyone else. I look at Mike, his eyes are wide with fear, and he's shaking with the anticipation of the pain.

Mike nods.

I don't know what Elle said to him, but he seems to be on board with what's happening now and has stopped fighting us.

I raise the rock high above my head—it's almost too heavy for me to hold there—and I take a deep breath.

This is it.

There's no going back after this moment.

I bring the rock down…

The first blow breaks the skin but barely does any internal damage to his bones. Thankfully, Mike immediately passes out from the pain, and I can only hope that he stays that way. The less aware he is of what's happening, the better; maybe it will spare him some of the pain.

The second blow fractures the bones, and the third breaks them completely. I step back and draw my first deep breath since we started. My entire body is shaking. My face, chest, and arms are covered in Mike's blood. It's soaking into me, just another reminder that I will carry with me forever.

After a moment catching my breath, I decide to try to cut off as much of the leg as I can by using the large rock method to smash through everything. I make it through most of the amputation, but eventually I resort to using my rock knife to cut through the rest of Mike's leg.

I'm completely exhausted, mentally and physically. My arms are so tired I can barely lift them, and my hands are cut up from the rock knife. It's taken me a few hours to cut through Mike's leg and completely amputate it.

I'm covered in his blood.

There's more blood on me than Mike has left in his body.

Looking down at the ground, it's covered in his blood, and I'm covered in blood that should still be in his body. I did this. Every last inch of the ground seems to pulse with Mike's lifeforce.

I'm covered in his blood.

All the blood that should still be in his body is spilled everywhere else. It's all I can think about as I sit, exhausted, next to him. It's playing on a loop in my mind as I look down at my hands and arms.

My skin is red.

Violent red.

I can hear my heartbeat, myself gasping for air, but it's like I'm not even in my body. I'm here and yet completely removed at the same time.

Mike is drifting away.

He's lying here, shivering. I can hear his teeth clattering. I can't bear to listen to Elle's uncontrollable sobs or Wren's screams when she sees what I did.

What have I done?

I turn, getting up and stumbling away with my red-stained hand over my mouth in a futile attempt to keep the vomit from exploding from my empty stomach. The metallic smell of my hands exacerbates the issue.

I lurch to a halt, doubling over, and my insides heave, but nothing comes out, not even bile. I fall to my knees, heaving a few more times. My body is insisting on getting something out and, finally, it gives up when denied. The pain is horrible, but it's nothing compared to what I've just done to Mike.

I look over my shoulder at Elle, cradling his head and rocking back and forth. Her body jerks with every sob that tears its way through her body.

Mike is barely alive. The blood is still coming from the amputation despite my best efforts to stem the flow. I don't know what else to do. I feel like I'm in a movie. Everything is in slow motion; my senses seem to be in overdrive, yet everything seems dull.

The way Elle's ratted hair falls forward, covering her grief-ridden face, the way her sobs fade into a dull roar. Mike's blood is an unbelievable color of red. I feel as if I'm seeing color for the first time. My ears can almost hear his heart slowing, straining to listen to the final beat before it stops.

I look down at myself. My skin is permanently scarred by the violent red of Mike's life. I can smell the copper metallic of his life seeping into the ground and my flesh. I can taste it in my mouth.

Mike is going to die.

I will carry that for the rest of my life.

The sun is now setting, and I know that tonight will be another sleepless night. My guilt and shame keep my mind and body from resting. Instead, I watch as Elle tries to make Mike's final moments in this world as comfortable as possible. She uses pieces of her shirt to wrap the wound, hoping to stem the flow. Elle, Lily, and Wren huddle around him, holding his hands, brushing his brow, and making sure he knows that he's loved before he goes.

I keep my distance, not wanting to disrupt them in their grieving. I'm sitting not far away, and I watch as Mike's breathing becomes shallower with every passing minute. As his skin becomes paler, his body grows cold, and the remainder of his life seeps from his leg.

I know the moment Elle's grief becomes anger because her sobs become sniffles, and then they stop.

Mike doesn't make it to sunrise. He passes quietly in the night, greeted by Death in a hallway of doors.

We all sit in silence, trying to process our loss the best we can. My chest feels heavy, and my heart feels like it's trying to claw its way out of my throat. It's beating so fast that I can't draw a full breath. The massive amount of guilt, mixed with my anxiety, makes me immobile in my panic.

We stay this way, silently holding a vigil for Mike until the sun comes up, and then the morning turns into the afternoon, and none of us has moved. We're all exhausted. It's funny how emotions can do that.

The grief and sadness are taking a toll on all of us: a weariness seemingly sinking into my bones, a pain I can't express, a tightness in my chest.

It settles into my soul, leaving me breathless.

It's midday when Elle moves for the first time. I don't approach her, and I won't. I'll let her come to me. I don't want to push or provoke her anger. She looks over at me, her skin blotchy, her eyes almost swollen shut from crying. I wait for her to lash out at me, but instead, she only nods.

"Can you deal with the body?" she asks as she gently lays Mike's head on the ground, taking a final look at him, kissing his cold lips, and then walking away. Lily and Wren are going with her, creating a comforting buffer and leaving me to bury Mike.

I can't bury his body in the ground because I don't have anything to dig with, but I do have a lot of rocks, and I decide that a cairn is my best option. I start collecting the larger ones and create the burial foundation. I work my way around his body, building the rock enclosure throughout the rest of the day. To think, we rescued Mike from a rockfall, and here I am burying him in the rocks he once escaped.

My hands are bloody by the time I finish, skin scraped raw and left weeping. My blood mixing with his, staining. I stand over his grave, looking at my stained hands as the sun sets.

I'm almost numb.

I don't know what to do from here. What to say, how to act. Nothing seems to make any sense anymore. Everything is so muddled in my brain; a fog. I should say something, or maybe that I should be feeling more than the ever-present guilt and shame that are my constant companions.

I stand over Mike's grave for a few more minutes before I go to rejoin the others.

We live in a world now where death is always lurking around the corner, just waiting for someone to slip up. We never should have left the underground. At least that was a cage we understood; out here, everything is an unknown.

We are always in danger.

Walking up to Lily, I see that Wren and Elle are both cuddled against her. They remind me of how a cat would curl up next to its person. There's a heavy silence hanging in the air as I look at them. Elle is fast asleep as Lily runs her hand over her clumped hair in a calming motion. Lily doesn't say anything; she won't even look at me as I settle on the ground across from her. She's untangling herself from me and has been since Rachel's death back in the forest. Lily is slowly disconnecting her heartstrings one at a time, as a surgeon would cut one nerve at a time.

I understand why, but it doesn't make it any less painful. Lily has realized something much quicker after Rachel died. She knew that the moment would come when I would be permanently pushed out of the group. It's easier to disconnect and shut off the feelings over time than deal with the shattering of emotions all at once. Lily had been building walls while I was still trying to live with one foot in and one out. She was brilliant at protecting herself from the inevitable. I was the foolish one, living in the hope that everything would be fine.

That we would all be fine.

As the realization of the end sinks in, I wrap my arms tightly around my knees, rocking myself gently to comfort the chaos that is surging inside of my body. Everything I know and love is going to end tomorrow, as soon as the sun comes up.

Chapter Thirty-Two
Singular

"What loneliness is more lonely than distrust?"
— *George Eliot*

I watch as dawn breaks and the group begins to stir. I stay seated as Elle, Wren, and Lily get up and start packing up our meager belongings. Elle hands out the small pieces of bark that we have left over from the trees we passed a few days ago, giving some to each person, including me.

I'm surprised but gladly take it from her, looking at her hands instead of her face. Her nails are dirty, a mix of blood and dirt embedded under them. She's just as stained as I am.

Having passed out food to everyone, Elle starts walking, heading in the direction we had been going before Mike. She leads, and I fall into place at the back of the group. Maybe she doesn't hold me responsible for Mike's death. Perhaps we will all stay together as a group.

I'm lost in my thoughts until Elle stops, turning to me.

My gut drops.

My body understands what's happening before my heart and brain do. The hair on the back of my neck stands up, my stomach tightens and it starts to churn.

Elle pauses for a moment, looking at me, and then turns away. She can't even look me in the face when she says it. But it doesn't matter, I can hear the determination in her voice.

"You're not coming any further with us."

Those seven words blow up my world.

My breath catches in my chest as if I've jumped headfirst into a glacial lake. I struggle with the little black monster clawing its way out of my chest cavity. I can't form words. I'm scared that if I open my mouth, my heart will tear itself free from the cage of my ribs and spew forth with a desperate cry. I stand still, as if frozen, except for the gulping of air into my starved lungs.

"You're a monster. I don't feel safe with you. None of us do." Another nail in my coffin. I bend over, hands on my knees, mouth open in a silent cry for help. I can't breathe.

Elle turns around now and walks slowly toward me, with Lily behind her. She kneels in front of me, placing her thumb and pointer finger on my chin, lifting my face so she can look me in the eyes.

"Don't follow us. Don't even think about following us." Her eyes are dead, just like her tone.

I can't even nod to acknowledge that I've heard her. I can't look away. All I see in those dead eyes is resolve, determination, and seething hatred, and myself reflected.

Elle turns away, dropping my chin. I risk a glance at Lily as I try to straighten, but I can't quite get there. All the air has been knocked from my body, making me want to curl in on myself as if I can stop the pain. Lily stands there, holding onto Wren's hand. Wren. She's crying. Please don't cry.

Lily looks at me, not saying anything, before slowly turning and walking away. There are no parting words, no last "I love you," no tears. She walks away. Pulling Wren with her. Taking my family, my life, with her.

There is a numbness that precedes the panic.

My little black monster rears its head, threatening to consume what is left of my tattered resolve. I try to focus on a single stone in the mud as breathing gets harder. Knowing that the panic is setting in only makes it worse and makes me panic more. I try to clear my mind, to think of anything besides the fact that I'm entirely alone, that they have given up on me, that they are better off without me. Tears flood my eyes, burning and blurring my vision before they hit the ground and disappear into the soil.

I'm giving in again. Why am I so weak? Why can't I stop this? My body begins to shake as my only companion, my little monster, settles right in the center of my chest. Squeezing my heart with its tiny, clawed hands, as if to resuscitate it. A body-wrenching sob rips through me as I fall to my knees, then onto my elbows. Sob after sob ricochets through my body, burying themselves in the soil with my tears.

How has this happened?

Panic, fear, and hopelessness are dangerous, one feeding into the other until my mind and body are completely overwhelmed. Everything I've fought to save is gone in seconds, and I have been left behind.

Discarded like an unwanted toy.

My body is shaking uncontrollably as my chest continues to grow tighter and tighter, my monster driving itself further into my chest. Its bloody hands are gripping my heart as its body wraps my lungs in a hug.

The world pitches beneath me as the dizziness takes hold and the darkness starts to seep into my vision. There isn't anyone here to help me this time. Lily isn't here to bring me back from the edge. I flop onto my back, and the sky above me spins sickeningly as I dig my hands into the ground on either side of my body, trying to anchor myself in reality. I start to hyperventilate, then the tingling and numbness start, and I welcome it. The dizziness worsens as I take quick, loud gasps of air. No matter how hard I try, the air isn't enough to fill my lungs.

The darkness closes in, pulling me down through the hole in my chest.

I come to slowly; I'm groggy and feel like shit. The usual pounding in my head is a thumping, but at least I'm still alive. I need food and water.

My panic attack has left me completely exhausted, with a dry mouth and feeling hungry. I think about standing up for a brief moment but decide against it. I still feel shaky and weak and don't want to push my luck.

I look around, trying to get my bearings. I feel like I've been transported to a different dimension. The sun had set while I was out, and I have no idea how long I was unconscious for. I still have my pack and have a little water and tree bark left to eat.

I gather my strength and crawl over to a large boulder that I can sit against and try to relax my body. I drink a little of my water; I need to ration it and the bark now more than ever. After drinking and eating a little, I start to feel better. More anchored; solid.

Leaning against the rock, I take a moment to reflect on everything that's happened since we came to the surface. How the people I considered my family cut me out of their lives without a backward glance. It's tearing me apart that they made the decision so quickly. Did I ever matter to them, or had Lily been the one anchoring us all together?

Had they kept me around because Lily and I were a bonded pair?
And Lily.

Did Lily ever actually love me, or was it just hope and trauma that bound us together? A relationship created and held together by convenience and fear?

If I look at it in this way, everything seems to make sense. It makes it easier to swallow, at least. If I pretend like all of this isn't real, that will make it easier to move past, right? None of it ever actually mattered; an illusion created from desperation.

My chest tightens, and tears threaten. I close my eyes and lean my head back against the rock. Exhaustion, confusion, and sadness drag me down into an uneasy sleep.

I'm aware on some level that my eyes are closed and that I'm asleep. I'm expecting to see my old friend Death standing in a door-lined hallway waiting for me. But it isn't Death that's waiting there. It's Mike.

He's covered in blood, the infected lower half of his leg hanging grotesquely from the smashed part of his knee. The hall's floor is covered in a mix of dark blood and greenish-yellow pus that leads from me to where he stands. His face is whiter than a blank white page, his lips are bluish-white, and his eyes are milky. The only color comes from the bright red blood on my hands as I look down.

He flashes his teeth, which are yellowed and blackened from his time on Earth. I don't run, like I do when I meet Death here; I can't. Instead, I stand. I'm ready for my punishment, and I know that this is something that I can't run from. This will be with me until I'm bequeathed to the ground I stand on. There's no more running.

I'm still aware that I'm dreaming and am caught in a weird state of half-consciousness and the dream world, where Mike waits for me to run like I do when Death chases me. Running is what usually wakes me up, but if I stand here and let Mike catch me, what will happen? I remember as a kid someone told me that if you die in your dreams, you die in real life. I wonder if that's true.

Neither of us move. The stench of Mike's infection and the rotting corpse is seeping into me, making my stomach churn. Is this real? Have I died? This feels pretty fucking real. It smells real. Is this what the end looks like for me?

I glance up from the '70s hotel carpeting the hallway to meet Mike's milky, unseeing eyes. He moves toward me in a halting, jerking motion, hopping on one leg while dragging the other behind him, his hands on the hotel walls to keep balance. Mike opens his mouth as he somehow gains speed.

"Run!"

That single word shoots from his festering mouth and hits me in the chest, driving through me, like a harsh, cold winter wind.

Gasping, I jerk awake only to find that my nightmare has followed me into reality. I struggle to sit up, realizing that my hands are bound behind my back. My nostrils flare as the smell of death blasts them. A dark figure looms over me as I struggle to make sense of what's happening around me.

Is this real, or am I still dreaming?

As the man in black grabs my arm and drags me to my feet, the truth starts to sink in. The group that killed Oliver has found me.

I struggle to my feet as the large man half-drags me over to where the others are waiting. They've formed a semi-circle, and the man pulls me into the middle of it. As much as I struggle, feeling the sting of the rope around my wrists, nothing I do is enough to free me from them.

He lets go, pushing me forward.

"You have a choice. You join us, or you die," he says, stepping back.

I turn in a slow circle, looking at each of the masked men. Every mask is different, carved from the wood of the trees we walked past a few days ago. Their clothes are intentionally made to look like rags—an illusion.

The only face I see is that of the man who brought me here. It's surprisingly clean, lean, tan, and bearded. His eyes are green, flecked with something darker. He sees me looking, sneers, and pulls his mask down over his face.

I reflect on all the moments of my life that have brought me to this specific moment in time. Is this where my life was always going? Is this how it's supposed to end?

The thing about survival is, you adapt, or you die.

Acknowledgements

Echoes of Us has been more than a book. It has been a companion through grief, healing, and survival. This story has lived with me for over fifteen years, taking shape in the long shadow of my father's death. In many ways, this book exists because of that loss, and because I needed somewhere to put the echoes it left behind.

To my family and friends: thank you for your patience, your encouragement, and your willingness to hold space for me when the work, and the grief, felt heavy. This book would not exist without your steady presence and belief in me, even when I struggled to believe in myself.

Most importantly, I want to thank Gina, my therapist, and the many therapists who have supported me since I first began therapy in 2018. I came to that work overwhelmed, fractured, and carrying grief from a recent loss that felt impossible to survive. Through your compassion, skill, and unwavering support, you helped me learn how to live with my loss instead of being consumed by it. This book is, in many ways, a testament to that healing.

Thank you to English Proper Editing Services for treating this story with such care and respect. Your thoughtful, meticulous work helped protect the heart of this book while making it stronger.

To Montrez, thank you for encouraging me to keep writing *Echoes of Us* after the developmental edits, when it would have been easy to walk away. Your belief in this story mattered more than you know.

And to ApexVerse: thank you for everything, from the stunning cover art to your guidance, support, and belief in this book at every stage. You helped transform an idea I carried for years into something real, tangible, and alive in the world.

Finally, to everyone who has ever carried grief, loss, or love that refuses to fade, this book is for you. Thank you for being here.

273

About the Author

Arden Coutts is a queer, trans author, retreat host, and creative entrepreneur based in rural Nebraska. They write emotionally rich stories that explore grief, resilience, identity, and love—often through the lens of romantic suspense, post-apocalyptic fiction, fantasy, and horror. Arden's work centers queer characters navigating fractured worlds, chosen family, and the quiet, stubborn hope of survival.

With a background that spans archaeology, environmental compliance, disaster recovery, and digital storytelling, Arden brings a grounded, human lens to every story they tell. Their writing is known for its emotional intimacy, morally complex characters, and tender moments set against high-stakes backdrops.

In addition to writing, Arden is the founder of Wandering Creative Life, where they host inclusive writing and wellness retreats for LGBTQ+ creatives. When they aren't writing or creating, Arden can usually be found planning their next retreat, making suncatchers, drinking too much coffee, or chasing moments of queer joy wherever they can be found.

Connect with Arden Coutts

Instagram: www.instagram.com/ardencoutts

YouTube: www.youtube.com/@wanderingcreativelife

Website: www.ardencoutts.com

Patreon: www.patreon.com/ardencoutts